built in a day

Also by Steven Rinehart

Kick in the Head: Stories

built in a day

a novel

steven rinehart

 doubleday

new york london toronto sydney auckland

PUBLISHED BY DOUBLEDAY
a division of Random House, Inc.

DOUBLEDAY and the portrayal of an anchor with a dolphin are
registered trademarks of Random House, Inc.

Book design by Chris Welch

Library of Congress Cataloging-in-Publication Data
Rinehart, Steven.
    Built in a day: a novel / by Steven Rinehart.—1st ed.
        p.   cm.
      1. Underachievers—Fiction. 2. Failure (Psychology)—Fiction.
    3. Father figures—Fiction. 4. Stepfamilies—Fiction.
    5. Teenagers—Fiction. 6. Twins—Fiction. I. Title.

    PS3568.I564B85 2003
    813'.54—dc21
    2003041968

    ISBN 0-385-49855-1

PRINTED IN THE UNITED STATES OF AMERICA

July 2003

First Edition

10 9 8 7 6 5 4 3 2 1

For Barbara, for everything

acknowledgments

I would like to thank Fred Leebron, Geoff Becker, Emily Chenoweth, Kim Campbell, and especially Barbara Jones for their patient and generous help with early drafts of this novel. For technical expertise and general encouragement and support, Judy Rinehart, Charlene Rinehart, Lois and Charles Jones, Elizabeth Cuthrell, Maria Jones, and Eric Schermerhorn have my deep gratitude.

Finally, I'd like to thank Eric Simonoff, Deb Futter, and Anne Merrow. Without their attention, expertise, and wisdom, this book would not have been possible.

Acknowledgments

There is a great difference between **still** believing something and believing it **again.**

—G. C. Lichtenberg

built in a day

part one

1

Isabel and I got married in her backyard, on a cold fall day under a tent that had once had banners sewn on it advertising cheap tequila and now just showed the outlines of the letters "Santa Rosa."

All the guests were from her side; a couple of her physical therapy patients were there, along with her boys, Russ and Alex, Russ's beautiful girlfriend Jule, big old Rosie, and a few others I couldn't really place. We had one very expensive bottle of champagne that we managed to hit every glass with, even mine, although I didn't drink it, I just toasted Russ's bang-up job as best man and carried it around the tent afterward. At that point I had been sober for a year and was still being extra cautious.

"Assembled guests," Russ had said, his teenage voice artificially grave. All of us stood with our glasses and listened. Russ was only fourteen but he had that effect on people.

"It falls upon me to say a few words about the couple before you. First, it's been a long road, a very long road. Many of us thought it was too long . . ." A few of us smiled; others nodded. I looked at Isabel next to me but she was staring at her son.

". . . but they persevered." He stumbled on that a bit and this clearly irritated him. Isabel's hand tightened on mine.

"They hung in there and now they stand before us, husband and wife. Please join me in saluting them."

A cheer rose up from the happy little bunch. One of Izzie's physical therapy patients even said Huzzah. The other, a guy named Carl, made a big show of tilting his plastic champagne glass vertically above his mouth and shaking the last drops off the lip.

"I should have been a scientist or a chemist," Carl said to me later, both of us hovering near the edge of the tent. Izzie was dancing with the younger twin, Alex, next to Russ and Jule. Rosie was loaded and had dragged some stranger out onto the parquet.

"My best class in high school was Advanced Chemistry," he said. "Do you remember oxidation-reduction reactions? I could do those in my sleep."

I'd been bored by advanced-placement chem and had kept myself occupied by cheating on my yields while designing elaborate water pipes. At that point in my life my questionable morals had gotten me passed over for valedictorian and kicked out of the Honor Society and I'd be damned if I was going to weigh out crystals and read thermometers like it meant something. Even now, at thirty-two, it seemed ridiculous.

"Doesn't high school seem like an old, really long movie you once saw?" I said. "Like *The French Connection* or *Barry Lyndon*?"

"Did *The French Connection* have Telly Savalas?" he asked. "Do you remember him, Telly Savalas?"

"Yes, I do. I don't think he was in it but I remember him. Wet lips, right? Sort of bags under his eyes?"

He nodded. "And bald as a cue ball," he said, as I knew he would.

"I don't think so," I said. "Not the way I remember him, anyway."

Carl looked as if he hadn't heard me right. "I'm sure he was bald," he said. "That's what I remember most."

"I bet we're just mixing up two different actors. I'm usually wrong about stuff like this, so let's just go with bald."

But he couldn't leave it alone. He just waded right back in. "You know, he had that Popsicle all the time." He began to look distressed and searched the tent for someone to back him up, but there was no one handy.

"Definitely the guy," I said, "but it was a lollipop, I think, not a Popsicle. Lollipop with the little white stick always wagging back and forth. And an Afro. A big natural with a comb in the side."

He seemed to squeak a little. "I think that was someone on *Baretta*," he said.

"You're right," I said. "I bet it was. And he always said, 'Who loves ya, baby?' "

Now he was wringing his hands. His ailment had been a kind of psychosomatic paralysis and he'd gotten attached to Isabel at some point in the eight weeks she pumped his legs up and down and made him walk between the parallel bars.

"That's him, but he's bald, I swear," he said. "It's a trademark." Just then Isabel showed up and took my arm.

"What's up?" she said. Her grip on the sharp bone of my elbow was something she must have learned as part of her training.

"Carl and I were reminiscing about high school," I said. "He remembers it a lot better than I do."

"Was Telly Savalas bald?" he asked Isabel, slightly out of breath. "He was, wasn't he?"

"I think so," she said.

"And white, right?"

"Definitely," she said. "Excuse us, Carl, we've got to do a few things." She steered us away and toward the card table holding what was left of the cheap cake.

"Honey," I said. "He was asking for it. You weren't there, he was really being awful."

"Like last time?"

At the engagement party I'd convinced him that vanilla was an element, on the periodic table and everything.

"I'm worried about Russ," I said.

"Baloney," she said. "Don't change the subject."

"Okay, I'm not worried about him but I'm afraid he's growing up too fast." This was true. A lot of things about Russ worried me, and the fact that he might catch up and pass me was somehow not a ridiculous thought. That toast was typical. That kid had his shit together way too much for fourteen.

Isabel took the champagne glass out of my hand and sniffed it.

"Still there," I said. "Still smells just as awful."

"I know we don't say things like this but I'm crazier than ever about you," she said. "It's our wedding so I thought I'd take a chance and get mushy."

"Oh, Izzie," I said. "You can say whatever you want anytime you want. I will too."

"You will?"

"I'll try." I meant it, even though I'd proposed to her in tears, blubbering, practically speechless. Afterward I'd laid my head in her lap and hiccuped, feeling as if I'd been plucked from the surf by a helicopter and deposited in a soggy pile on the beach.

Under the tent Isabel was looking at me the same way she had that day.

"So try now," she said. "Say something."

"Okay," I said. "I'm absolutely nothing without you. I'm less than nothing. My whole life begins today."

"Hmm," she said. "Not really romantic for a wedding." But she had colored a bit, so I was not far off. "Keep going."

I could tell I was scrunching up my face, like a child squeezing out the answer to his mother's possibly entrapping question about his whereabouts or the smoky odor lingering around his clothes.

"When you're not around I think for a second that my life hasn't changed, and that I can go back to the way I was. Then I realize that Holy Shit you aren't around and I panic a little and think, Why isn't she around? Where is she? So I go find you or find something that reminds me of you." I licked my lips, they had gone dry.

All of it was true—what I usually did if I couldn't get to her was look for Alex, twenty minutes the baby of the family, but sometimes it seemed like twenty years. The boys were fraternal twins—Russ stocky and handsome, Alex thin and boyish. I'd find Alex and we'd play Nintendo or backgammon or throw a football around until I got it out of my system.

She didn't say anything for a moment.

"That's maybe all for today," I said. "I'm sorry."

She put the champagne glass down on the cheap card table. She took one of my hands and moved close, and I could feel her start to move her hips, and I instinctively started to move away.

"No, come on," she protested, pulling me back. "You said."

We started to dance, and everyone looked at us. We danced the way we had practiced to the video we had rented, a modified swing. I tried not to count out loud and stare at my knees and actually succeeded for seconds at a time to look like I knew what I was doing.

"All my life I thought I was better than everyone else," I said. "And now I feel like a failure because I can't dance at my own wedding with my own beautiful new wife."

She pulled me a little closer. "You are better than everyone else. You could be President. Why do you think I let you badger me into this marriage?"

Badger. She'd said yes even before I started blubbering.

Then we fell into the groove and we actually danced like

regular people, loosening up, working it a little the way the freaks on the tape had, ballroom pros with waxy expressions and colitis, both of them.

But God they were good dancers. They were fabulous, whatever I thought of them personally.

Izzie had been married once before, at eighteen, her boys born that same year. Her husband was an orphan raised by the high school librarian. All he ever wanted was a family so he wooed Isabel all through junior high and high school and he succeeded in knocking her up after a homecoming hayride. When the boys were five he moved them all from Kansas to Iowa City so he could take a job at the Procter & Gamble factory making Pert Plus. She got a job bartending at Rosie's where she could go to work after he got home. That's where she met me. The first time she saw me she stared at me so long I thought I must have known her or done something to her drunk and not remembered. I had been taking a poetry workshop and had been ostentatiously scribbling on notepads and coasters for weeks at one corner of Rosie's fake-Irish bar. I still remember the first thing I said to Isabel, one of the best things I ever said to her, a jewel among the turds of things I would end up saying to her for the next year or so. I said, putting down my pen and shoving some frayed papers into my jacket pocket:

"If you're going to be working here now I think my old life is pretty much over."

She went deep red and it was one of those things that happened like a natural phenomenon, like an explosion of flowers or a meteor shower.

At least, it seemed to be like that. Most of the time I saw her I was in the process of drinking myself sick. I had no idea what she saw in me—she was dark and very intensely sexy and I was a goateed slacker with a scraggly soul patch and a few crappy piercings—but it took only about a week for us to take up with each other. Once we even made it in the walk-in, in the middle of her shift, right there on the cold cardboard next to the half-barrels, and worried the whole time that Rosie would walk in on us.

Some months later she left her husband and I got a job at Starbucks running the blenders. The twins, fishing in Alaska with their old man, had no pity on me when she called them crying after I'd insulted her or threatened to break it off.

"Dump him," the boys would tell her from their end. "Just dump the fucker." They were thirteen then and apparently thought that the lives of adults were simple that way. "He's a loser," they said. "He sucks."

I know they said this because Izzie told me after she hung up.

"They're right," I said. "What have I got to show for myself?" At that point I'd been an Iowa University undergraduate for over twelve years and had been through four advisers, seven majors, and five department chairs. The Guaranteed Student Loan people had me on speed dial.

"You're brilliant," she said. "You're strong and handsome and we were made for each other. I knew it the minute I saw you."

"You should listen to your kids," I said. I was probably drinking her liquor when she said this stuff.

At the end of that first summer Russ and Alex dropped by Starbucks on their first day back from Alaska. I recognized them right off, even though I had seen them only once before, when they had come into the bar after school to show Isabel something.

They stood in front of me, on the other side of the counter, and pretended to look at the bagged beans on display behind the Plexiglas. They were all done up in lumberjack shirts and Doc Martens, with gray hoods resting back on their shoulders.

Arlene, the assistant manager, asked them to step over to the register.

"We're just looking," Russ said.

"I can help you over here," Arlene said firmly.

"They're friends," I said. Arlene glared at me and retreated into her office to roll quarters. She hated me, I suppose for my general goateed slackerness. She was only twenty-two but was already saving for a house.

"Hey," I said to the boys. *"¿Qué pasa?"*

They didn't answer. Alex picked up a pewter coffee press and turned it upside down.

"Can we sort of get some coffee?" he said.

"Sure." I started up a couple of Frappucinos. "I'll take a break," I said. "We'll all sit down. You want a couple of biscotti or something?"

They just blinked at me. We all stood there while the blenders screamed.

At the corner table they sat with their feet out, knees spread. They sucked on their Frapps and stared at the customers.

"You guys catch a lot of fish up there?" I asked.

"Pravda," Russ said.

"That means yes," said Alex.

"Well, technically, it means truth," I said. "If I had said, 'You guys sure caught a lot of fish up there,' then '*pravda*' would have been right."

They both shrugged and their eyes wandered around the store again.

"These flatlanders must seem weird after hanging with the Russians all summer," I said. They ignored me. Russ was eyeing a couple of lesbians at a far table who could easily have been twice his age.

I made a motion in my chair, the kind you make to recapture lost attention. Their heads swung back to me slowly, as if on casters.

"Me and your mom? We've been having some problems, you know. Rough spots. She probably told you."

Russ vacuumed the last of the Frapp off the bottom of his cup. *"Jah,"* he said.

"Did you say *Jah?*" I asked.

"*Jah*, Rastafari," his brother chimed in.

"You know," I said, "in that context *Jah* means God, not yes."

Then Russ stood up. His hand plunged into his front pocket. "We've got six thousand dollars," he said. "A sixteenth share."

"Wow," I said. "Nice work."

"Dad's going to buy his own boat."

"That's fabulous. Bully for him." I wiped my hands on my green Starbucks apron—a loaner, as I'd not been able to purchase my own. They left dark smears on its waxy surface.

Then Russ pulled out a tight handful of cash and held it in his fist directly in front of me. "We'll give you four bills to break up with Mom."

"Four what?" I said. "Do what?"

"Four thousand bucks," he said. His hand was a foot from my nose. His voice had somehow taken on a little echo. "Four thou—"

"I fucking heard you," I said. Conversation at the surrounding tables subsided. Russ stood over me, arm extended, elbow locked, holding the money like a porpoise trainer.

I lowered my voice. "Why don't you just sit down, Russ," I said.

"Dude . . ." Russ said.

"It's Andrew. Sit down please."

". . . it's four thousand dollars, Andrew."

"Please."

"Mucho dinero."

"God damn it, enough," I said. Everyone in the place heard it.

I stood up quickly and backed away from the table. Russ just held out the cash, defiant, the entire restaurant staring at him. At the next table a pimply grad student's fingers hovered in the air above his laptop. Arlene herself watched from the office doorway.

"Just enough, already," I said, my voice fading at the end. "This is ridiculous." But still nobody moved.

I untied my apron, somehow. I draped it over the chair and

turned my back on Russ and his brother and the fistful of *dinero*. I walked across the sperm-motif carpet and out through the double set of doors and onto the pedestrian mall.

Outside I sat down on the band platform and smoked my last seven cigarettes. When I went to the machine at Rosie's pub I discovered I couldn't even scrounge a pack's worth of money out of my pants.

I went to my apartment and called Isabel at home and broke it off with her, just like that. I can't even remember what I said, but I didn't mention the boys or the money. I threw away all of my liquor, upending scotch bottles in the sink and filling the air of my little kitchen with the heavy smell of what seemed like orchids. I stayed in my apartment for three weeks, living on Top Ramen and frozen orange juice, and when the first of October rolled around, I walked outside, a little unsteady but sober. I plugged my phone back in, bought some groceries. But I avoided the pedestrian mall and Rosie's and anytime I saw any kids any-where near the twins' age I crossed the street or cut through a yard to avoid them.

I found a new job, amazingly enough, at a sign painter's shop out by the Coralville strip. It was owned by a Korean bachelor who spoke very little English and spent most of his time ignor-ing the ringing phone and heating up vile-smelling lunches on a hot plate. Mostly I cut vinyl for window signs—insurance bro-kerages, lawyers, the Ford dealer. It was close work, the kind of work you can do just as well with the radio turned up loud, and it suited me.

Once I had to put the vice principal's name on his door at the high school. The proximity to fourteen-year-olds concerned me at first, but it turned out there was nothing to worry about. It was Christmas break. I got my materials out quickly, though, and squeegeed the glass and ran my level line with the red wax pencil. Too quickly, it turned out. The plastic was the cheap kind my boss liked—a fake gold leaf that was prone to creasing. Plus

the vice principal was the kind of guy who liked to use his ini-
tials, which were a problem with letters that small—the periods,
mostly. At any rate the vinyl slowed me down and after twenty
minutes I was sweating and rubbing and thinking I'd have to go
back and cut another strip when I heard the boots clatter down
the hall. I dropped my squeegee.

But it wasn't the boys; it was Rosie, Isabel's boss, all two hundred fifty pounds of her. She was huffing from the stairs, pluck-
ing here and there at her running suit. When she got up close
she was still panting.

"Hey," she said, putting one hand on a drinking fountain for
support. "New job?"

"Yeah," I said. "I guess. A couple of weeks now."

She nodded at the door. "This asshole sends me a letter a
week before Christmas telling me my kid might not graduate in
the spring. I already spend two hours a night with him on his
fricking homework."

"Nobody's in there," I said. "A bunch of them came out about
a half hour ago. Nobody's gone back in."

She squatted down, still out of breath, her hands hanging in
front of her. "School still gives me the creeps," she said.

"Here," I said, pushing my portable stool over to her. "Sit on
this."

She straightened up and eyed it warily. "I sit on that thing I
might be taking it with me when I leave, if you know what I
mean."

"Oh, no," I said. "Go ahead."

She sat on it and looked me over.

"How much do you pay to get your hair cut that way?" she
said.

"That's classified."

She nodded.

"How long do you stare at that soul patch in the mirror every
morning?"

"The same amount of time as every other poseur, if that's what you're driving at."

"Take it easy," she said. "I'm just giving you a hard time because I miss you."

"Oh," I said. I didn't know how to respond to that.

"While I'm here," she said, "I should ask you if you know why Isabel gave her notice. If you knew any way I could talk her out of it."

"Her notice?"

"That's what she said. She didn't give a single other detail."

I sat down against the door. "I don't know anything about it," I said.

"She didn't mention it?"

I just shrugged. "She talked about finishing her physical therapy training, but that's all I know."

She nodded. "Word on the street is that you quit drinking. You do that on your own?"

This time it was my turn to nod.

"Good for you," Rosie said, her skepticism barely contained. She watched me work for a while.

"Hey," Rosie said. "Is that hard what you're doing there?"

I looked down at the strip of vinyl in my hand. It had already begun to dry and curl. It wouldn't be going on anyone's window. For some reason disappointment swelled against the wall of my chest.

"Yeah," I said. "It's hard. I was surprised how hard. I thought it would be a breeze to pick up."

Rosie stood up and unstuck her pants from her thighs. "That must be why they call it skilled labor, Pancho," she said. "What the hell did you expect?"

It was a Saturday morning the following spring when I knocked on Isabel's screen door out on Prairie du Chien. It had

taken me about forty-five minutes of pacing the block before I'd
gotten up the nerve. Russ answered in baggy shorts and a black
T-shirt. He had a drop of milk on the point of his chin. Some
very bad music blared from somewhere within. "Dude," he said.
"What's up?"

"Hey," I said. "Your mom home?"

He shook his head. "Nope." We stood there for a moment and
stared at each other.

"Yeah, well," I said, "if you could tell her I stopped by."

He didn't answer; he just stood behind the screen. Then the figure of a woman appeared behind him. My heart gave a panicked
kick, then the figure stepped closer to the screen and the image
coalesced into that of a young girl. She was wearing a heartbreak-
ingly short white T-shirt and cutoff jeans. Her hair was freshly
slept in. She was holding a spoon in one hand and a *TV Guide* in
the other. That was the first time I'd set eyes on Jule.

I looked back at Russ. "How's your brother?"

"He's all right," Russ said. "He's asleep." And that was it; I
left the two of them in the doorway.

I had reached the mouth of the alley when Isabel's car pulled
in. She almost hit me with her old Renault. There was a lot of
glare from the low sun. When she rolled down her window the
glare still hit me from the side mirror and I couldn't see the expression on her face.

"Hey," I said. "You got a job on the graveyard shift or something? I hope that's what this means."

I couldn't tell, but I don't think she smiled.

"I'm getting my certification," she said. "A few nights I work
at a nursing home for credit."

"Rosie said you quit. Where are the groceries coming from?"

"Savings." The car started easing forward. I followed along-
side.

"I quit drinking," I said. "Cold turkey." She cruised a little
faster.

"Stop," I said. She didn't. "Stop," I pleaded. I stopped walking. "I want my money," I yelled at the rear window.

The car jerked to a stop at the house. She opened the door and clambered out of the car, throwing a scarf onto the seat.

"You want what?" she said.

"My money," I said. I could feel the conviction draining from my voice.

She just stared. The kids appeared, silently, on the other side of the screen door, all three of them this time.

"They owe me four thousand dollars," I said. "I have witnesses."

"You're kidding me, right?"

"It's true," I said. "Let's talk about it inside. Let's just see."

She stood there next to the car, arms crossed, and set her head a bit to one side. "I've got news for you, Andrew. I took the money," she said. "The whole four thousand. It's gone."

I was seeing the wad of bills again in Russ's palm. I was hearing his boots.

"I lost my new job," I said. "I'm out of money and I basically don't have the rent."

She took a couple of breaths. "So it's true? That's what you really came here for?" The anger had drained from her voice; she looked and sounded heartbroken.

"You don't understand," I said. "This was a stupid job, and I tried. I tried hard, I really did. I should have been able to do it but I couldn't. I have no idea why."

"God, I do," Isabel said. "Stupid me, I absolutely do know why."

"Izzie, nobody ever said you were stupid."

"I'm going to bed," she said. "I've been working all night and I'm tired." She opened the door and pushed past the kids. "Ask the boys if you want to know why your life is the way it is," she said to me. "They're smarter than both of us put together." In another second she was gone.

The three of them watched me from behind the screen. I started to walk away. "Dude," Russ said, opening the door and waving me inside. I followed him dumbly into the kitchen. I could see Isabel's shoes heading up the stairs. "Let's look at it this way," he said. "When people hit the bottom they got no choice, right? They have to start over. It's like you die and start a new life. Like Jule did."

"I don't know what you mean," I said, but the words had sent a chill into my chest. I looked over at the girl.

"Why did you start over?" I asked her. She just stared at me.

"Her folks died when she was ten," Alex said. "She lives here now. We got a court order and everything."

"That's terrible," I said. I didn't feel any better at all. I really wanted to sit down.

"Dude," Russ said. His arm was now draped over Jule's shoulders. "Don't look so whacked out. It's not so totally hopeless."

"It's not?" I said. I stole a glance at the top of the stairs. The hall up there was mostly in shadow but a soft light came from the near end where her bedroom was.

"Absolutely," he said. "A guy told me it's easy to get jobs. They're everywhere. It's a college town." He dug into his pocket and pulled out a wad of money, significantly smaller than the one he'd flashed months before.

"How much," he said, "do you need to get you going again? Would five hundred do it? No strings attached this time."

I looked at the bills peeling from his fourteen-year-old fingers, at the beautiful young girl holding on to his arm. Did he really know what he was doing? How could he? It didn't seem possible.

Directly above me I could hear Isabel getting ready for bed, her soft footfalls and the opening and closing of drawers.

"What do you say?" asked Russ, the bills curling around his fingertips.

"*Jah*," I said. I left Russ there and walked to the stairs, and climbed them up to where the light was. Isabel met me at the top, and I fell to my knees at her feet.

"Oh God, please marry me," I sobbed.

"Oh, baby," she said, over and over. "Hush, baby . . ."

2

That first winter I was on a kind of probation, I knew. I'd moved into the house right after the engagement but I was still a guest. Russ could cosign for the mortgage if the bank would only let him—I was lucky to be sent for stamps.

But all in all I didn't mind—it was something of a rebirth, the fresh start that others in my situation had gotten from AA or Narc Anon or whatever. I was living my second chance every day in front of them and there was no pretending about it. And, amazingly enough, they smiled at me with genuine affection when I walked through the door, when I made them all scrambled eggs in the morning before school. When I carried armfuls of wet towels to the basement and armfuls of warm stacked ones back up. When I changed the almost empty roll of toilet paper with a new roll even though there was a little left just so nobody in the house would be stuck there without enough. When I started Izzie's car up for her ten minutes before she left for school so it would be warm inside and the vinyl soft. When I shopped for bargains at the Eagle store, sneaking my lunch as I went along to save money that day.

Of course I looked for work every day that first winter. Russ had been more or less accurate when he said there was very little unemployment in our town; there was only enough, apparently, for me. I filled out a dozen forms at the university, at the county job bank, at the Coralville Mall. I got exactly one call, a woman who immediately asked about my typing speed. I told her it was in the high thirties and she thanked me very much. Before she hung up I told her that if I only had two hands it would be in the seventies at least. "Good one," the woman said. I wondered how she could be so certain I was kidding until Izzie asked at the dinner table if her friend Becky from the nursing home had called me.

"Oh, she called," I said. "But it seems I couldn't pass muster on the typing front."

"Damn," she said. "She was probably just humoring me."

"Probably," I said. "Where was the job?"

"At the Teen Scene," she said. "She's friends with some lady who works there."

Alex snickered, and we all knew why. The Teen Scene was the town outreach center, housed in a crappy Victorian between the sporting goods (guns, knives, and mitts) store and the Plasma Donation Center. I'd never been inside but I could picture it: sprung furniture, lame video games or pinball machines or foosball, a refrigerator full of Pepsi and Sunny Delight, a counselor with bad breath and cheap wire-rims who called everyone Dude or Homie or Girlfriend, a pay phone scratched with obscenities, and a bathroom heavy on deodorant to cover the fact that it was "cool with everyone" if thirteen-year-olds smoked there, as long as it was only tobacco.

"Maybe you should call her back," Izzie said.

I nodded slowly and took a few bites of my grilled cheese. "That's a good idea," I said. "Maybe the typing thing isn't so important. I bet I could cram and get up into the forties." I took another bite. "Only . . ."

"Only what?" she said. It was quick, and everyone at the table caught it—Alex, Jule, Russ. There was a noticeable shifting of gears.

"I don't know," I said. "Maybe they wouldn't care, but I wonder about the whole drinking thing."

"But you don't drink. They'd love that, are you kidding?"

"Well, there was the arrest." I'd gotten the one D&D about three years before—a stupid incident I'd instigated with some frat types and was lucky to have survived.

Izzie shook her head dismissively. "I don't think—"

The phone rang and Izzie tilted her chair back and picked the receiver up from the wall.

"Becky," she said, her eyebrows high and significant. "Hey, honey." The rest of us spooned our soup in silence.

"Uh-huh," she said. "That was fast. Wow, great."

Jule gave me an encouraging look from across the table and Russ followed it with a thumbs-up.

"You want to talk to him?" she said into the phone.

I waved my hands and made exaggerated chewing motions.

"What time?" she said. "Let me check." She put her hand over the mouthpiece, then removed it a second later without saying anything. "That's fine. He'll be there. Bye."

After she hung up and tilted back to the table there wasn't any talk for a solid four or five minutes. Russ broke the silence.

"The Teen Scene pretty much sucks, though," he said. "I mean, it's a good idea and all but they need an underground entrance because nobody would be caught dead going in or out of there."

Jule objected. "It's only when they do that stuff with the posters and the buttons. They think we're stupid or something."

I'd seen some of those. One big advertised event had been the Teen Smash, where they'd put an old junked Ford out on the lawn before a football game and sold whacks with a sledgehammer for fifty cents apiece. It was mostly a bust, since only some college drunks paid and they all took five or six whacks for their money and once it was clear that the guy in charge didn't have the stones to object to a guy with a five-pound mallet in his hand all remaining decorum fell apart. When I left three phys ed majors were jumping up and down on the car roof yelling Hoo Hoo Hoo and making obscene gestures at passing cars.

Another school spirit–type event was the Haunted House for Diabetes. They hired private security that night and everybody was on their best behavior. The setup was very elaborately gory and well done and the whole thing would have been an enormous success except for an eight-year-old girl who went in the front door and never came back out. Her mother got hysterical and they turned on all the lights and tore the place up looking for her and finally called the police. The cops showed up and looked around—fake blood and headless corpses and viscera of all types strewn everywhere—and stretched their yellow tape across the doorway and bleated at each other on their shoulder-mounted microphones until four in the morning when someone called up saying that they'd found the girl screaming her head off in their garage. She'd crawled into the backseat of a car in the parking lot—not her car but one that looked just like it to an eight-year-old—and had gone to sleep.

"Don't you have to be a social worker or something to work there?" I said. "I mean, to deal with the suicides and incest cases and issues like that?"

"I don't know," Izzie said, without meeting my gaze. She'd kept her eyes on her dinner since she'd gotten off the phone. "But you can find out tomorrow at ten. Ask for Dwayne."

I nodded. "Dwayne," I said. "Teen Scene Honcho and Typist Extraordinaire."

Jule giggled and Alex followed suit but Russ glared at them both and they quit.

"Hey," I said. "If nothing else I can make their signs for

them, right?" I winked at Jule. "Don't miss the Nude Teen Dance for MS!"

"Teen Spirit Car Wash for Really Bad Sprains!" said Alex.

"Teen Psychic Fair and Pet-Neutering Festival," said Izzie.

"Teen Electrolysis and Pancake Breakfast," Jule said. "Get Ready for the New Summer Fashions!"

Only Russ didn't get into it. He might have really had his shit together but he couldn't think on his feet to save his life.

I wore Russ's leather jacket to my interview the next morning at the Teen Scene. His clothes were much nicer than mine, and we were about the same size. Dwayne turned out to be a forty-year-old hypertensive with a shy smile that partially offset some alarmingly untended nostril hair. He talked to me from behind a chipped wood-tone Formica desk strewn with yellow Post-its and assorted small change, mostly nickels. I'd be damned if I was going to work there.

"Pushy," he said. "Pushy absolutely doesn't work. I figured that out a long time ago."

"That makes sense," I said. "That would make them feel not . . . I guess . . . at home or whatever."

The feebleness of this response clearly was lost on Dwayne.

"That's right," he said. "And you know why? Because all homes, no matter how different or broken or whatever, have one thing in common."

Roof? I thought. Family? Love?

"A credo. A code of conduct, an understanding of the baseline so everyone can feel comfortable enough to stake a claim to the territory."

"Like a room—a bedroom?"

"Exactly!"

I realized around this time that for all intents and purposes the interview was over, and had been over before it even started.

We had come to terms, somehow, before I had even gotten in the car in the morning. It seemed silly to even ask about details of salary and hours while Dwayne was explaining the credo of the Teen Scene.

"I mean, you can't get everyone on the same wavelength if nobody's built the radio station. You can't tune in if nobody's on the air."

I looked around. "There's a radio station here?" Dwayne seemed to be the kind of person who could bring out the moron in anyone.

He didn't skip a beat. "No, but that's not a bad idea. We get a license for a small-range station, just the city limits. We'd be able to announce our events and hours, send shoutouts to troops we're worried about, asking them to stop by."

Dwayne called all the clientele of the Teen Scene "troops," I discovered. He called the staff—which was him, me, and Becky's friend, a middle-aged lady named Charlene Farley—"wranglers."

But he was already losing steam on the radio station idea. "Of course we'd have to play music or something and that means CDs and that means money and we don't have it."

"Well," I said, "we could just set the microphone down next to a radio playing someone else's station. I mean, when we weren't doing our own thing."

"Okay," he said, tilting forward in his chair. "Let's get the details out of the way. We're paid by a private fund put together by an old widow, so your paycheck will actually be a regular bank draft, even though you're technically a city employee. It's a bit odd, but it works. It's full-time, but you can sort out your hours with Charlie. She's here all the time and all we need, really, is one person here at a time, so you may be coming and going whenever you want. We have some outreach stuff and Charlie doesn't like to do that all that much, and since she has seniority you'll probably do most of it."

"You mean like go to schools and stuff? Talk to kids about drugs or whatever?" It had returned to me that if I could demonstrate complete inadequacy in some necessary skill, such as communication or empathizing with teenagers, I still stood a chance of leaving the Teen Scene in the same amateur state I had entered it.

"You know, that's a good idea, going directly into the schools," he said. He looked around him as if for a pencil and gave up. He picked up a nickel instead and tapped it on the desktop metronomically, nodding his head. "Might be a nice thing to get a message to them before they get launched out the door in the afternoon to drive around aimlessly. Remind me later about that."

Dwayne went on to explain the outreach missions they had done in the past. For instance once, several months before, Dwayne and Charlie had locked up early and driven in Dwayne's Honda to Marshalltown to see if they could initiate a Scared Straight program at the penitentiary there. It turned out there was already a program in place, a fact that was shouted at them by a guard in a tower who wouldn't even let them near the visitor's entrance without an appointment or a law degree.

Another time Charlie had showed up by herself at the multiplex in Cedar Rapids with a large box of condoms, planning to hand them out after a showing of a teen slasher film. She made a clever sign that said PROTECT YOURSELF. IT'S BETTER THAN GETTING DISEMBOWELED. But as soon as she set up her table a couple of professors from the university mistook her for an anti-abortion activist and descended on her with a ferocity they'd perfected at rallies. She left almost immediately, in tears and minus her box of Rough Riders.

"So, clearly, we're always open for new ideas," Dwayne said.

I nodded and we were both silent for a moment.

"You mean now?" I said.

He stood up and reached out his hand. "Welcome aboard.

Let's go meet Charlie and I'll let you go on home and come back Monday all rested and sharp."

I trudged after him up a back staircase, an old servants' stair from when the place was a private home, narrow and twisting. At the top, Dwayne stopped and knocked on an overpainted white door, set up ten inches or so off the floor. Without waiting for an answer he pulled the door open and revealed another set of steeply raked steps to, apparently, the attic. I followed him, this time carefully, his ass practically wagging in my face.

At the top was clearly, to any impartial observer, an apartment, complete with bed, dresser, nightstand, throw rugs and pillows, and a small desk. Seated at the desk was a middle-aged woman with wild—almost tattered—hair, a scarf against the chill, and a ski sweater. She watched us materialize through the floor with a serene expression, the kind you find on posters of people claiming to be in love with their HMOs.

"Oh, wonderful," she said as we reached the landing, both of us stooped over awkwardly due to the sloped ceiling. I waited for Dwayne to move farther into the room but he stayed there, on the fringe, near the stairs. "That was easy," she continued. "Becky knows absolutely everybody."

Dwayne made an awkward presentation-type motion with his hand. "Charlie, Andrew. Andrew, Charlene."

"Hi . . ." I had already started to respond when my brain took in what he said, and I stumbled, ending up saying "Charlene" with a hard *ch*.

She regarded me warmly, then raised her eyebrows at Dwayne. "About the you-know-what?" she said.

He nodded quickly—even, it seemed, guiltily. "Sixty, I believe it was," he said.

"Oh?" Her tone seemed to verge on disappointment.

"That's strictly for manual," I said. "I'm probably a bit better on electric."

She beamed and Dwayne seemed to let out a pent-up breath

and started crowding me and pointing down the steps. I clutched the poorly attached handrail and tried not to brain myself on the floor joist while taking the steps down.

"See you," I called up into the space.

She answered, "Ta-ta, now."

At the bottom I stopped to let Dwayne take the lead again. "Does she live up there?" I whispered.

He shook his head firmly. "Oh, no," he said. "She lives somewhere outside of town with her son."

Through the ceiling I heard a telephone ring and, faintly, Charlene's voice answer, "Hello?"

"How old is her son?"

Dwayne pushed past me. "Gee, I don't know," he said on his way down to the first floor. "High school or college by now, surely. I'd have to stop and do the math."

"That's okay," I said. Do the math, I thought, and fifty bucks says he's forty. His mom lives in the attic at the Teen Scene and he's been working for Lockheed in Long Beach for eleven years.

I followed him all the way through the first-floor hallway and out to the front stoop where he shook my hand again. "So, Monday?" he said, almost jocularly. He seemed to breathe easier outside the Teen Scene, even if we were still on the front steps.

"I apologize," I said. "I really should ask what the salary is. It just seems unprofessional not to." Whatever it was, I would ask for more, even double, I had decided. It was my last chance.

"Of course—you mean I didn't tell you? It's twenty-two an hour to start, with a review after six months."

I nodded. The sign maker had paid seven seventy-five. There was some silence there on the stoop.

"I know what you're thinking," he said. "It's the old charter I'd mentioned before. At your level you're supposed to have at least an MSW, but we're more interested in someone young that the kids can identify with."

"I don't especially——"

He cut me off. "You should know, since you're going to be here. We need to keep the whole lack of an MSW thing under wraps, so to speak. The town needs this center. It's really the only place with the kids' welfare at heart. It's important what we're doing."

"Who would care?" I said. "Really, would anyone really investigate whether or not I have a degree?"

He nodded with his whole head and shoulders, it seemed. Then he reached out and seized my hand with both of his, his whole torso stiffened, and he leaned up close to me again. I could feel the vowels as he spoke them.

"I'll level with you," he said. "I'm looking to get out. I need a new me, someone to take over. I want to get the hell out of Iowa City while I have some life in me."

I froze, my entire arm pulled stiffly out in front of me like a pump handle. After a moment he let it go.

"Becky said you could be trusted," he said. "That you didn't have . . . a lot of options, so to speak. It'll be easier for you than for me, since you don't really have a calling—at least according to Becky, that is." He leaned forward again. I quickly put my hands in my pockets.

"The twenty-two an hour is my salary," he said. "I'll be taking yours. Nobody"—he glanced skyward—"has to know. It's between you and me."

"Do I really have to learn to type that fast?"

He nodded grimly. "You learn to type Charlie'll believe you've got a Ph.D. in social work. And she's the only one you have to convince."

"But——"

He held up his hand. "Just start practicing, and for the first few weeks come in the back door and stay out of the attic. If any kids show up, just chat them up, keep them around. Simple." With that he stepped back and disappeared through the front door, leaving me standing on the porch amid a half-dozen faded copies of the weekly shopping circular.

I stepped off the porch and slowly made my way to the sidewalk. Russ's comment about the Teen Scene came back to me, about how all it really needed was an underground entrance.

If only.

3

When I was a kid my parents swapped partners with my best friend's parents. My dad was this kind of military badass and my best friend's mother was pretty hot as those things go, so they probably were the instigators. My own mom—a college professor—and the other dad probably never had their hearts in the deal all the way. It took me years to figure out that my parents and their friends weren't the kind of people I'd ever choose to be around.

"Andrew," my mother said to me once, "get your head out of your ass. If you're going to be in college, at least study Shakespeare. Why waste your time?"

I had been pursuing a degree in chemical engineering at Washington University in St. Louis, across the river from where I'd grown up. I had a full-ride ROTC scholarship my grades and my old man's connections had gotten me. But I managed only C's and D's and refused to wear my uniform, and after only one semester the Air Force pulled the plug on the whole relationship.

But before they did I met a guy from Chile who managed to introduce me to the girl with whom I lost my virginity. His name was Julio. Mostly what he talked about was soccer and girls' asses. He told me he planned to be engaged to an American before his freshman year ended, and he was, to a Jewish girl who hated the plain sight of me. She had brown eyes which up close were the size of small apples and I started attending her classes, too. They caught me in a midterm when there wasn't a test copy with my name on it. When the teaching assistant asked me to leave, to my utter amazement, the girl gathered her books and walked out with me. I wasn't even sure up to that point she'd known I was in the room.

"Andrew," she said to me out in the dusty marble hall, "let's cut right to it, okay?" Her name was Elaine and already I was afraid she was too smart for me.

"That's cool," I said.

She just stared. "Do you have any idea what the fuck I'm talking about?"

"Can I get a drink before I answer that?"

"Do you screw only cheerleaders or something?" she said, but she was already leading me away.

We bought some wine in the village and went to her apartment. It had a fireplace and everything. She had candles. She had a poster of the Clash on the wall but only music by women on the shelf. Her body was white with scarlet bands where her underwear had crimped her. She was wet and impatient. She did all the work, all the talking, then lit me a cigarette and drank my glass of wine.

"If you're thinking of leaving now, no way," she said.

"No, no, I'm good," I said.

"I wish I could smoke but I quit," she said. She sighed and looked around her place. "Tell me about farming," she said. "Horses and bulls and steers. I'm really interested in that kind of thing."

"Well," I said. "I can only tell you what I've read." This wasn't quite true. Friends of mine had been farmers' kids. My high school across the river in Illinois had a 4-H club and a Future Farmers of America club for the Christians. I'd gotten drunk on farms all through school, but I couldn't tell you how they worked.

"Whoa," she said, sitting up and pulling the sheet over her chest. "You didn't grow up on a farm? Julio said you grew up on a farm."

"Julio lied," I said. "I grew up on Air Force bases. My dad grew up on a ranch but that's him."

She slid down a little. "Really?"

"Truly. My dad was a major before he got out."

"A major," she said. "My dad is a fund-raiser. When I was ten he took my brother and moved to the other side of town."

"That's awful," I said.

She slumped down even farther in the bed.

"I think you better leave now," she said.

Back home my mother just laughed at me. "In Shakespeare classes nobody would give a flying fuck if you were enrolled or not," she said. "Take the early histories, learn something."

"She wanted me to be a farmer," I said. "Some sort of weirdass slumming, I guess. If I'd told her I was a National Merit Scholar she'd have called the cops."

"She sounds like a head case," my mother said. "You're better off."

"I don't know. Education isn't everything." Look where it got you, I wanted to say.

"Hey," my mother said, "I'm not a social worker. If people don't want to better themselves it's no skin off my fat pink ass."

"Not a social worker" was my mom's favorite line. My mom was a classicist, a short and chunky chain-smoker who was convinced of her own brilliance and played folk songs on her acoustic twelve-string guitar when my friends came over. My dad always took that opportunity to tune the pipes on his Indian in the garage. They were really a couple of show-offs. Why I told them everything that happened in my life is beyond me.

So when my dick started to sting in the bathroom a few days after sleeping with Elaine, I should not have mentioned this to my mother. I see this now.

"Oh, man, Jezebel gave you the clap," she said. "That's just unbelievable."

"I don't know what to do," I said.

"It's the eighties," my mom said. "You call her up and tell her and get a shot. After that you carry rubbers with you, stud."

Of course I called her and she went to pieces. I should have waited until I'd seen the doctor and he gave me a prescription for NGU—nongonococcal urethritis. I also should have called her back and told her I'd made a mistake. But I didn't. I was a coward and I'd already made a fool out of myself enough for one year. I finished the semester without ever setting foot in Washington University again. I never even sent for my transcripts. I moved myself to Iowa City the next summer with a fresh start. My parents, their last child finally gone, moved back to Oregon, where they had both grown up.

My mother called me out of the blue that afternoon after I'd met with Dwayne. It was just me and Jule home. We were watching the *Boy in the Plastic Bubble* movie.

Jule had been talking all through the film. She was nervous lately because she and Isabel were going to meet with the school vice principal in a few days. She was convinced he was going to make trouble, maybe try to have her taken out of the house.

She twisted her fingers around each other and through the locks of hair that fell on either side of her face.

"Do you think he'll ask any questions about me and Russ?" she asked suddenly.

"I don't know," I said. "Maybe. If he does just change the subject to your grades." Jule was a straight-A student, always had been. Blissed out, depressed, in a coma, abducted by aliens, she'd still be a straight-A student. Grades would never be a problem for her.

"What are you most afraid of?" I asked.

Just then the phone rang, and Jule reached over and picked up the handset.

"Hello. Hi. Fine. Yeah. Yeah. I do." She furrowed her brow and listened. John Travolta gazed at her from inside his bubble.

"I don't know, *Hamlet*, I guess."

I reached for the phone and she gave it up immediately, mouthing the words "your mom."

"Hey," I said. "Are you like William Shakespeare's fucking agent? You're worse than a telemarketer, for Christ's sake."

Her voice was mild over the phone—without her intensity and grith in plain sight she sounded a lot like someone's long-suffering roommate.

"Your father is missing," she said.

On the television a baby cried. "Missing?" I repeated. "Is he flying? I thought he wasn't flying anymore."

"He was hunting. He wasn't flying. Maybe he's still hunting. He's only overdue two days."

"Where is he hunting?"

"Alaska. Georgette called me this morning." Georgette was my father's common-law wife. Younger than me, an Indian of some kind of extraction. The three of them had lived together for a while. I never inquired after the details, but at some point my dad and Georgette had moved out to a farm outside of Ashland, Oregon. They called it a farm but really it was a compound, the kind of place you'd expect to operate hate cells. The only electricity was in the shop via a generator. My mom lived in Yreka, just over the California border.

"How will you know he's back?" I asked. My dad and Georgette had a cell phone, but they had to hike a mile up a ridge to use it.

"I'm staying at a friend's in town here," she said. "Town" was Medford, where the airport was.

"The airline will call here when he checks in. That's the only thing we can think of. Georgette doesn't even know where they're hunting. He and fucking Otto just said they'd be back day before yesterday."

"Otto," I said. "That's great." Otto was Georgette's drunken white brother or father, I couldn't remember which.

"He got free tickets to Juneau," my mom said. "All they had to pay for was freight on the way back for the coolers."

"Just call me when he gets back," I said. "Call anytime."

When I hung up the phone Jule was watching me with expectant eyes. The television was off.

"I'm really really really sorry," she said.

"It's okay," I said. "My parents are good at taking care of themselves."

"You're sweating," she said. "You look really pale. Isabel will be home soon." She put her hand on top of mine and I couldn't help but stare at it. My father had walked away from spectacular motorcycle accidents, had crashed an ultralight plane into a metal barn, and had three fused vertebrae from a terrific ass-kicking by a Portland Trailblazer after a postgame heckling.

The phone rang again and I grabbed the kitchen extension. The caller ID reported Isabel's work number.

"Teen Scene," I said. "Can I take your birth control order?"

"Yes!" she said. "You got it? You rock."

"Your sources are very good," I said. "Too good."

"What do you mean?"

"I mean I could have had a ham for a head and gotten that job. It smells like a setup to me."

"How much do they pay?" she said. "Becky said it pays really well."

"Let's put it this way," I said. "We're getting the all-beef bologna now. No more of that store brand."

Isabel started to laugh and I couldn't talk to her for nearly thirty seconds over the snorting. She had a really loud bray and it was generally very sexy but sometimes made me glance around a room to see if anyone noticed.

"Isabel," I said, "it's too weird. We can't count on it to last too long."

"Gotta run," she said. "See you at dinner?"

I looked over at Jule. She sat in front of me with her head bowed. She had blue jeans with holes in the knees and no socks on her feet. Her slender neck was partly covered by her hair and I could make out the ridge of her nose, just barely.

Jule would always get straight A's, always skitter along the edge of perfection. But she'd never understand the way she would make the poor fifteen-year-old bastards' hearts fibrillate when she turned her head or laughed at a passing thought.

"Okay," I said. "See you." I had forgotten what we were talking about, but it didn't matter. Izzie had hung up.

I hung up the phone and sat down next to Jule. I reached out with my index finger and lifted her chin. I was no fifteen-year-old. I was sweating, my heart was racing, but I knew what I was doing in a way no fifteen-year-old possibly could.

"Jule," I said. "Thanks for being here for me."

It was that easy to go to hell, it turned out. At least, it seemed so at the time. I leaned forward and put my cheek up against her cheek. She trembled next to me but didn't move.

When Isabel and the boys got home they were flushed and laughing. Russ plopped down on the couch next to Jule and she gave me several furtive looks before they left with each other for the night. Russ's baggy jeans dragged on each step; Jule's jeans revealed the curve and dimple of the small of her back. When their door clicked shut I realized that Izzie had been watching me the whole time.

In bed Izzie ran herself all over me, culminating in a blow job that left my feet tingling. She fell asleep facing away from me. I started thinking about the first time we had been together, when she had been married and had given me drink after drink and the way she moved behind the bar and washed glasses and laughed with the regulars and the underage farm-state frat boys. She had a small tattoo of a rose on her neck, the stem bent in a small arc the circumference of a dime. I'd show up around eight-thirty trying not to seem as desperate as I felt, slide into the stool by the waiter's station that they discouraged anyone else from using by moving the setup tray and napkins in front of it; when I sat down Isabel moved them to the other side of the brass rail, even if someone was sitting there.

"Hey," she'd say to me with the Maker's Mark already cocked in her wrist. "How's my boy?"

The first time we touched was a fabulous, dangerously frantic night when she let it be known that her boys and her husband had gone to Chicago for the weekend to spend two days at the boat show. She didn't have to close; I lingered as she rang out, trying to both make it obvious but cover myself if I had to. When she came from the back with her coat on and I was getting to my feet it was as smooth as it possibly could have been. It reminded me of the perfect shoplift.

In her car. In her driveway. In my apartment. Her skin smelled like fruit and sweat. She liked to pull her lips back across her teeth a lot, like she was grinning but then dart the tip of her tongue out, like a tiny lure. She liked to raise her chin up and expose her throat, then bring it down in a sudden twist. She liked to grab my hair, then release it, then grab it again. Her hair was dark, her nipples were dark, the skin under her arms rough like a cat's tongue.

"I guess this makes me your bitch," I said after. "What a great setup for you. You get me drunk and then use me for sex."

"Rosie's gonna freak," she said. "She talks about your ass all the time."

"That's a chilling thought," I said. "But we're not going public with this, right? I mean, for obvious reasons?"

She shrugged. "I suddenly don't really give a shit," she said. "If it wasn't for the boys I would have changed my life years ago."

"That's the spirit," I said. I fought the urge to look at my watch. I wondered if she expected to stay over. I suddenly needed to be back at Rosie's. Or anywhere else.

A week later she came to my place for lunch and I told her to leave her skirt on, put her hair in a ponytail, and wear my tennis shoes. I don't know; it made me crazy and I came so hard I ached afterward. We never got tired of it, never. When I dropped everything and broke up with her I was surprised how easy it was to believe that it hadn't meant anything.

In the middle of that night I woke up suddenly, stupidly and insistently hard and in a light sweat. Isabel was snoring slightly, turned away, her rump tantalizingly near. I could have awakened her; I knew how to do it perfectly by now. Instead I got out of bed and went down the hall to Russ and Jule's room. I stood outside, baggy-assed in my gym shorts and losing steam steadily in the chill. Some light played across the ceiling from a car in the alley outside; a door slammed somewhere and the lights moved off and disappeared.

I pushed the door open as quietly as I could; Russ lay in their bed alone, spread-eagled. I looked around the room quickly and slid the door shut. At the end of the hall the bathroom door was closed, but no light came from under the door. As I walked up to it the door swung in and Jule started to slide around it. She gasped when she saw me, and drew her hand across her mouth quickly.

"Sorry," I whispered. "You all right?"

"I had a bad dream," she said. "It's all right."

"You're sweating," I said. "It must have been bad."

"My dad was in it," she said. "And your dad was in it."

"Oh, no, I'm really sorry you had to hear all of that," I said, and as I said it I found myself really wishing it were true. She stood and shivered in her T-shirt and underwear and I got to hold her again; twice in one night. It was dark in the hall, no more lights from the alley, and something made me feel like one of us was glowing.

I spent the next morning at the law library reading up on youth center–related cases; I was searching for lawsuits involving inexperienced youth center counselors and wealthy irate parents. I didn't take any special notice of him at first—a bland-featured guy with a vacant expression. I thought he was someone I recognized from somewhere. Whoever he was, he was watching me from the Lexis-Nexis terminals. I nodded at him and then realized who he was. It was Dwayne, my new boss. I couldn't tell if he had been having similar trouble placing me, or if he'd just locked eyes on my table and had lost himself in reverie. I waved a little at him, and got nothing in response. I checked behind me for a clock, a movie screen, a belly dancer—nothing.

I tried to concentrate on my own screen and for a few minutes succeeded—the next time I looked up he was typing furiously and the time after that he had disappeared.

On the way out the door I ran into my old Farsi professor and we talked for a while about dope, which was always the thing we talked about. Ganja Boy I called him—shit, he was two years younger than me.

"So, how's married life?" he asked.

"Creamy," I said. It was the adjective we'd long ago chosen for the best bud. He seemed impressed.

"That good," he said. It wasn't a question.

"How's tenure?" I asked.

He shrugged. "Maybe not the best time to ask. Care for a lightup?"

I shook my head. "Can't afford the groceries anymore." I knew he knew I'd given it up. He was offering the same way you ask the triple-bypass survivor if he wanted more bacon—in the end, behind so many relationships, there was only empty hospitality.

I stopped in to see Rosie on the way through the ped mall. She was in the office in the back, flipping through invoices. The Budweiser delivery guy was standing in his shorts (forty degrees these guys wear shorts) and baseball shirt, a fairly beat-up bill in his hand.

"Hang on, stud," Rosie was saying. "I'm getting there." She pulled out a yellow bill. "Why the fuck is this yellow?" she said, holding it up in front of the delivery guy.

"I gave you the yellow one because you said you couldn't read the pink one," he said. "Remember? I caught shit for that, too."

"I thought it was because you shorted me and said you'd make it up next time."

"No, you said I shorted you, and I gave you the yellow copy so's you could see I only had nine and that's all that was on the paper."

Rosie started to nod by bobbing her entire torso thoughtfully. "Got it," she said. "Danka shane, stud."

When the Bud man had left with his signature I sat in the chair across from her desk. "What are you going to do next week, drop a pencil and ask him to pick it up? That dude is thick but even he has to be catching on by now . . ."

She shrugged. "I already offered him money to help me move some furniture. He didn't take."

"Hire him at the bar."

She snorted. "That guy? I'd sooner hire you. I got enough farmers working for me." She rolled up the sleeve of her enormous blouse.

"I got a new tat. Look at that."

In the middle of a large tan- and olive-colored bruise near her elbow was a cartoon of a guy sitting on his ass, bracing himself with two hands on the ground behind him, his pecs sticking out. It was the same pose you saw sometimes on the mud flaps of semitrailers.

"That's hideous," I said. "It's temporary, right?"

She rolled her sleeve back down. "Izzie told me about your dad. From what I heard he's probably just hunting beaver. I bet he turns up."

"You'd like my dad," I said. "He'd like you."

"Send him over. My kid needs another terrible role model."

This made me laugh. The phone rang and she barked into it for a minute or two.

"Dude," she said when she hung up, "you want to know about the Teen Scene, right?"

"And how you read minds while you're at it."

She just looked angry. "My kid went there for a while but he said it's just a weird scene, like a *Lord of the Flies* minus the island kind of thing."

"They're supposedly going to pay me like a goddamn senator. It's too weird."

"Just take it, but keep your wits about you, as they say. You'll know soon enough if it's something bad. Everyone says you're smarter than the average Iowa City dumbshit."

"Can you ask around, though? Just let me know whatever you hear?"

"Sure," she said. "Hey, you want a burger basket?" She hauled herself up and I followed her out to the table next to the computer golf game. I ate a cheeseburger and beat her by nine strokes. On the way home I swore I saw Dwayne at the Citgo station and then again coming out of the Fiji house. Both times it turned out I was wrong.

4

When I was drinking at Rosie's I'd been officially in charge of the jukebox and there was a period in which I strictly enforced a tacit code that all music on the thing would have to be that of girl groups or bands with at least one openly gay member and preferably two—one of each sex was best. There were a few good examples of each but quickly I had to compromise and allow groups fronted by girls and bands with gay members who were, undoubtedly for financial reasons, mostly closeted. It was pretty good all around, even for Rosie, since the frat and sports types stayed away and left a lot of room for everyone else—people who could be counted on to not leave the place and break things or crash their cars.

Around this time I struck up a friendship with Aaron Gill, a huge black fag who admitted much later that he was never, for some reason, ever attracted to me. This was strange, he said, because over time he was attracted to just about everyone, even at one point the soon-to-retire president of the university. That one was so intense he spent an entire semester stalking the old guy and finding opportunities to run into his wife at the supermarket and bang into her cart.

Aaron was a lapsed music major who just couldn't find it in himself to actually give up the craft. He was a trombonist—a terrible trombonist if I'm any judge. He was the kind of trombonist who could never seem to actually hit a note dead-on and solid—his tone was always kind of wavery and carried a strange spit-buzz undercurrent that, if recorded, would make anyone listening suspect they needed new speakers.

But until he left town a few weeks before I quit drinking he was my best and pretty much only friend. He would stop by my apartment almost every day on his way to the classes he was auditing and sip his tea in my kitchen. His stove always stank of gas, he claimed, even though it was electric, so he mistrusted it completely. And he was addicted to tea—no Japanese maiden commanded a stricter ceremony of stirring and pouring than he did with his strings and gauze bags and little perforated chrome balls. At that point I was taking a small amount of scotch every day with my bagel but Aaron never mentioned it—glass houses, maybe—and we often sat together, sighing and shivering a little with pleasure when we raised our cups to our mouths, like two old biddies at luncheon.

"It's insane," Aaron said one day, fitting the cup back onto the dead center of his saucer. He was a big guy, six-four at least, around two hundred fifty doughy pounds. "I mean I'm still growing. At twenty fucking three years old. Last year this jacket was big."

"You've gained weight."

"I have not. Plus that would not make my arms longer. Look at this."

"Maybe it shrank," I said.

"Leather does not shrink. At least it shouldn't."

"Did you get it wet?"

He rolled his eyes. "That's suede," he said. "And that's about spotting."

"So make a mark on the doorway," I said. "We'll look at it six months from now and see."

He thought about it and finally just shrugged. "By then I'll have forgotten about it."

"So I'll remind you."

"Who'll remind you?"

"I'll mark my calendar. I'll find my calendar and mark it down. April or May sixteenth or seventeenth or whatever. Whatever six months from now is."

Aaron gave me a very congenial smirk. "I'll set my watch," he said.

And that was the last time I saw him; he disappeared the following Friday, the day I quit drinking. He sent me a letter a few weeks later—his mother had had a stroke and he had returned to Des Moines to take care of her and would be back soon. It was only one hundred miles away but neither of us ever managed to close the distance. His wedding/best man invitation came back rejected by the post office.

So it was with some surprise that, the morning after leaving Dwayne on the porch of the Teen Scene, I had to stop my car at a pedestrian crossing to let Aaron pass in front. I almost didn't recognize him—he'd put on weight and his clothes were wrinkled and ill-matched.

I rolled down my window.

"Bijou," I called. "Hey!" Bijou was my nickname for him, since I'd caught him once necking with a teaching assistant in the back row of the campus theater. The film—I still remember it because of that—was that old chestnut *In the Realm of the Senses*. Even then I thought yuck, and the combination didn't help with my latent revulsion at the thought of guys getting that sloppy with each other.

Aaron stopped in the middle of the crosswalk and peered at my windshield skeptically.

I stuck my head out the window. "Aaron," I said. "It's me, man."

He stared for a moment and then crossed over to the passenger side and opened the door. When he climbed in he grunted and pulled in his trailing leg with his right hand, as if it were asleep. "Who makes this thing, Mattel?" he said.

"It's Isabel's," I said. "I think it's French."

"How do you say Stupid Little Car in French?" he said, staring ahead at the road.

"I don't know," I said. "I'd tell you but my font doesn't have that funny *c* with the tail on it."

"That letter you're referring to means Cat on a Window. So popular an image the French just assigned it its own letter in the alphabet."

"If it helps, Stupid Little Car in Serbo-Croatian is Yugo," I said.

"What kind of language needs a hyphen in the fucking name, anyway? It's an invitation to slaughter, if only to get rid of the extra typing. Winner gets the language."

But at that point I pulled up to another light and it suddenly seemed impossible to keep it up.

"You're back," I said evenly.

"You're married," he said. "Or that ring's just a cheap ploy to hit on baby-sitters." He raised his eyes then and I could see that he looked exhausted and older. His dark skin was powdery and loose under his jaw, even though he looked at least as big as the last time I'd seen him, if not bigger. He must have added a lot of weight and then recently lost it. His head was shaved and he now looked like a very bad character.

"Bijou," I said. "Where you been at?"

"Around," he said. "Where you heading to?"

"I mean it," I said. "People were worried. I wanted you to be in my wedding."

"Say maid of honor and I'll kick your toy car to shreds."

"Best man," I said. "Plus the orchestra was short on brass, so you could have pulled in some tips."

That made him smile for the first time.

"Really," I said, "what the fuck happened to you, Aaron?"

"I was entombed."

"Funny," I said.

"I was in jail. Or maybe prison. I'm actually not sure which."

I slowed the car down and pulled over to the side. I slammed the shifter up and turned the ignition off with a flourish that I regretted as soon as I did it.

"Shit," I said, "I wouldn't believe you for a second if you didn't look exactly like someone who just got out of jail."

"I didn't just get out. I've been out for two months. I was only in for ninety days."

"Ninety days? What did you do?"

"Killed my mom."

"You did NOT," I said. "You did NOT do that."

"Tell that to the state's attorney. His name is Marshall. He thinks I gave her about fifty times too much Demerol."

"You did NOT," I said.

"I'm hungry," he said.

I nodded to myself for a few moments. We sat there silently.

"Well," I said. "Come home with me, then. We'll have lunch. Izzie's got some pretty good tea."

"How about Kool-Aid?" he said. "I've acquired a taste for cherry Kool-Aid."

"Maybe," I said. "We've got pretty much everything."

Later on I would get some more of the story out of him, how the state's attorney was being picked on by the local paper and—as he even admitted to Aaron—was forced to seek time for what he felt was a mercy killing. The judge split the difference between the probation Aaron's attorney had asked for and the six months Marshall had come up with to satisfy the editorial page.

He'd served his three months at a place called Candlewood near Marshalltown, filled with meth lab operators, unsuccessful pimps, and the marginally retarded. He'd spent most of his time alone, under the protection of a "friend." All the new friend took in exchange was money, food, cigarettes, recreation chits, and telephone time. This wasn't so bad, Aaron said, since he didn't need money, needed to lose weight, didn't smoke, hated pool, and had nobody to call.

On the way to the house I remembered in quick succession a half-dozen times Aaron and I had kicked around together; like the time he'd taken me to the gay bar in Des Moines and had us both stuff a glove in the crotch of our jeans first. The clientele was on the old side, or at least I thought so then, and I didn't have to buy a drink all night. As the night wore on I told one guy sitting next to Aaron at the bar that I was his legal guardian since his mother offed herself because he was borderline autistic. I described the perversions I was planning for him when we got home in such lurid detail the guy excused himself for the rest room and never came back to the bar. A few minutes later Aaron got me to pretend to be fighting with him.

"You disgust me," he said, loud enough to carry.

"Oh, you're so pure," I replied. "You're so fucking tight. Well, one day you'll be like me and then you'll see, Bright Eyes."

"I should never have pulled over that day," he yelled. "I should have just left you there on that moped."

And so on. Another time we showed up at the famous presidential caucuses and bet each other who could control the most delegates by evening's end. We picked separate candidates and by the end of the night I'd won that one walking away.

The last time, just before he left, we were drinking tall cans of beer down below the dam when a dad who had been barbecuing outside his camper came over and sheepishly asked if we could temper the language since his little daughter was playing close by.

We both apologized profusely and Aaron struck up a conversation with him. We ended up drinking Old Style and watching black-and-white 12-volt TV with the family until after dark, when they had to leave for the RV park. The little girl tried to give us her toy pony and Aaron got upset and wouldn't take it. He was drunk and the father was drunk and I was worse than anyone.

"I have a real horse at home," he told the little girl, who might have been five or might have been ten. "He'll get mad if I bring home another one."

"What's his name?" she asked.

"Flaming Orifice," Aaron said.

The father looked confused.

"He's a retired Thoroughbred," Aaron said. "A gelding, so he wasn't worth anything and I adopted him."

"Sweetheart, come on inside," the girl's mother said from the door of the camper. She had been suspicious of us the whole time in that typically even, midwestern way.

"I saved his life and he's never forgotten," Aaron said.

"Let's go." I started to pull on Aaron's arm.

"He's a magic horse," Aaron called out over his shoulder as I led him away. "And they were going to turn him into Irish Fucking Spring."

In the car he was morose all the way back to his apartment. When I let him out he leaned back down to the window. "I really really really wanted that little toy horse," he said. "How fucked up is that?"

At the house only Jule was home, listening to her Walkman and watching television. When I came in with Aaron she slid off her headphones.

"Isabel called. She says she loves you. She says——"

"Jule," I said, "this is Aaron. Aaron, Jule."

"Pleasure," Aaron said. "Do you have a bathroom?"

"We just had one put in," I said, but he didn't even smile. I pointed down the back hall. "That way," I said. He clomped off, trailing his ragged coat behind him.

I sat down on the couch next to Jule. "Did you ever have a

best friend?" I said. "Then you went away to camp or something and when you came back they were someone else?"

"No," she said. "I had one best friend and it turned out later she was always in love with me. What a liar she was."

We were quiet on the couch after that and she slid her headphones back on. The earpieces pulled her soft hair back from her temple and showed off her near cheekbone, which was admirable, and the trailing edge of her eyebrow.

Aaron returned from the bathroom and went immediately to the refrigerator. He had to bend halfway over to see inside and his black coat hung off his sides like funeral bunting.

"Don't worry, I'm not going to take anything out," he said. "I'm just looking because I haven't seen a family refrigerator in about eighty years."

"Eat anything you want," I said. *"Mi Kenmore es su Kenmore."*

He emerged holding a jar of sweet pickle relish. "This has never been opened," he said. "You don't need to keep it in the refrigerator if it hasn't been opened."

I stole a look at Jule. She hadn't heard. "I think it has been opened," I said. "I think I used a little in some tuna salad."

He put the jar down on the counter. "Besides being disgusting that's untrue. You can tell by the dimple in the top." He picked up the jar again and, without even the slightest effort at concealment, slid it into his pocket. He walked over to the couch and sat down next to me. The couch was old and he created a serious lean. In order to stay out of his lap I had to angle noticeably over toward Jule.

"I can see auras since the whole thing with my mom," he said. "I know in the past I said that stuff was crap but here we are."

Jule slid off her headphones. Aaron was staring past me at her and he was looking for a moment like his old self, except for the broken teeth.

"What happened to your mom?" Jule said, the headphones buzzing on either side of her slender neck.

"She stopped using most of her brain and then she died."

Jule nodded. "Mine too."

"Jule," I said. "I thought your parents were killed in a car crash."

"They were, but she died later on in the hospital from an infection," she said, still looking at Aaron. "The last time I saw her I thought they had, like, bleached the pillowcases or something. Her whole head was all pearly even though it was really dark in the room. There was only this skinny bedside lamp with an old yellow tube in it but she was all pearly white."

"Maybe she had a fever," I said.

"My mother had violet sparks," said Aaron. "They would shoot out about three inches and end with this little twirl. I knew a guy in jail who said that toward the end his wife gave off a blue light when she slept."

"Did she die?" Jule asked.

"No," Aaron said, "but she left the guy and he never saw her again. She left a note saying she was going to live in the desert."

"She probably joined a cult," I said. "The order of the blue-glowing divorcées."

Just then Alex pushed the door open and slipped inside. He dropped his coat on the floor by the door and went into the kitchen. He was muttering to himself in that cute way that Izzie and I often remarked on. Even though sometimes if you listened carefully you could hear him swear, it was usually more like a benign argument with himself, the kind you'd find Linus having in a *Peanuts* cartoon.

"Alex," I said from the couch. "This is my old friend Aaron."

"Hi," he replied, his voice muffled by the fact that his head was inside the refrigerator.

Aaron got to his feet and stood next to the couch. Alex kept

his head in the refrigerator and Aaron remained standing, almost ceremonially.

"Have a seat, he's a minor," I said.

In the past Aaron would have cracked wise about that, saying
"I major in minors," or something like that. Not this time.

"I'm cured of all that," he said. "Those days are totally over.
That was someone else completely."

I nodded slowly. Who knows what he'd gone through?

He shook his head as if he heard my thoughts and sat down.
"It's not that," he said. "Homosexual sex is a base urge. The
Buddha gave it up by the time he was sixteen."

"That's lovely for him," I said. "But, you know, he was pretty
advanced. And a prince if I remember correctly."

"We're all princes," he said. I could see him fingering the jar
in his pocket. Jule was staring at him, the lashes of her eyes
spread like petals on an iris.

"This prince is ready for some lunch," I said. "Who's up for
grilled cheese?" Maybe it was the way I said it, maybe it was the
choice of entree; even Alex looked at me like I'd said something
loathsome.

"Okay," I said, "I'm open to suggestions."

"I ate," Jule said.

"Me too," said Alex, heading for the stairs. Aaron watched
him disappear down the hall. I thought I saw him shake his
head a little. For a strong moment I wanted him out of the
house.

Aaron stayed for about an hour. We ate warmed-over Chunky
turkey soup and talked about prison as if it were summer school.
Aaron showed me his tattoos—a horse head ("copied from a
kid's book") and a small shamrock. A friend had done them with
real tattoo tools he'd borrowed from a guard. The horse looked a
bit goatlike but Aaron was clearly proud of it.

"You know what was weird and humbling about that whole goddamn thing?" he said. "That I wasn't the smartest guy there. Not by a long shot."

"Did they have stockbrokers and guys like that there? Inside traders?"

"I think so," he said. "But the smartest guy there was this nigger preacher named—so help me God—Buck. From some shithole Davenport ghetto. He fucking crackled with smarts. I did everything that dude said. Without him I would have gone crazy."

Aaron told me how Buck had given him his prison name, Tommy D (for Doubting Thomas), and baptized him in the Church of the Total Consecration. Buck was serving a year for assaulting a security guard at an abortion clinic.

"Not battery," Aaron said. "He never touched the guy. Don't fuck with that lobby, let me tell you."

"Okay," I said. "I won't."

A few minutes later I asked him where he lived. "Greenwood Apartments," he said. "I think they should rename it Plywood Apartments."

"Are you working?"

He shook his head. "Last year's student loan. Social Security. That sort of thing."

"You can't keep that up forever."

"Do you get letters from the governor?" he asked severely.

"I do not."

"I do. 'Dear ex-fag convict nigger. We're watching you.' "

"Come on," I said.

" 'Dear scum. We caught you once and we'll catch you again. Dear shit—' "

"I get the picture."

"It's hard getting a job."

"I know."

"However, I got one today."

"You did. Where?"

"Lumberyard. Guy who runs it was a CO. Says he knows everything about convicts. He can read us like a book."

I started to open my mouth.

"Corrections officer," Aaron said. "He doesn't find me colorful at all."

"I do."

He shrugged. "That's your problem."

"I think that's a little harsh."

"So sue me," he said, but I could sense that he was softening up.

"Bijou, you remember I told you about my cousin, the Viet Nam vet? He went to about seven prisons and whenever I talked to him I felt like he was bullshitting me."

Aaron started to cry. He didn't sob but tears started to ease down his cheeks.

"But you don't sound like him, Bijou. I'm guessing that's a good thing."

We were quiet for a while. "I want to go back to school," he said.

"So go," I replied. "What's stopping you?"

"Can't afford it."

"Get another loan. Like last year."

"You never read the fine print, have you?" he said. "No loans for felons."

"You're kidding. That's stupid. Who needs loans more than felons?"

"The government didn't seem so choosy way back when, did it? Once on the application I wrote lubrication where it asked for major course of study."

"So lie," I said. "How will they know?"

"It's breaking parole to lie on employment applications or any government form that asks if you've been convicted of a felony."

I didn't say anything for a while. "Jeeze, Aaron," I said. "Why'd you do it? Was your mom in that bad a shape?"

It turns out she was, indeed. She was meowing like a cat and wetting the bed and worse. She was breaking out in hives and sores. She had rattling teeth. They were putting in a freeway ramp next to her bedroom window. Her husband was dead, her son was depressed, and her house was worth nothing. Aaron killed her with a prescription he'd refilled four times in an hour.

I dropped him off in front of the Greenwood Apartments. Someone in a knit cap was searching through the junipers next to the unmarked door when we pulled up; he started tying his shoes, deep in concentration, until Aaron passed through the front door and I pulled away.

That night in bed I had Isabel do the office worker thing—she put on a white dress shirt and tie and no pants and pretended to file papers on her knees up at the bookcase headboard, her hair pinned up and fake reading glasses on the end of her nose.

We hadn't done that in a while but it was a kind of celebration of my new job. While she was doing all kinds of sexy office mannerisms—cocking her head to one side, chewing a pencil tip—I made my move on her from behind.

"Mr. Bergman," she objected in a throaty whine, "I have to finish the Baker correspondence—"

I lifted the sides of the shirt and ran my hands up under her ribs.

"—and make copies and make it to FedEx by six."

"If you don't fuck me immediately you're fired," I said.

She gave a nervous little laugh as I traced my index finger across her belly. "I don't think it's right . . ."

"Bullshit," I said. "It's right. It's proper. You want it."

"Yes," she agreed. "I do want it. I've always wanted it. Ever since the first day."

"You only work here because of me," I said. She put the paperback books aside and, reaching down, helped guide my dick inside her.

"That's true," she breathed.

My breath started coming short. She braced herself with one hand on the edge of the headboard.

"This is the best job," I panted, "you'll ever have."

"I know," she said. I could see her tongue dart out and make the circle of her lips.

"Isabel," I gasped. "Help me." We stumbled back onto the bed with her on top of me. We writhed and clutched like two people going down one of those dark and crazy water slides, being thrown from side to side, up and suddenly pitched downward. At the bottom we were tossed into a warm pool and bobbed there effortlessly. Just like always we'd made it at the same time, at the same instant, in exact sync, in perfect tune.

5

Somewhere in the night I felt violently sick—the air in the room seemed foul and my ears rang with a dull humming. I made it into the bathroom in time to retch in the toilet—there was nothing there but some acrid slivers of gray meat. The linoleum behind the sink had started to buckle and curl and I tried to keep my eyes on it, my gaze steady.

At seven in the morning Isabel slid a mug of coffee onto the night table next to my head. She ran her fingers quickly through my forelock.

"I feel like shit," I murmured, my eyes closed.

She pulled her hand away. "What, you're sick?"

"Apparently." There was a quiet moment. "But I'm sure I can go in. They sounded pretty flexible. I'll rest until eight and then get going."

I opened my eyes. Isabel was looking doubtful. "Don't oversleep," she said. "Even if it's an easygoing place you have got to show up on time your first day. It's one of those unwritten rules."

"I think all of the rules at the Teen Scene are unwritten," I said. "I'll be fine."

She fingered the hair at my temples again, and sighed. Her shoes squeaked their way down the hall.

Isabel had taken the car so I walked the twelve blocks to the Teen Scene. I stopped twice to gasp and spit into the bushes. I'd skipped breakfast so there was nothing really to retch up, but this simple act seemed to give me a few minutes' health, a few blocks of clearheadedness. I passed in front of the rec center and the Realtor and the guns and knives store. Their little parking lots were almost empty—one or two employees' cars only. Employees—employed persons like me—people with jobs in small buildings, the heart of the American workforce. I leaned over behind a mailbox and pretended to be tying my shoe, my finger down my throat.

I went into the Teen Scene through the back door, which was built up on a wheelchair ramp. There were no stairs so you had to wind around a bit, like a Six Flags ride. Inside there was dusty fluorescent silence in the game room, stuffy gloom in the lounge. Dwayne's office was locked. I thought about going upstairs to Charlie's apartment, but then she stepped out of a bathroom door. She was dressed in dark wool from head to toe. Her short gray manlike hair poked out from under a watch cap.

"Andrew," she said. Her voice was surprisingly lilted, and my name seemed to float like an unanswerable question.

"Good morning, Charlene," I said. "Am I too early?" It was eight-thirty or so. The clock on the wall said three-fifteen.

"Oh, no, no," she said. She pulled the hat down over her head tighter. "I just had to step back out to get some coffee. I never seem to remember on the way."

I nodded. "I'll hold down the fort. I think I can handle the crowd."

She just looked puzzled, glancing out the window. "It might snow," she said. "You never know."

She went past me to the door I'd just come in. "Would you like anything, dear?"

Tall Cap with extra milk, I thought. "No, thanks. I'm good."

After she left I found a place for my coat on a wobbly rack in the lounge. I wandered around the first floor reading the posters thumbtacked to the dirty plaster wall. The best one was about the Heimlich maneuver, but someone had editorialized in the margins with a pencil. After the step entitled "Call for help" someone had added, "You think?" The rendering of a man wrapping his arms around a victim from behind had been helpfully annotated to a new Step 7: "Sodomize the unconscious victim." Someone named Zoe was advertised as a person not terribly likely to spurn advances, and Will was reported to be attracted to members of his own sex. At the bottom was a notice that the Teen Scene "blew chunks."

Another poster on recognizing depression had been almost completely edited. "Check for weapons" was now first on the list, followed by "Determine if both feet are swinging a few inches off the floor."

A pencil lay on a nearby tabletop. As a last warning sign for recognizing depression I added, "Be alert to acts of petty thievery, religious conversion, and abrupt changes in sexual orientation."

As I was jotting the period I saw a shadow out of the corner of my eye and quickly I flipped the pencil around in my fingers the way a drummer twirled a drumstick. It was Dwayne, I could tell without looking. I forced the tip of my tongue out the side of my mouth he could see and bore down on the poster. As he shut the door behind him I brushed some eraser lint off the poster with the back of my hand. He came up next to me, his coat still on.

"JJ wrote most of those," he said. His voice seemed a little sad.

"Oh. Did something happen to JJ?" I asked.

Dwayne shrugged his coat off his shoulders. "No," he said. "I just liked it."

"I'm sorry," I said. "I was just trying to be useful. I can still make it out if you want me to put it back."

"I don't know," he said. "Do you think you could?" He leaned a bit closer. "But not that last one. I don't know where that came from. We try to not deal too much with religion or sexual orientation here. Very volatile."

I carefully traced the wisdom of JJ back onto the depression poster.

Dwayne was wearing corduroy slacks and a white oxford shirt. His parka stank of plastic. My nausea returned.

"Well," he said, a few minutes later when he had unlocked his office. "How are we doing so far?"

"Pretty good," I said. "I woke up with a little bug but it seems to have worn off."

Just then he sat up behind his desk. "I should give you the Cook's tour. There's quite a lot to remember at first—at least I guess there is." He pushed in his chair. "Petty cash," he said. "Top drawer with the lock. Charlie cashes a check once a week for fifty dollars. There's a MasterCard for bigger things but Charlie holds on to it pretty tight. If it were up to me we'd be broke, so that's good."

"What kind of things do we buy with the petty cash?"

"Let's see," he said. He pulled a wad of receipts out of a drawer and thumbed through them. "Not coffee," he said, and put one aside. "Ping-Pong balls, a screwdriver, ibuprofen, something called bakery item (he put that one aside as well), sixty-watt lightbulbs, misc. electrical."

"We could go to the Shopper's Club for some of that stuff," I said. "Probably save a bundle. I'm a member."

He nodded like he was on some sort of internal syncopation. "Absolutely," he said, then he froze slightly. "You have a car, right?"

"Yes," I said. "I'll probably walk but I do have a car, or my wife does."

"Is it insured? I don't think you should ever let any troops in it, regardless, but if you use it for yourself on the clock you need insurance."

"Liability," I said. "It's pretty old."

But he was already onto the next thing.

"Lights," he said. "Our light bill is pretty high but we have to leave some of them on all night—there's something about having this place too dark that invites trouble. The floods outside come on and off automatically. Janitorial comes Tuesday and Friday morning. Usually it's Lourdes and she has a key but if it's someone else you'll have to let them in."

"How early do they come?"

He looked at his receipts absently. "Eight? Eight-thirty?"

"Do you want me here by eight? I can do that."

He stuffed the paper back into the drawer and stood up.

"Do you have a cell phone?"

"Not really," I said. "I mean, no. I have e-mail."

"You can have a cell phone if you want one." He opened another drawer and pulled out what might have been the fattest cell phone I had ever seen. He pushed it across the table to me. "It's not a company car but it's something. Who said nonprofit couldn't be hip?"

I hefted it. It was like something out of *Rat Patrol.*

"Go ahead," he said. "Try it. Charlie won't use it because of the whole brain tumor thing." He pulled a warped piece of tinfoil out of the drawer. "You can wrap it in this if you want."

"It's out of juice," I said. I put it down on the desk.

"Did you say you had insurance? I think you said you did but I cut you off."

"Yes," I said. "I have liability. It's not much of a car. My wife is a physical therapist so she'll probably use it most of the time."

Dwayne stood up. "Do you hunt? Own firearms?"

I had started to rise but sat back down. He must have seen something in my face because he immediately sat back down himself.

"That was just out of curiosity," he said. "That's none of my business." He looked like he'd just asked me if I masturbated.

"It's okay," I said. "I don't hunt or own firearms. The question just made me think of something."

Just then Charlene came in, three Starbucks cups in a holder.

"Hunting is God's work," she said, putting the cardboard tray on Dwayne's desk. "I'm not a Christian but that's in the Bible."

I thought of my dad and Otto stomping around Alaska in their padded camouflage doing God's work: loading their coolers with blessed venison, anointing themselves with Wild Turkey, and cruising Juneau for teenage prostitutes.

I don't know why I told them. I don't know why I tell everyone everything, but I do. Dwayne started rubbing his jaw.

"How many days, dear?" Charlie asked. "They're fine, I'm sure. The weather in Alaska is unseasonably warm lately. I'm a Weather Channel groupie."

"Three days, I guess," I said. "So that's not so bad, right?"

"They're probably on the plane right now," said Dwayne. He pushed one of the coffees my way. Americano, Tall. I used to joke at the store when someone ordered one that I was spoken for.

"What do we do when the kids are in school?" I said. "Must be quiet in here."

They looked at each other. "Good question," Dwayne said. "We've never had a third before. It's new territory for us."

I looked around. "Can I clean something? Make a Laundromat run?"

"How are you with a hammer?" asked Charlene. She and Dwayne exchanged another look. "The ramps," she said. "They're a disgrace."

Two minutes later I stood in the backyard storage shed looking down at three plywood skateboard ramps. The wood was streaky and mostly gray, and the ramps had separated from the arched supports in several places, the drywall screws having ripped out. They were a total loss.

"This will take a trip to Home Depot," I said. "I think I can save the sides but the surface has to be replaced."

Charlene looked doubtful. "Can't you just bang new screws in there? They don't use the sides."

"I don't think it would be safe," I said. "Plus I don't think I can get the old ones out, they're all stripped there, see?"

Charlene shot Dwayne an unmistakably dirty look and his face flushed.

"Who built them originally?" I asked.

"JJ," they both answered.

"Andrew." We all turned around. Jule was standing outside the shed door, peering inside. She was wearing her red parka, but it was unzipped. It was a bit dirty—she hadn't let me wash it.

"Jule," I said. "What's wrong?"

She let her shoulders drop and I pushed past Charlene and Dwayne, who were staring at her like the Teen Scene had never witnessed a depressed sixteen-year-old before.

I stepped up close to her and zipped up her parka. She kept her head down and I tried to see her face. "What's going on?" I said.

"Your mom called," she said. I could see her jaw move from above. I could see the part in her hair and the blush of scalp underneath.

"What did she say?" Dwayne and Charlene moved up close, I could feel them behind me.

"She said to tell you Otto called."

"Listen," I interrupted. "I'll just go home and call her. You don't have to tell me anything. This isn't your job."

Then she grabbed me around my shoulders, tight, and

mashed her face against my sternum. I could feel her mouth moving right where the thudding had begun in my chest.

"Isabel talked to her. She's crying and everything. She's all upset and this afternoon is our interview with the vice principal. She was still crying when she went to work."

"Okay," I said. "It's okay. You go to school and go to your interview and I'll call my mom back. I don't want you to talk any more."

She shook her head. "My dad was always saying how he wanted to be cremated all the time," she said.

Jesus, I thought. Otto shot him. He got drunk and fell off a cliff.

"They think it was a bear, she said," whimpered Jule. Charlene gasped and Dwayne whispered something under his breath. I sat down on the edge of the nearest rickety skateboard ramp.

"A bear what?" I said. "Is he dead?"

Jule's eyes were flooded. "They haven't found him," she said.

"I need to call my mom," I said, standing right back up. "You need to go to school and I need to call my mom."

I took Jule by the arm and walked her down the driveway and to the front sidewalk.

"I'm sorry but you're squeezing my arm," she said. My hand had compressed her parka so much that when I let go a ring of wrinkles was left near the shoulder. We stood for a moment and just as I was about to turn and go she threw her arms around me.

"I love you," she said. Then she ran for it. I watched her run all the way down the street until she turned at the movie store to cut over to the school. I walked slowly back to the shed, but Charlene and Dwayne met me outside.

"Some first day, huh?" I said.

"Hush," said Charlene. "Just go on home and call your mother. She needs to talk to you right now." Dwayne nodded dumbly. For some reason before I stumbled away I shook his hand.

When I was ten my dad took me out to the trotters in Cahokia, Illinois. He had met a guy who knew a guy who knew who was going to win the second race. He bet a bundle and won and when he collected a guy came up to us in the parking lot and said my dad had to go with him for a few minutes. He nodded at me the whole time he was telling me my dad would be right back. He told me at least four times my dad would be right back. When my dad came back he had a dislocated finger. He let me help steer and we went to the base hospital to have it set. I was only ten but I remember wondering if I would ever see my father again. I wondered how I would get home. I remember wishing he had given me the keys, even though I didn't know how to drive.

My mom was not crying—Jule must have been referring to Izzie. Two minutes into the conversation we were both laughing.

"Otto gave me the name of the detective up there and when I called him he said they were treating it as a missing persons. There was no bear—they were in a motel, for Christ's sake, and he went out for beer. For beer."

"Oh God," I said. "So there's no bear, no body, no funeral, no all of us standing around looking stupid?"

"Not right away," she said. "Who knows, now? Maybe he is gone. All I know is I have been on Pam's couch long enough. I'm teaching my *Henry Five* today and going home."

"But what else did Otto say? Where is Otto, by the way? Is he back?"

"He's at the ranch with Sacajawea. I'm stopping by there on the way over the mountain."

"What else did he say? I mean, looking at it another way, it does seem a little suspicious. You own half that shit on that ranch. Maybe you should ask more questions."

"You question him, Sherlock."

"Mom," I said. "On the way over here I thought of something and I wanted to tell you."

"What," she said. Her voice had changed. "Tell me."

"I'm sorry you guys weren't invited to the wedding. I'll probably—I will—be sorry about that for the rest of my life."

"Oh," she said. "Forget about that. Your father would have embarrassed you and I wouldn't have come."

I was stunned. "You wouldn't? Why not?"

I could hear her breathing for a minute before she answered. "My marriage sucked. And we loved each other. I don't know if I could gear up to forget how much that kind of thing could do to hurt my kid."

"But . . ."

"Look, I'm not making any sense. I should have been a dyke, right? I gotta go."

I protested a couple more times but she hung up. I didn't even get the number of the cop in Alaska.

I looked up at the clock and realized I desperately wanted to know what happened at Jule's meeting. I dialed Izzie at work. Her service answered.

"She's at the clinic until one. Then she's on personal."

"Can you put her home number on the pager?" I said.

Thirty seconds later the phone rang.

"I'm a wreck," she said. "I have to talk to the stupid vice principal and worry about you, too."

"Izzie," I said. "Jule thinks my dad got eaten by a bear. You should try to calm her down first. The two of you will make quite an impression if you don't."

Izzie started laughing. "She was listening to my end. I swear I told her to just say you needed to call your mom. I swear . . ."

"Jule said you were crying."

She stopped laughing. "I was . . . I was. It was something else."

"Anything you want to elaborate on?"

She took a second to answer. "Not right this second, okay?"

"Okay," I said. "When do you see the vice principal?"

"Three. He's up to something."

"Remember, don't talk about Russ unless he asks you. It's supposed to be about Jule. If you bring up Russ he'll have more reason to believe they're together. I don't know the law but that might be trouble."

"Andrew," she said. "Where do you think your dad is?"

"I don't know," I said. "Alaska is a big state."

"Maybe Kenny . . ."

"Honey, I just said Alaska is a big state. I don't think your ex-husband can do anything if he doesn't want to be found."

"I know," she said. "I was just thinking that if it turned out he was in trouble or something Kenny might be able to help. Put him on the boat. Get him out on the water."

"Look," I said. "Let's concentrate on keeping our Jule at home. One lost soul at a time."

"She's not a lost soul," Izzie objected.

I meant me, I wanted to say. I meant me.

When Izzie and Jule got home the three of us men were sitting on the couch in a row. I'd made a meat loaf and it was in the oven staying warm. I'd realized a half hour in I'd forgotten the egg so I was in no hurry to dish it out. Neither of the boys had mentioned my dad so I assumed they didn't know a thing.

"Hey," I said in a hearty voice. I jumped up and took their coats. Jule shivered noticeably and didn't look me in the eye. She kept her head down and went down the hall to the bathroom. Russ didn't look at her. I'd missed something, clearly.

I pushed Izzie's hair back from her temple and kissed her. "Momma told me there'd be days like this, huh?"

She shrugged. "Momma's a mind reader, then."

I stole a glance at Russ. He was staring resolutely at the blank TV.

"It was just weird. He fell all over himself to be nice. We ended up talking about the Simpsons. I actually told him I thought I wanted a baby. Stupid stuff like that."

"That's not stupid," I said. "We talked about that."

Jule came back into the room. "I'm not hungry," she said. "I don't even know what time it is."

"It's five," I said. She walked back upstairs.

"Did you go back to work?" Izzie asked. I shook my head. "I'll go back tomorrow. I had a lot to do around here that I'd forgotten to do before I started at that place."

We ate dinner in silence. Izzie was distracted the entire time. Nobody said anything about the vice principal or Juneau, Alaska.

In bed Izzie squirmed up against me a lot but backed off when I went for her ass with my hands. "Andrew," she whispered in my ear, "do you have any idea how much my body wants to have a baby?"

"No," I said. "What is it like?"

"Invincible," she said. "I feel like a superhero. Wonder Woman."

"I'd like to have a baby," I said, even though I'd scoured my mind for a shred of desire anywhere and failed repeatedly.

"I'm finally feeling old enough," she said. "Thirty-four is like totally optimum."

"We can't count on the Teen Scene to cover us," I said.

"I can work up to the last two months," she said. "I'll go back right away. We'll pump, we'll use formula. I don't give a shit."

"I wonder what Kenny would think," I mused out loud. I immediately wanted to clap my hand over my mouth.

She turned over and faced me. "What does that mean?"

"I don't know," I said. "To me I guess he still seems like the dad and I'm some kind of big brother. I mean, look at me. I'm not exactly what you'd think of as a stepfather, right?"

"That has nothing to do with you and me. You've already taken care of this house more in six months than Kenny did in ten years. He's the last person you should feel inferior to."

"He owns a business. He has people working for him. He adds to the economy. He has two guys calling him Dad."

"Unbelievable," she said. "I don't believe I'm hearing this." She rolled onto her back and looked up at the ceiling. Her chest rose and fell and I knew her well enough to know what that meant.

"These are just feelings," I said. "That's all. He always knew what he wanted; I never knew what I wanted. People like that seem to be better parents, that's all."

"My parents were right out of a magazine ad," she said. "And I got knocked up at seventeen and they wrote me off. You're worth ten of them, and twenty of Kenny."

There was something flat about how she said it, though. It sounded rehearsed, I decided. It had the sudden odor of convenience and propaganda.

"You think the vice principal really thought you should get pregnant?" I asked. "I mean, Jesus, if the school board's all for it who am I to back out?"

She didn't even look at me. "One of these days you're going to learn that words mean something." She turned her back to me and we didn't touch again.

6

After two weeks at the Teen Scene I had adopted the
two to ten P.M. shift, which probably wasn't what Dwayne had
had in mind but it was the busiest shift—in fact, the only time
anyone but the three of us was in the building.

I'd gotten to know most of the regular kids—JJ was the only
one I knew by name, though. Jule and Alex showed up twice
that first week for moral support. When Jule walked into the
room most of the girls and all of the boys stared at her. The girls
got quieter and the boys got louder. She kept close to Alex,
though. Russ never came by even once.

Mostly the kids hung out and played handheld video games or
used the two PCs to send each other messages and to chat on the
SceneNet with other Teen Scene centers spread out around the
country. Teen Scene was more or less a nonprofit franchise out-
fit. The money may have been private but just about everything
else, it turned out, was done by the book, a book written by some
Ph.D.'s in the Teen Scene nerve center in Kansas City.

The first night I introduced myself to any kid who walked in the door. The second night I tried to casually insert myself into conversations without much luck. The third night I stayed in the office most of the time, watching through the glass. Like drunks, the kids seemed to be able to just hang out and talk for hours about absurd trivia; time stood still. At ten minutes to ten I stamped some Killer Kards. Killer Kards were like library cards that were filled in with date stamps—a lot of the kids needed them stamped for probation or just for their parents. A stamped Killer Kard was the only way some of these kids were able to stay out at night. Why they were named Killer Kards became apparent when a mother called me once, nearly hysterical, wondering if her son was there, or if he'd been killed by a drunk driver or a drug overdose. I stamped no more than six or seven Killer Kards a night. I figured at my salary each Killer Kard stamp netted me forty dollars.

The first night Aaron came by he brought ice cream sundaes from the Kum & Go store. He sat across from my desk in his dark coat and we spooned Cool Whip and idly watched the troops hang out on the couches through my observation window.

"What are they talking about?" he said after about fifteen minutes.

"Beats me," I said. "They always shut up when I get close enough to hear. They could be talking about fisting as far as I know."

"I doubt it," he said. "These kids may be sexually active but I bet they're too cool to talk about it."

"The girl there in the red top chews the shit out of her fingernails," I said. "She probably needs therapy."

He watched her for a moment. His enormous black head was turned to the side and I could see a bit more of the old Aaron. I'd forgotten that he had been a good-looking guy way back when. Once when a famous poet had come into town to do a reading at the fancy graduate school, Aaron and I had crashed the party and he'd managed to take the famous poet in hand in under twenty minutes. When they started walking to the door together the anorectic grad student hostess started to object and Aaron stopped her in her tracks with the Black Power salute. Later he told me he'd just seen it for the first time the night before on the History Channel. The grad student looked like she'd had a run-in with the Shining Path.

"What are the rules?" Aaron asked, whipped cream on the corners of his mouth. "What's off-limits at the Teen Scene, anyway?"

"Well," I said. "No sex, no petting, no French kissing, no fondling, no rubbing of private areas, no drugs, no profanity, no gambling, no Latin dancing, no water sports, no hacking, no MP3 downloading, no breast-feeding, no animal husbandry, no Swedish massage, and no herbal supplements."

"How many of those did you make up?"

I watched the girl in the red top chew her index finger. "All of them," I said. "As far as I know there are no rules. It seems that you can do here what you could basically do in a schoolyard. If it gets beyond that, I figure I'll have to deal with it one incident at a time."

From above us came the sound of Charlene moving around on the second floor.

"That boy there is using," Aaron said. He was looking at JJ. JJ was like a nervous tic with tattoos. He was clearly some kind of anxious budding genius—he was twice as quick as anyone in the room but afraid to miss any acknowledgment of this on the face of whomever he was talking to. He annoyed the shit out of me.

"Did I ever tell you about my high school band teacher?" Aaron asked.

"Yes," I said. The year before he'd found out his high school band teacher had died of cancer. He found out by going on the Internet and finding out they'd changed the name of his high school to the name of his band teacher. He'd picked up the

phone book before it even occurred to him that they didn't name
schools after band teachers because they won State every year.

"If you're loved or feared," Aaron said, "you get remembered.
FDR and Hitler, Jack Benny and Roy Cohn."

"Who was Roy Cohn?" I said.

"I'm not sure, but he was in *Angels in America.*"

"Feared, then?"

"When I talked to his wife she remembered me, and it had
been ten years. What does that mean?"

"Loved, clearly," I said. "You're thinking what, that she was
just being polite?"

"I didn't remember her. I barely met her. Why would she remember me?"

"Her husband must have been really fond of you, then. Or did
you scare the crap out of her once?"

He shrugged. "Not that I recall. I never was a particularly
scary person." As he said this he scratched his Shaft goatee and
rubbed his Shaft bald head with the small bumps and scars and
narrowed his Shaft eyes.

Aaron had somehow managed to figure out his teacher was
dead before he asked if he could come to the phone. At least that
was the way he had told the story.

"The girl in the red is in love with the motormouth Jew," he
said.

"I don't know," I said. "I don't see that."

Aaron shook his head a little. "You can't see that? She's clearly
fucking him. Look at the way her knees are working."

"Does she have a sex aura?" I asked. To me they were kids,
only kids. They shouldn't be having sex, they had plenty of time
for that. Russ and Jule had sex and that was hard enough for me
to take. Honestly, I couldn't have been more poorly suited to
work at the Teen Scene if I were a Bushman.

"Did I tell you about the dreams?" he asked.

He had. Prozac dreams, very colorful, violent spectacles of he-
donism and terror.

"Last night I was attacked by demons in the Malebolge and I tore them to pieces but they rematerialized. The sky was one of those red ones right out of early *Star Trek*—big papier-mâché rocks and that fake sand under my feet and everything."

"What circle are the Malebolge again?" He had been reading the *Inferno* for about the fiftieth time. He was sitting in on a grad Dante seminar and pestering the professor with all kinds of Florentine footnote issues.

"Eight," he said. "Hypocrites and sycophants in a lake of boiling shit. They crawl out, they get the lance. But," he said significantly, "one guy gets out and makes the demons look stupid right in front of Dante and Virgil. So, you know, goes the big difference between art and religion."

"What?" I said. "It's art because someone gets a chance in hell?"

He nodded. "In my dream that girl right there is writhing around and a demon gets distracted and she pulls him in and they all drown him."

"That girl there?" I said, nodding without pointing at the girl in the red with the torn nails. "You dreamed about her?"

"I dream about her every night."

"Bijou," I said, "that's possibly just normal."

"Dreaming about a white girl swimming in a lake of boiling feces surrounded by devils?"

"Who are you in these dreams?" I asked. "Who's the narrator? Are you Dante?"

"I'm me," he said. "I'm me, in the shit."

Just then Alex and Jule wandered in. They came immediately back to the office and stood by the door. Aaron stood up.

"We're going to the movies," Alex said. "Russ and Mom are at the mall buying shoes. She said she was tired of waiting for you to do it."

"What movie?" Aaron and I both asked together.

"The long one," Alex said, looking at Aaron. "With the elves and shit. It's at the mall for two bucks."

"Watch when all the Orcs attack," Aaron said. "You'll see the same troll go by like twelve times."

Alex scowled. "Someone told me that they put a wristwatch on one of the computer-made trolls just as a joke."

"A digital anachronism," I said. "That's very funny."

"Out of time," Aaron said.

Alex stared him down. "I know what it means."

"Isabel said she's going to buy you some nice shoes, too, whether you like it or not," Jule said. Everyone looked at my shoes, which were propped up on the desk, and nobody said anything. Outside the window the boys were looking our way. One of them was punching another one in the arm without even paying attention to what he was doing. JJ was listening to headphones and moving his lips.

"If you don't mind," I said to Jule and Alex as they walked out of the office, "burn this place down when you leave." Aaron cracked his knuckles and watched them all the way out the door.

"You could have gone with them," I said.

"Fuck that," he replied. "I've seen that movie three times. All the Negroes except that fucking HBO comedian are flesh-eating monsters."

"It's got good special effects."

"All I need to get special effects is to take a nap. If I could be the art director of my goddamn dreams I'd be Hollywood A-list."

I took another look at the girl in the red. She was chewing away at a pinkie. She looked up suddenly and saw me, then dropped her eyes. JJ stuck his hand out and squeezed her knee very quickly and I felt like I'd just witnessed some sort of anthropological phenomenon.

"Bijou," I said. "When the hell did we grow up?"

I beat everyone home and found an Iowa Power truck in front of our house and no lights inside. A guy in a cherry picker worked on the transformer that hung directly in front of my bedroom window.

After about two hours the candles were getting low. The walls pulsed with the reflection of the truck out front. There were some shouts from outside and then the phone rang. The caller ID didn't work and the voice on the other end was distant.

"Yes, hello, this is Sergeant Lawless of the State Police."

"You found him?" I said. "This is his son."

"Excuse me," the voice continued, "I'm trying to reach the home of Isabel Miller."

"That's me," I said.

"Sir . . ."

"Hold it," I said. "Isabel Miller? That's my wife."

"I'm sorry, sir, can I have your name, please?"

"Andrew Bergman."

"You're Miss Miller's husband?"

"Yes," I said. "What's wrong?"

"Mr. Miller, I'm calling from Mercy Hospital. Do you have a son, Mr. Miller?"

I pictured them both climbing into the Renault. "Russ," I said. "He's my stepson. Has there been an accident?" The candles had dimmed and the room had focused down to simply the area between my head and the kitchen countertop.

"Mr. Miller, if you could please come as quickly as possible to the hospital, and please bring a copy of your marriage license or medical power of attorney for both your wife and your stepson."

"I don't have that," I said. "I don't have a car here, I don't know where my marriage license is, and I don't have guardianship of the boys."

"I'll come get you, sir." He read my address to me and I hung up.

I pushed a few buttons on the caller ID but it was still dark. I clawed through the notes tacked one on top of another on the bulletin board. Near the bottom was the scrap of envelope. I plucked it off and stabbed the rest of them back onto the board.

The cop had disappeared with his lights flashing just after he'd driven me up to the ER's wraparound driveway. My guess even then was that he'd set up a call in advance so that he wouldn't have to come in with me. Even that early in the game I'd known it was bad.

"56 control," he said as he pulled under the canopy. "Control 56," they answered. "38 main five forty-one. 48 is ten minutes."

"56 two minutes," he said into his fist, and flipped his rolling lights on. I stepped out of the car and the lights hit me in the eyes. He stood up next to his door and talked to me over the roof of the car. "Desk is to the right. You need to see Dr. Fotsie. Tell them your stepson's name."

A half-dozen bruised and bored patients sat in the first waiting room by an open door. Inside the door sat a frizzy-haired volunteer with a PC and a roll of translucent wristband tape.

"Where do I go if my family came in in an ambulance?" I asked her.

She quickly pulled out a pad of paper and wrote on it, ripped out a sheet, and handed it to me on a clipboard. "Please just write your name on the bottom and leave the top blank. All I need is a real quick peek at an ID."

I handed her my driver's license and put my name at the bottom of the piece of paper. The top was insurance information.

"Am I consenting to anything?" I said, handing the clipboard back to her.

"No, no," she said. "There will be all of that soon enough, I'm afraid, but for right now we just want to get you where you need to go." She stood up and took me by the elbow. We walked about ten feet down the hall, where she stopped. We were opposite the chapel.

"Down through the double doors," she said. "You'll see a station there. If there's nobody there just wait. I'll page them and you won't wait long."

There was someone at the station. She was young and black-haired and very pretty. She was on the phone when I walked up. She made eye contact and said, "Just a moment" into the phone. Her voice was soft and nearly perfect.

"Mr. Miller?" she said. "Your son and daughter are on their way. I'll just tell them to come straight back, okay?"

I nodded. While I was waiting for the cop I'd called Rosie and asked her to find them at the movie.

She turned back to the phone and spoke in a perfectly normal voice but I couldn't understand a word. When she hung up she asked me to please come into a side room and sit in an oak chair with padded armrests. While I sat she told me that Isabel had been critically injured in a collision with a tractor-trailer down the street from the VA hospital and had died in the ambulance. Russ was in the operating room and he was in very serious shape. She had an incredible nose and eyebrows that seemed too dark for her hair.

"Did the police talk to you?" she asked.

"He brought me," I said.

"I can take you to your wife or we can wait for the rest of your family. Or we can go and then you can see her again with them. Either way is up to you."

"This is probably strange," I said, "but could I just see the room?" I started to stand up and then didn't. "If I could just see the room or place where she is and then I think I'd be better when everyone . . . when Alex gets here."

"Sure," she said. "Your son is—"

"Stepson."

"—stepson is of course in the operating room now so there's nothing I can show you except we'll need some consents fairly quickly for him."

I reached into my pocket and pulled out the scrap of paper

from the bulletin board. "Here's the boys' father's number. It's an Alaska number. It's a satellite or cell phone or something."

"Why don't you use this," she said, pushing a thick tan phone toward me. She pressed a button and I could hear the dial tone even before I put the receiver to my ear.

It rang only once. "Hello?" Isabel's ex-husband's voice was quiet.

"Hello," I said. "Is this Ken?"

"Yes," he said.

"Ken, this is Andrew Bergman, Isabel's husband."

"Hey," he said. "Hey, what's up?"

"Ken, there's been an accident and Russ and Isabel are here in the hospital. The nurse needs to talk to you about Russ."

His voice never changed in pitch. "Okay," he said.

"Okay, here she is," I said. I passed the phone back to the pretty nurse. She took it and spoke again in a perfectly normal voice and again I couldn't make out a word. She spoke for a while and wrote on a pad and spoke some more. A minute or so later she put her hand over the receiver and said that perhaps I'd like to speak to Kenny again.

"Kenny?" I said. "How are you doing?"

"Good, man. Thanks." He went on and told me that he was going to check flights but was pretty sure that he'd be there the next day and to have Alex call him as soon as he got to the hospital.

"Okay, buddy," I said.

"Thanks, man," he said.

I handed the phone back to the pretty nurse, and we stood up to preview the room with the curtains. She was incredibly beautiful, that nurse.

Isabel was down three halls and in a corner behind a curtain. In the far corner there was another dead person behind another curtain, it looked like. Isabel was covered by a sheet. The nurse said no identification was necessary but I could see her if I wanted to. I didn't, but I asked them to uncover her neck, just enough to see the dime-sized rose.

"Okay," I said. Alex held my hand tight and we stood for a while with the sheet over her face and a different nurse with a strange hat padding in and out of the room ferrying equipment from someplace beyond the rear door.

Alex looked like someone who had been punched while he slept. His hair was matted here and there and his pants hung low. He kept moving his head forward slightly and then bringing it back as if he were struggling to hear in a crowd.

We stayed for either ten minutes or an hour.

Jule sat in one of the orange armchairs next to the gift shop window. She kept her feet up under her and her parka on. With her eyes closed anyone seeing her might have thought she was asleep, until they made some noise with their shoes and her eyes opened just long enough to identify them as not being the trauma surgeon or the nurse and then resolutely closed. She came off as the expert at all of this that she probably was.

Later in the dull ringing hours past two in the morning they unhooked Russ from one room's machines and wheeled him into another room, plugging him into a completely different-looking set of equipment. What little I had seen of the electronics in the ER reminded me of soft ice cream machinery. The equipment in the ICU looked more like submarine gear. His face was covered with tubes, taped this way and that. His right arm was splinted with what looked to be a paramedic splint. Some cross-hatched bandages on his skull bulged out frighteningly. They reminded me of overmatched wrestlers straining to keep their opponents pinned to the mat. He died a few minutes before sunup. Jule had her head buried in Rosie's lap. Alex sat next to me gripping the metal armrest of his chair.

"Your dad will be here tomorrow afternoon," I told him.

Rosie nodded on the other side of me. Her face looked brilliant with fury. Only if you knew her would you know she wasn't in a murderous rage. Between Rosie's huge lap and Jule's parka there was practically none of Jule to be seen.

The trauma doctor sat with us quietly for nearly half an hour without anyone speaking to him. He was exhausted and everyone knew he wanted to be reassured that we knew he'd done everything he could, but all I could do was wonder unfairly how long they had waited and how much they had stumbled and if they had argued or forgot something or infected him with staph or hepatitis or drilled in the wrong place or moved his neck too much. He'd said something about an inquest or autopsy and that we'd talk later the next day. And then he sat there.

Not long after that the pretty nurse took me back to the little office and asked me if I needed to use the phone.

"No," I said. "No, thanks."

She looked at me without breaking eye contact. She looked at me not like I was making a mistake but like I'd told her to watch while I did a trick with my eyeballs.

"Is it better to be stuck in a plane knowing the worst or to have some hope?" I said.

"It's better to have a familiar voice tell someone very bad news," she said. "You lost your wife and had to have a stranger tell you."

But you're not a stranger, I thought. You're too beautiful, and we've been through too much together. I slumped in my chair. I resolved to begin my breakdown. I did lose my wife, I thought. I had no fucking responsibilities here, I was in shock, someone had to take care of *me*. Nobody would blame me if I couldn't tell the guy whose life I had ruined just two short years before that now even the pieces he'd left behind had been thoroughly trashed on my watch.

A light blinked on the phone in front of us. The nurse picked it up and spoke, looking suddenly very tired. She pressed a button and made the light blink again.

"It's the boys' father. He's calling from the plane. I can tell him if you like. It's completely understandable. But he's asking for you."

In that moment something happened to me. The best I can describe it is when you've been walking around with water in your ears from the beach and suddenly they clear; or you'd been listening to a Walkman with the plug half out and bleating in half-ass mono, and you push it in and the music is suddenly absurdly particular and realistic.

The beautiful nurse was tired and probably lonely, perhaps she had been a fat child and had been teased and now read romance novels and was turned off by oral sex. The room had been painted recently, the drop ceiling was installed poorly, the cheap plastic phone had more buttons than the department had lines, the desk drawers were full of rubber bands and loose paper clips. The hospital was run by people who'd long ago given up on the idea of Mercy and operated primarily out of Desperation and Pity. Iowa City itself was really just a cleverly concealed way station squatting between Chicago and what people call the West, selfishly clutching its children and their history-addled tutors to its scrawny chest. My wife whom I barely knew and whose share of misery I'd never get a chance to whittle down was dead; her son was dead; and the survivors could not have been more aptly named.

I took the phone. "Ken," I said, "I'm sorry, I couldn't have worse news for you." I could hear the plane roaring around him, at least that's what I thought it was. He gasped into the phone, all his cool gone. "I'll pick you up, buddy," I said. "You wait by the bags and I'll find you."

When I gave the phone back to the beautiful nurse, she and I had become equals.

"I'm so sorry," she said. After a few minutes of silence she told me about her day; about the baby who had died in OB that morning, not enough lung to ever take a real breath. The parents had suffered through three miscarriages and had prayed in the chapel for a solid week. She explained it all in a perfectly normal voice, and this time I understood every word.

part tWo

1

Cedar Rapids' airport had once been interesting and funky but around 1986 they boxed it up and lined it in mauve carpet and now it looked like a half-empty shopping mall. I'd seen so many people off at that airport never to return that part of me believed it was a point of emigration instead of the regional transportation hub its designers promised was just around the corner. Today there was, inexplicably, a girl singing folk music next to the car rental counters with a small amp and acoustic guitar. I was profoundly happy to see her there. I needed a melancholic accompaniment for my afternoon business. I needed a sound track. She was perfect.

I'd driven Alex to the airport to pick up his dad in Rosie's sedan DeVille with the dirty steering wheel. She'd insisted I use it as long as I needed to, as she had another car. We passed underneath Kenny's plane as it circled in to land from the east over the truck stop. By the time he trudged down the only gate ramp we'd listened to two ballads by the girl with the guitar. She took a break and left her gear with the kid at the Avis counter and I was sorry to see her go.

Kenny was a big guy. I'd forgotten how big. He was black-haired and wore a sharp-edged beard and ponytail. His chest was lean but his shoulders were wide. He immediately reminded me of someone I couldn't place. It would be hours before I realized he reminded me of Russ.

Alex ran up to him and hung on to him with his eyes closed. I stared at them shamelessly, as did the sweatpants and windbreaker crowd waiting for their loved ones there with us by the divider rope. A flight attendant gave them a heartbroken look as she wheeled her cart down the ramp. Why did I stare at her navy blue ass as she passed? What kind of absolute lowlife shitheel was I?

Just then Kenny and Alex came up to me, and we successfully gripped hands and passed something (Christ, an aura?) between us and that moment was over and I hadn't cried onto his shoulder.

"Andy," Kenny said, "you doing all right, buddy?" His eyes were wet pits.

"Hanging in there," I said.

"These are the times, man," he said. "This is when it hits you, right?"

"I guess," I said lamely.

He put his hand on my shoulder. "I'm sorry, man. I'm just blathering."

"It's okay, Dad," said Alex. "Andy didn't mean it."

We both looked at him. "Mean what?" I said.

His face darkened and he looked at his feet.

"There's my bag," Kenny said. He looked around him as we walked the twenty yards to the luggage carousel. "This place sure looks all nice and fixed up," he said. Alex followed us silently.

In the car I gave it until the interstate before I brought up the lodging issue.

"Ken," I said.

"Kenny. Ken always sounded like the gay doll."

"Okay. I thought I'd give you the choice about where to stay. I thought maybe you'd want to stay with Alex at the house, unless that's too much too soon. I can stay over at Rosie's with Jule. Or you can stay at Rosie's with Alex if that's more comfortable. There's about a million combinations including we put you and Alex up at the Ramada Inn."

"Shit," he said, rubbing his beard where it met his sideburn. In the car I could smell the travel on him. His hand shook a little and I guessed he hadn't slept or eaten for twenty-four hours. "I don't think I'm going to be feeling good about putting you out of your house. What if me and Alex get us a nice room with a Jacuzzi and you and the girl stay put?"

"Dad." Alex's brow was furrowed. "How long are you going to stay?"

It was everything I could do not to apologize for him—that would have been a lovely moment. But it was nice to have the question out in the open.

Kenny slumped a little in his seat and rubbed his neck. "Buddy," he said to Alex, "I stay too long and the boat goes all to hell. Can I answer you later on that one?"

"We can help out on the hotel if that's something you would consider," I said. The "we," once I realized I'd said it, burned to a crisp as it hung in the air.

"Thanks, man," he said. "But we had a good summer so that's appreciated but no go. You got so much else to take care of you don't need to worry about me and Alex."

It was only then that I noticed the watch on his wrist and remembered the checks he sent every other month that covered everything Izzie's lousy salary didn't. I noticed his boots and his gold ring and his coat. I was suddenly overcome with panic and it was all I could do not to hyperventilate.

"He . . ." I began. I started over. "Have you thought about when Alex should go back to school?"

"Hey," protested Alex from the backseat. "Don't fucking talk about me like I'm not here."

"I'm sorry, Alex," I said. "I was just thinking I had to call the school. I have to call the school and a lot of people. I just wondered what I'd tell them and if they would need to talk to your dad." I was quiet for a moment. "Shit," I said. "Fucking shit."

"I can call them, man," Kenny said.

"I was thinking about Jule," I said. "Who speaks for Jule now? I call the school—who the hell am I? I wouldn't take my word for anything . . ."

"I'm sure they'll be cool about it," Kenny said. "Just get Rosie to make the call. As long as a woman makes the call you can buy some time."

"Is Jule going to have to leave?" asked Alex.

"No," I said. "Nobody leaves. We have a home."

Everyone in the car was silent for a good chunk of time. I was remembering what Isabel had told me about Jule's aunt—her legal guardian. Her name was Tana; she was old and not terribly interested in Jule. She lived in Cedar Falls and had been only too happy to let Jule live with Izzie when the idea had surfaced. Surely she wouldn't press for Jule to come up to Cedar Falls, would she?

And then I realized what I had just said. "You know I mean you guys make your own call on that," I said, but my voice caught at the end. Kenny reached over and gripped my shoulder. I was aware of how skinny my shoulder was in his grip, how much I was like one of his kids. I used the back of my hand to rub my face dry.

Alex would be going home with Kenny; Jule would be sent away. I would be left with Dwayne and Aaron and Charlene in the attic. I hadn't even buried Isabel and already I'd lost the rest of them. Maybe Alex would stay and finish the school year; maybe Jule would be all right with, say, Rosie, until she turned eighteen. Maybe they would let her stay with me. Maybe Kenny would sell the boat and stay here and share custody. Maybe Rosie and I would get married. Maybe I could sell myself to everybody as the kind of person to depend on in a situation like this.

Kenny had asked to go straight to the hospital. By then I knew where to park and which hall to go down and which station to sign in to and which chairs to wait in. After about a minute an older volunteer came and collected Alex and Kenny and I offered to come along and he'd said, no, buddy, thanks. He was shaking and scratching his beard and Alex was holding him by the hand but with a lot of contact along the forearm the way I remember people standing with FDR sometimes in photos. They disappeared down the hall past the chapel and I sat with my sour stomach and turned over the sad tunes from the airport singer in my head.

While they were in there I called over to Rosie's. Nobody answered so I started to leave a message for Jule. She picked up the phone a few words in.

"Hi," she said.

"Hi," I said. "We're here at the hospital, then I don't know. We'll probably get a hotel for these guys. Then I got an appointment at the funeral home at two. Lots of things."

She was quiet while I went through my immediate future.

"How are you doing?" I said. "Do you want me to come by? Do you want to get out of there for a while?"

"Yeah," she said. "Can you come by and get me? I don't want to go out but I don't want to be here by myself."

"Did you get your stuff from the house? Did you go by?"

"No," she said. "I didn't go in and she just took me home."

"We'll go by," I said. "I'll go in and you just tell me what you need."

When Kenny and Alex came back I was on my feet. We climbed back into Rosie's Cadillac and on the way over to her house we made a plan for stopping by the house and for the next day and for where everyone would sleep and for dinner that night and for phone calls and for an extra car and getting groceries. We picked up Jule and I steered over to the house and parked in the alley.

A note was taped to the alley door—a note in a small envelope. I carried it in unopened. Inside, the house was blank, strange, muted. After a moment I realized that the power was still off. I crossed to the fuse box and threw the master breaker; it always tripped when power from the city came back on. The house hummed to life; the answering machine clicked, the refrigerator whirred, the little radio in the bathroom that stayed on most of the time started musing in the flat monotone of the public radio station.

Kenny and Jule and Alex stood in the kitchen.

"Something went bad in the fridge," Alex said. "Or the garbage."

"I'll get all that later," I said. "Why don't we all go upstairs together and you guys can get some clothes. There's a bunch of clean stuff on my bed I never got a chance to put away."

We all headed for the steps together, except for Kenny, who strayed a little behind. At the top of the stairs I slipped into my room and quickly grabbed Jule's and Alex's clean things, shoving everyone else's out of the way. Kenny and Alex were already opening drawers in his room so I crossed the hall quickly and found Jule sitting on her bed alone.

"Here are some clean clothes," I said. I handed her some underwear and black jeans and socks.

"Okay," she said. She looked at the clothes. "No shirts?" she said. "I'm out of shirts."

I went over to the bureau and sorted through the drawer she and Russ shared and weeded out some shirts I knew they both wore. I got an old abandoned backpack from the hook in the closet. It had crumpled paper at the bottom and pencils with snapped-off leads.

I put it on the bed next to her and stepped back a little bit. I had no power in my soul to go near her, no way to conceive of how I could touch her now. She put her elbows on her knees and stared at the floor.

"This is your house," I said. "This is my house and Alex's house and it's their house, too."

"I know that," she said. "Why are you saying that? Do I need to know something?"

"No," I said. "What do you mean, 'know something'?" She was sitting there looking up at me, her throat exposed. I could see the little vein throbbing in her neck. She might have been a baby swallow.

"I don't want to leave," she said.

"It's too soon to talk about all this," I said. "We don't even know what we're going to do for the next couple of days. Let's get through that first."

"I don't want to stay at Rosie's," she said. "I want to stay here."

"Okay," I said. "You and I can stay here, Alex and his dad will stay at the Ramada Inn. We'll hang in there."

"I want to sleep in your room."

"Okay," I said. "Okay, then. That's . . . you can't do that. I mean, if you mean you want to switch rooms, sure, that's fine. Is that what you meant?"

She reached forward suddenly and grabbed me around the waist and buried her head in my stomach.

"I'm afraid of hospitals," she said. "Doctor's offices, and hospitals. I won't go there."

All my arms could do was hold her around the head and neck awkwardly.

"Okay," I said. "Sure, you don't have to do that."

Kenny and I dropped Alex and Jule off at the library and drove to the funeral home around two o'clock. He'd showered and shaved and straightened his limbs and combed his beard and this time he drove.

Eddie the mortician was a slightly swollen twenty-two-year-old with pink scalp showing through his thin white-yellow hair. He wore an extremely nice suit and made it look like it was not his only one. His shirt was so white it hinted at lavender; his tie demonstrated compassion, his shoes dispatch. He was, I am quite sure, born to undertake.

Izzie and Russ were there before us, somewhere in the basement. The funeral home was a converted Victorian, the top level probably where the proprietors lived. Kenny and I walked a long hall with Eddie beside us to a small showroom with some loose-leaf binders and silk flowers and a few pieces of lace on the arms of the chairs. We sat and Eddie asked us a few questions about the accident. I told him where it had happened, how the truck had taken the curve too wide and crossed over.

"I'm so sorry," Eddie said. "I heard about it on the radio this morning."

The truck that had smashed the Renault into the side of the overpass went on to end up in the Iowa River. I had heard it too and only that second did I realize that it was the same accident. The main thing about the radio story had been how the rig had to be winched out. The dead people may not have been mentioned at all. But Eddie had picked up on it. That was only natural, I suppose.

We looked at pictures of caskets, talked about money, talked about a joint service, decided against a viewing. Kenny and I were picking some maple boxes with chrome when an old woman walked into the room and raised her hand a little like someone who was afraid to interrupt.

Eddie's solid professionalism suddenly pooled around his feet. "Oh, Jesus fuck," he said.

She was wearing only a flimsy, dirty old nightgown. Her feet were bare and her nose was bleeding slightly. Eddie leapt up and

took her hand and waist and led her off, but not before I noticed
him check her legs and feet. I don't know how but I knew he
was making sure she hadn't peed on the floor.

Kenny and I watched them disappear around the corner to
where steps led to the top floors. "Shoot me before I ever get like
that," he said, still watching the hall.

"I have this friend," I said. "His mother was past that and he
helped her along."

"Should be legal," Kenny said. "This is a fucked-up world
where something like that is not allowed."

"They put him in jail," I said.

"Like I said," he answered. We bent back down and checked
out the hardware. It was fine that Eddie was gone. This was the
hard part.

"Kenny," I said. "I have no idea what I can even afford."

He looked grim and shook his head. "I don't know if this is
gonna be good news or bad but Izzie's got life insurance. I know
because I bought it on her. It's paid up and I was going to do
something about it when I got the bill this year but I never did."

"Why isn't that good news?" I said.

He shook his head. "It is, it is, buddy. It's just that, you know,
I'm the beneficiary. Nobody ever changed it."

I didn't say anything for a second. "Is it enough for all this?"

"Yeah," he said, "but not much more. I think maybe we
should take that and pay for half and I'll pay the other half out
of pocket..."

"Whoa," I said. "Look, if there's insurance money she'd...
you guys would have wanted it for this, right? Why don't we just
use it up? That way you don't have to go out of pocket."

Kenny looked back down the hall.

"Yeah, okay," he said. "But, I got to ask you at some point—
doesn't have to be now—I mean, you're working now, right?"

I wasn't able to answer him for a few seconds. The smell of
the carpet seemed to fill my head.

"Yeah," I said. "I'm doing really well now." I might have been addressing a parole board the way I felt.

But Kenny didn't get a chance to answer. Movement down the hall caught our eye. Incredibly, it was the old lady again, this time in a robe. She padded up to us in slippers and stopped. We stood up.

"Are you Democrats?" she asked. Eddie motored around the corner before either of us answered. His face was red and his hair mussed.

"I'm a county delegate," I said, and immediately wished I hadn't.

Eddie was about to take her in hand again but stopped. "You caucused," he said to me. "I remember you. You were incredible."

"Thanks," I said. "I got carried away, I think."

Eddie turned to his mom. "You remember I told you about him?" He looked at Kenny. "We had about forty-five undecided and a few guys tried to get them to commit, talking the same old shit, and then . . ."

"Andrew," I said.

". . . Andrew got up on a chair and just, I don't know, just started in."

Aaron and I had originally decided to pick different candidates and see if we could drum up votes for the sheer comic absurdity of it. But after a half hour I'd decided on a different approach and eventually got an entire high school gym full of Democrats to reject the party retreads and send five delegates to the county convention with a sworn mandate to nominate me for President of the United States. When the county convention came around I'd forgotten all about it, and I assumed my delegates had been absorbed into the traditional machine by then.

"I used to drink a lot," I said. "I'm embarrassed by it now." But I hadn't been drunk that night. I hadn't had a drop, for some reason.

"People talked about it for weeks," Eddie said. "Everyone wondered who the hell you were. I'm amazed I didn't think of it when you walked in. Someone was just mentioning it to me the other day."

"We should get back to this," I said, sitting back down.

"Cabbage," the old woman said. "That's what they feed me here."

Eddie started to steer her away again. "She thinks she's in a nursing home," he said. "All because we put in new fixtures to take care of her and hired a day nurse."

"Lyndon Johnson shot those colored people," she said. "You put that in your pipe and smoke it." She leaned forward with narrowed eyes. "In China," she whispered, "they eat rats just like gingersnaps."

Kenny and I watched her go, Eddie's arm around her back, holding on to both of her hands with both of his.

"What do you bet," Kenny said to me, "all the money's still in that old broad's name?"

"God, money," I said. "Take money out of the equation and I wonder how many people you'd ever want to talk to? You know?"

"What do you mean?" Kenny had been about to turn over the contract to read the back.

"Nothing," I said. "I was trying out a thought. Sometimes I think I would have made a good monk."

He shook his head. "All that praying," he said. "What have they got to pray about in there? They're protected from everything. Get them out into Prudhoe Bay and set them praying, maybe it would do somebody some good."

"What do you need for the insurance?" I said. "You need anything from me?"

He shook his head. "Not a thing, buddy. The hospital will have everything notarized and ready tomorrow. Then it's just the paperwork. The agent who sold me the damn thing is still here, I'm sure. I'll make him earn his commission." He put down the contract. "You, though, have to go through probate. You should get some help with that right away."

Eddie had returned just then. "One thing you should look into right away," he said to me. He'd picked right up on our conversation. "Your auto policy maybe has medical payments on it. Have them pay the hospital before you do anything, particularly before you give them a credit card. The other guy's policy definitely had medical, too, since it's commercial. Call them today. Get the police report. Call the coroner to get a copy of the death certificate as soon as it gets to the registrar or whatever they call that lady in the office above the ambulance bay. Medical payments go out regardless of fault starting with the owner and then paying out to occupants and other vehicles."

"The truck driver wasn't hurt," I said. "He swam out of the window and ended up down by the power station."

But Kenny and Eddie had moved on, leafing through the flower arrangements now. I looked over at the corner every few seconds, and it took me a few minutes to realize I was hoping the crazy old lady was coming back again. There was something to her situation that I liked thinking about. To be able to float like that, unmoored; how bad could it be?

That evening I was too tired to attempt to keep the little group together and let Kenny take Alex off for dinner and bed at the Ramada Inn without much of a protest. Rosie wanted to keep Jule over at her place again, and then amended that to both of us; I didn't like the expression on her face when I insisted Jule and I were fine on our own.

She let us off and took her Caddy back home, I think as punishment. When we got in the door Jule went immediately to the bathroom and I went to the phone. Next to it was the unopened envelope that had been taped to the door. I sat at the table and tore the end off and blew into it. It was from Aaron, and it simply said "Whatever you need."

Over the next two hours Jule sat on the couch and I dialed the phone. The machine had been full of messages; Rosie had called everyone for me, except my mother, even Carl the client. I called them all back and mercifully got a lot of machines. At eight o'clock I sat down next to Jule and put my arm around her; she leaned in and rested her head against my ear. A few minutes later we got up and trudged up the stairs to my bedroom. Inside she pulled off her socks and her jeans and climbed under the covers. I lay down, fully clothed, next to her, my head close to the bookcase headboard I'd loved banging Izzie up against. She turned away from me and I positioned my face about an inch from the back of her head, just outside the range where her hair would tickle my nose, and went to sleep with one hand on the bedspread covering her perfect thin hip and the ceiling light burning above us.

Sometime in the night I got out of my clothes and into my gym shorts; but then I couldn't get back to sleep with Jule there. The bedspread had come off her shoulder, and one leg and thigh lay exposed up to the line of her underwear. Her lips were open and her eyelashes were flat against her cheeks. Her face looked flushed and I put my hand awkwardly on her forehead; she seemed a little hot. I covered up her leg and her shoulder with the bedspread and lay down tight against her. I lay this way for hours, claylike. At that point I'd been awake for thirty-six hours; my entire body hummed and curlicues flared on the inside of my eyelids. Jule slept without moving a muscle all night long.

The cast at the funeral was about what I'd expected. I hung by the basement door where nobody could see me. Kenny and Jule and Alex and Rosie waited in the pastor's office. I spoke with Eddie once or twice and he was completely in his element—

keeping his hands behind his back seemed like an enormous effort. He'd brought the caskets an hour before the ceremony and upstairs in the sanctuary they sat, head to head, while a grim, hard-smiling crowd filed through the doors.

"Eddie," I said. "How do I look?" He was carrying stacks of the little notices that I hated and refused to use until Kenny explained them to me as just charms that people hang on to during the funeral so they don't have to look at the caskets. Kenny had provided all the material by memory.

"You're doing good," Eddie said. "Better than most. Some husbands can't even dress themselves in this situation."

I gave him an appreciative nod. He was good. The guy you give bodies to so something can be done with them has to be the first link to the taking-out-the-garbage, cleaning-out-the-dresser, picking-photographs Beginning of the Rest of Your Life. His future was set.

I went upstairs and waited next to a half-open door behind the altar. I could see into the sanctuary and watched a little from there. Arlene from Starbucks was there, my Farsi professor, lots of kids, Aaron, a couple of people I knew worked with Izzie, Carl the client, the old guy who cleaned up Rosie's every morning. A friend of Isabel's from the clinic—another porker nearly the size of Rosie—was all set to sing some Bach. I only realized later that this was the famous Becky who'd interceded so adeptly with the Teen Scene position. She sat in the front and tried not to keep looking back at who was coming in. What did it matter who came? I thought. Sit still, Fatty. The rest of the front row was left for the five of us—six since Rosie counted as two.

At ten minutes till eleven I went back down and hooked up with everyone else. I'd helped Jule get ready and she'd picked the same dress she'd worn at the wedding—a kind of sexy number with a lot of black in it. Today she wore it like a ravished novice. We walked into the sanctuary and sat next to the singing nurse. The pastor started, the organist played, we rose and sat a few times. The friend sang, terribly, and noses blew. I studied the stained-glass windows, which struck me as disconcertingly modern. I held Jule's hand. I shared a hymnal with Kenny on my other side. I prayed different words, though, when the prayer started.

Dear God (you hideous fuck): What you didn't figure when you did this was that it TOTALLY gives me an out to do whatever I want to with your servant Jule (knocking off her parents was also key, come to think of it). So maybe you should stick to reducing old ladies to piss-covered tea cozies from here on out, that is if you're not too stressed by the plagues of flies you apply to the lips of the basketball-bellied infants in the Sudan.

I wished I had a pen.

While I'm thinking about it, how about taking Kenny to your bosom so I can keep the rest of the family I have left, huh? Send a perfect storm his way some trip when Alex is not on the boat. And send my old man a message in the form of a bleeding ulcer or something—anything to remind him how old he is supposed to be. Or if you've already gathered him up, pinion his wings so he flaps around heaven like a grazed mallard. Take my word for it, he's high maintenance.

And then, sooner than I thought possible, we were on the doxology:

Praise God from whom all blessings flow,
Cornhole us creatures here below,
Praise Him above the Heavenly Host,
Praise Father, Son (unless you're toast).

It was everything I could do to keep from giggling. I ground my teeth and squeezed my eyes shut. I knew I was close to hysteria. Jule gripped my hand; God knows what she thought. I tried to slow my breathing but it was catching in my throat. I had the sudden overwhelming desire to flee—the same desire, I was sure, that the murderer feels when the foreman is about to read the verdict. I prayed one last time as we rose to leave:

I'm sorry, God (you vindictive asshole). Forgive me, I have not a single clue what I'm doing.

2

It would be exaggerating to say that Alex hated my guts after that, but not by much. I'd love to say that I understood why but I didn't.

He and Kenny and I made an appointment with the vice principal at his school and we spent the first fifteen minutes on four-guys-sitting-around-acting-grown-up baloney before I had a sneezing fit that got so bad the vice principal started to look alarmed. I spent the rest of the meeting with a box of Kleenex on my lap twitching my nostrils.

In one of those predetermined administration deals it was decided that everyone was fine if Alex finished his sophomore year with me as long as his dad checked in on the phone with the vice principal every two weeks. It smelled suspiciously like parole to me; just who was under suspicion was clear. But that wasn't the worst part; just as that little confab was breaking up, the vice principal asked me to stay a moment, if I would. I sat back down and Kenny and Alex shook hands and smiled grimly and exited the vice principal's office like members of the school board. I put the box of Kleenex on the chair Alex had left, and then found I had nothing to occupy my hands. I folded them on my lap.

The vice principal, with Alex and Kenny out of the room, assumed the other of what was probably his complete set of daytime facial expressions.

"Julianne Bradshaw," he said.

"Yes," I said. I moved my hands around a little and nodded.

"I don't want to pretend to know all of the details of her custody. I'm sure that, for the time being, there's some..." He stopped with his eyebrows raised.

I'd started to tremble a little. Back when I actually attended high school I was so completely hip to these little power games I might have laughed in his face. But that was when I was living to get high and life meant nothing more than a buzz and a tankful of gasoline.

"There's insurance," I said. "Is that what you mean?"

"Confusion," he said. "I was just acknowledging it's to be expected there will be some legal questions and transitions and those kinds of things."

"Well," I said. "I haven't really looked into it. My wife had an agreement with her guardian to be her custodian, at least until Jule went to college—we always assumed she would go to college."

He nodded. "She's going to do fine. I don't think anybody here is terribly worried that she won't be able to put this behind her."

"God knows she has experience enough with this," I said. "I may end up leaning on her for a while."

The vice principal frowned and nodded again and I knew I'd said something I shouldn't have. He drummed his fingers on his desk and looked over my shoulder out his window.

"Do you have any advice?" I asked. "I mean, she's asked if she can stay with me and Alex. She's . . . numerous times she's asked about it."

He stopped drumming his fingers and tilted his head at me. "There's something you should know. God knows you've had enough to worry about this week but I think if you genuinely want the girl to stay in the house with you, you ought to know that I had already been making some inquiries about the suitability of the situation in your house. Nothing personal, just part of the job."

"Yes," I said. "You were concerned that the relationship between Jule and Russ wasn't appropriate. I agree." The air in the office had gotten cold suddenly, it seemed. My head was clearer, clear enough to read the disappointment in the vice principal's face. He'd expected to shock me.

"Well then," he said. "I'm sure that you can see how this situation is—"

"Very different now," I said. "My stepson is dead, and that relationship no longer exists."

"Well, yes, but—"

"I fully expect Jule's guardian to transfer her custody to me."

The vice principal did not try to hide his skepticism. "You do?"

"Yes," I said. "With my background and current supervisory position as a youth counselor, I'm pretty confident." I made motions in my chair to indicate I was ending the meeting. The vice principal didn't move.

"Let's do this," I said. "I'll call Jule's aunt and ask her to contact you if she has any concerns. In the meantime if you'd like to meet with me and Jule to discuss the next two months I think that would be fine." I'd gotten to my feet and I held my hand out to him. He considered it for a moment and then stood.

That was when I saw him clearly; he, like Alex, hated the very sight of me. Behind his fashionable wire-rims his eyes practically sparked with rage. He was a fortyish educator on the long downside of the exceptionally easy course he'd chosen for himself. He saw, every day, the fresh fates of dozens of Jules, and wondered again how his had soured. Halls full of better choices, clearer paths, finer luck, and higher blessings. He probably wanted to bang every girl in the school just to prove to the world that they could settle for as little as he did.

"Thanks for your concern," I said as I gripped his fist. "It means a lot to us."

I left him in his office with his mouth slightly open. Out in the hall Kenny and Alex stood by a double door, bent toward each other in conversation, while students crisscrossed in front of them.

"Asshole," I said as I approached them. Alex looked a little shocked and almost smiled; instantly, though, he assumed the look he'd plastered on his face at the hospital.

"I got sociology," he said. "I'm here, I might as well go." He said this to his dad; he knew that I'd tell him to blow it off. But Kenny nodded at him. They looked at each other for a moment and then Alex waded into the hallway traffic and disappeared through the double doors.

Out in the car—a rental Kenny'd had delivered to the hotel— he turned up the radio and we didn't say anything until he got back to my house.

"I'm going to pick him up after school. We'll come by after dinner, then I'm off to the airport."

It had been gradual, but now, after four days of morgues, funerals, and hospitality the situation had finally matured. We were not friends; we were civilized men who'd needed each other's help in an emergency. We were anxious to expunge as much of the last few days as fast as we could. Identifying the last time we'd have to occupy the same space was a relief to both of us.

"I'll try to make the place seem as natural as possible," I said. "I think he'll do okay."

"I'll come back in about three weeks," he said. "By then I'll have some things taken care of and can let my hair down a little. And I can spend some time here in the fall after the season."

"You stay with us next time," I said. "I insist."

"Sure, buddy," he said. "You got a deal."

In the middle of that night, after Alex had gone to bed in his room and Jule in mine, after we'd said goodbye to Kenny and eaten some ice cream, I walked out into the dark hall and opened the door to my bedroom. Jule lay in my bed with the light on and her Walkman headphones over her ears. She lay perfectly straight, like a victim waiting to be transferred to a stretcher. In the cream-colored light her hair looked dark—not nearly as dark as Isabel's but pretty dark all the same—and her sharp chin, maybe her only flaw on an otherwise perfect face, pointed a little upward. She might have been asleep except for the tapping of her index finger on the plastic side of the tape player. When I sat down on the edge of the bed she peered at me from under her eyelashes and smiled.

"Back to school tomorrow," I said. "I talked to the vice principal and warned him if he so much as blinks at you he'll be selling mattresses over the phone."

She took off her headphones. "What?" she said.

"I asked if you had everything you needed, clean clothes, all that. For school."

"I'm dropping out," she said, looking away from me toward the dark window. "I'm going to be a blackjack dealer in Reno."

"They don't play blackjack in Reno. They play keno. Keno in Reno."

"Then I'll deal keno."

"There's no dealing in keno. It's a machine."

"Then I'll go to Atlantic City. Do they deal blackjack in Atlantic City?"

"Yes, but you need to have keno experience to get those jobs."

Good Lord that smile. She lay on her back in her wife-beater and boxers in my bed and beamed at me. Alex hated me but Jule loved me. My wife and stepson were dead but nothing proved that maybe life might just turn out a fabulous fairy tale more than this girl, fresh into her exceptional personhood. Jule, head and shoulders shoved out of the womb, just needing a tug to be out here with the rest of us.

"Two months and then it's summer vacation," I said. "Then we'll put your ass to work, if it's employment you want."

"I'd like to make films," she said. "But they don't teach that in high school, do they?"

"I know the head of the UI Film Studies department. I'll get you an internship." It was true, I did know him. I'd fucked his wife in an earlier life. His interest in me was not the kind that would lend itself to favors.

"I could go live with Aunt Tana," she said. "It would make it easier on everyone. Alex is going to be going away soon and they'll never let me stay here without all kinds of meetings and interviews and lawyers."

"I think you should stay here at least until the end of the school year. They won't move you until then. They'll appoint someone to check us out and meet with you a lot and crap like that. Bureaucracies don't move that fast, they just throw more overworked drones at a problem until it goes away."

"Internships don't pay any money," she said. "I can get a job right now if we need the money."

I shook my head. "You've got to study. You and Alex both."

"There's a bunch of stuff I need to tell you," she said. She put her arm over her eyes, like she was shielding them from the sun.

"Okay," I said. "You don't need to do it now if you don't want to."

"There's money in the bank," she said. "Kind of a lot."

"There is?" I said. "You have a savings account?"

"Mine and Russ and Isabel's," she said.

"Then it's yours," I said, pretending I knew all about banking law and minors.

"It's nine thousand dollars," she said.

"Wow," I said. "That's great."

"I've got four hundred thousand dollars in my trust from my parents' insurance," she said. "Aunt Tana's in charge until I'm eighteen."

"Jesus," I said. "Did Isabel know?"

"She got a thousand a month from Aunt Tana and she just gave it to me to save. That's where the nine thousand came from."

It was so like Isabel; she worked her ass off and took in this girl and didn't even take the money. My Isabel. I almost laughed. Maybe if it hadn't been a secret from me I would have. I moved a pillow and lay down beside Jule.

"She always said that if things got really desperate she might ask for it," Jule said. "I think maybe things qualify now as desperate."

"Hardly," I said, looking up at the ceiling light. "I've got a good job and we've got a little insurance money and if we need money Alex can work at Orange Julius."

"Shhhh," she said. "He'll hear you."

"He used to have a sense of humor," I said. "I hope he comes back. I hope we all come back, Christ."

"Where are we?" she asked.

You're sixteen, I thought. Isabel was thirty-four. For God's sake don't get knocked up. "We're in Iowa," I said. "Where things like this don't happen."

We were lying on our sides, facing each other.

"Things like what?" she said. I was starting to ache. Next to my head were all of Isabel's crappy paperback novels. Her pencils and Kleenex. God help me I started to cry.

"I'm going to take care of you," I said. But I was sobbing and it came out as a statement and not a question.

"I know that," Jule said, hiking herself over to me. She stroked my forehead with the tips of her slender fingers. Her unblinking beautiful eyes fixed on my face. Isabel's eyes had been more stunning, no doubt about that, but in them she'd carried something of her scarred heart. Now her eyes were walking around in someone else and Jule's were focused on me, and only me. God, what exactly was she thinking about Russ now? She had lost both her parents; she knew he wasn't coming back. She knew the family court didn't care about her. She knew what the girls *and* the boys at the Teen Scene were going through. She knew that planes crashed, houses burned to the ground, lovers killed for nothing more than wounded vanity and that ninety percent of the people in the world would sell their organs just for a house and a steady income. She knew all these things at sixteen and didn't have a cynical bone in her body. I'd have been a fucking fool not to want her in my life.

The next morning we woke up early and I got the hell out of the room before Alex woke up. When he came downstairs he had that stare firmly planted on his face and I wanted to smack him two minutes into the day.

I'd put a glass of orange juice out with a toasted frozen bagel. He drank the orange juice and pushed the bagel away like it was an insult.

"Did you find your gym stuff?" I asked. He shook his head. "It's on the dresser. I'll go get it for you."

"No," he said. "I don't need it."

I waited a second. "It's Wednesday," I said.

"I know what day it is. I don't need it today." He didn't look at me. When I'd first moved in we'd had this really great scene one day about gym, how he felt stupid and how the bull dyke bitch who taught volleyball hated him. We'd gone to the sporting goods store and gotten him some nice gym stuff that made his narrow shoulders not so narrow and his thighs not so Shoah-like. Russ had put on weight the year before without even trying but Alex still looked twelve, especially in comparison.

"If they changed the schedule just tell me, so I know when to go into your bag and wash the crap," I said.

He shook his head. "Don't you have to go to work?" he asked.

"Yes," I said. "I do. You guys will have to fend for yourselves for a while. I think maybe it would be a good idea if you and Jule hung out at the Teen Scene since I have to be there."

"You're kidding, right?" Alex gripped his orange juice glass, his face openly contemptuous.

"It's not a rule," I said. "I just thought you'd get lonely being here alone every night."

Jule just then walked into the dining room. She was dressed for school, wearing clothes I'd washed a hundred times. The shirt was my own.

"He won't be alone," she said. "We'll be all right."

"Fine," I said. "Whatever." I chewed my bagel and didn't look at either one of them. I'd called the Teen Scene the day before and told Dwayne I'd be coming back and he'd said, "Take your time" but then made sure I meant it.

"Did you call your mom yet?" Jule asked significantly. She'd taken a seat across from me and close to Alex.

"No," I said. "It's always too early and then I don't get to it."

"Call her at one before you go in. That's what, ten o'clock in Oregon?"

"What if she wants to come out and visit?" I said, and I was instantly sorry.

"Who cares?" Alex said. "Why are you asking us?"

Jule started to say something and then stopped. Maybe like me she'd done the math. I'd lost a wife and stepson. She'd lost a boyfriend and the boyfriend's mother. Alex was down one mother, one brother, and his father was three thousand miles away. I had no idea what I was going to do with him except keep my mouth shut and let him work it out. It would be all I could do to remember not to ask him to support me, the way he had been for a year. I felt sorrier for him at that moment than I had ever felt for anyone.

"Do you need any money?" I asked him. I remembered the Orange Julius remark from the night before and hoped to God he hadn't been eavesdropping.

"No," he said. "Dad left me some. I'm cool for a while."

"Good," I said. "Just let me know."

He stood up and slid his backpack over one shoulder. It needed to be washed, I noted as he went out the door. It had turned to April at some point in the last week but I still wished he'd worn his warmer jacket.

Jule was picking at her bagel. "When my parents died I treated my Aunt Tana like shit. I stole money from her. I canceled her magazine subscriptions, stuff like that."

"How about you?" I said. "Do you need cash for anything this week?" She shook her head. We were quiet for a few minutes.

"I like that shirt on you," I said.

She looked a little embarrassed. "I've always wanted this shirt," she said. "It was there on the chair."

"It's yours," I said.

"I'll come by tonight," she said. "I don't mind it there."

"Yeah, well, maybe for a second."

She immediately went red and I let her feel discouraged for a few moments.

"I think it's different if the two of you hang out there," I said. "Just you and you'd either have to spend the whole time with me, which isn't a good idea, or hang out with the fleas."

"I don't mind those guys," she said. "I've seen them around and stuff."

"Come by," I said. "Definitely."

After she left I called a lawyer I'd met once when I had spent the night in the drunk tank and left a message with his secretary. I talked to the billing department at the hospital and with my insurance company and spent forty minutes on hold with the Social Security Administration. When that was all over I called my mother at a time when I knew she'd be away from the phone.

"Hello, sweetheart," she said. I almost hung up.

"Hey," I said. "I'm glad I caught you."

"Oh yeah?" she said. "That's nice to hear. I was just about to go buy some dog food. We lucked out."

"Why aren't you at school?" I said.

"It's spring break," she said. "Don't you remember Easter?"

"What?" I said. "Sure I do. When was it?"

"Four days ago. You ever get out of the house?"

"Mom," I said. "I've got to tell you some stuff. It's all pretty bad."

"You're divorced," she said. "Jesus, what did you do?"

"I didn't—"

"Did you mess around with that little girl?"

"Mom . . ."

"I shouldn't be surprised, I guess. Look at your father . . ."

I hung up on her. I started to pick up the phone again and then threw it against the wall. It split in half like a big black peanut and dropped its guts against the floorboard. A piece of green circuit board spun up into the air, pinged lightly off my temple, and landed on the counter next to me.

I unplugged the base from the wall and before I got my jacket and left I could hear the extension upstairs bleating.

Outside the sky was the color of manure. I walked to the Teen Scene cursing everything I saw (fucking grass growing in the curb, goddamn rotten branches lying in the gutter, bitch use your turn signal!).

Charlie was in the office when I got there. Lourdes the cleaning lady was sitting in the office with her, her standard blue windbreaker on. I hung my jacket on the rack and stuck my head in the doorway. Lourdes blanched a little and glanced at Charlie.

"You're bleeding," Charlie said, pointing at my head. I backed out of the doorway and went into the bathroom. The piece of phone had cut my temple and I'd somehow smeared a small amount of blood in lots of places on that side of my face. There was a brown clotted streak on the back of my right hand.

I knew that I could turn around and go home and I'd still have a job the next day. I'd never really worked anywhere but I knew this much. I cleaned myself up and then sat on the toilet lid for ten minutes before I switched off the light and closed the door behind me.

"I was going to get coffee and forgot," I said to the two of them before they could say anything to me. "Okay if I run back out? You want anything?"

Charlie shook her head.

"Lourdes?"

"No, thank you," she said in her Ecuadorian accent that reminded me, conveniently, of Starbucks.

Of course Arlene was working when I got to Starbucks. She was still in funeral mode, though. "*Hey*," she said with her head to one side. "*Good* to see you."

I smiled grimly at her. The grim smile was my acknowledgment of their acknowledgment that it was me and not them that got smacked around recently by God.

"We got fresh scones," she said. "And that new Sumatra you like is COD," by which she meant Coffee of the Day.

"You talked me into it," I said. "Give me a Venti drip and a scone, room for milk."

I sat in the corner by the single wall outlet just for kicks. That seat was coveted highly by the roving laptoppers, and sure enough within three minutes one of them came in, his head swiveling to a hard right when he got through the door. When he saw me sitting there he did a fast mental calculation, noticed all the empty tables, and dropped his knapsack and laptop bag on the table closest to mine. All the time Arlene was waiting on him he kept glancing back over toward me; maybe he was just keeping an eye on his bags. Sure.

I tortured him for about ten minutes—let him bring his drink over, stare at it, pretend to be interested in the *Daily Iowan* someone had left on his chair. I sat there with my coffee covered up and my scone still enwrapped in its wax paper sleeve. I sat and stared out the window at the pedestrian mall. It was turning out to be one of those dramatic spring mornings with fast clouds and encouragingly warm flashes of sun. Kids were going to class, the UPS guy was hopping in and out of his truck. A couple leaned against the kiosk with all the fringed flyers stapled to it and had a conversation that should have been about birth control but undoubtedly wasn't.

When Isabel and I first knew that she was going to leave Kenny, I took advantage of her in the worst ways. The only time we could reliably see each other was at Rosie's so I often stayed away and drank elsewhere. I made offhand comments about her clothes ("How old *is* that?") and if someone I knew came into Rosie's I made a point of not introducing her to them, even if they sat up at the bar right there with me—often I'd get a table if that happened. She was the pure professional during all of that; but the next time we could sneak into my bed she'd start off petulant and I'd have to assure her I was just trying not to blow our cover. I'm sure the idea of my being the reason for any-one to change anything about their lives—much less end a marriage—was as absurd to her as it was to me.

And just last week after the funeral when we all went down to the church basement I was sure everyone was looking at me and Kenny at opposite corners of the place and wondering whom to give the lion's share of their sympathy to. Kenny seemed to rec-ognize everyone and have no trouble with the grip and the hug and the heavy nodding look of gracious acquiescence. I stood by myself and greeted the occasional mourner the way the strange old guy with the darkened porch stiffly rewarded the odd trick-or-treater on Halloween. I spilled two cups of coffee before I gave up trying to use my hands and mostly stared at Jule, who stuck close to Rosie. I wished Alex would come stand with me, or I could stand by him. I wished I could sneak out back to the little church school play area and swing with him or kick a ball around. Alex just stood next to his dad and nodded dumbly at everyone who came up to him. I noticed then that he'd forgotten to fasten the little buttons on his collar. How could he have remembered? It was Russ's shirt, after all. His father should have noticed.

I gathered up my Venti and scone and vacated the plug table. The lapper didn't even wait for me to push in the chair; he leaned over and dropped his limp backpack on the table with a smirk of triumph. Jesus, I thought, what dreck was he so hot to flick his keyboard at? What specimen would stumble through the door next and blanch like a flashed virgin when he saw the precious plug table occupied? Didn't these people notice the part in the undergraduate orientation that mentioned the goddamn *library*?

Dwayne never showed that day at the Teen Scene. Charlie hung around until about four before putting on her jacket and trying to hide the fact that she was merely climbing the stairs to the attic. All of the usual kids showed up right about on time, and I was absurdly glad to see them. They all nodded at me a bit strangely and after about fifteen minutes JJ came over and knocked softly on the doorjamb.

"Hey," I said. I had been doodling on a pad of graph paper someone had left lying around.

"Hey," he said. His face was bright red and his eyes blinked furiously. If I didn't know that this was his standard nervous behavior I would have been tempted to pump his stomach.

"We were all talking and we wondered if there was something we could do to help out."

"Well," I said, "you could burn me some CDs."

He blinked a few times in rapid succession. "Yeah?" he said. "I could do that, dude, sure. What do you want?"

"Whatever you like," I said. "I don't listen much to music anymore." I wanted to add "because it's crap," but I didn't. Most of what I heard on the radio was so derivative it should have an extra track to explain the provenance. The indie/alternative stuff was worse, four guys standing in front of microphones abusing their instruments the way someone would hack a computer.

JJ looked a bit apprehensive. "I mean, maybe you should name some bands, because I might make you a lot of shit you hate." He started to rattle off a couple of names and I stopped him.

"It's okay," I said. "As long as you think it's good I'm sure it will be. Impress me."

He nodded and went back to the gang. They all leaned forward when he told them what we'd said. He was their scout— he'd approached the Dude Who Stank of Mortality and had returned with the good word. "All he wants is music," JJ was no doubt saying. "We give him some choice cuts and Quetzalcoatl stays in the volcano."

Aaron came in around nine. He stalked in the back door and dropped into the chair on the other side of my desk. He was panting and sweat beaded on his forehead.

"Been jogging?" I asked.

He nodded three times, catching his breath before answering. "A mile," he said. He was wearing black work boots and jeans and the kind of jacket you see on losing football coaches.

"Bijou," I said. "You could hurt yourself running like that."

"I stretched," he said defensively.

"I mean you could get arrested," I said. "You look like you're fleeing the scene."

"That's why I pump my arms," he said, demonstrating. "Your common Negro purse snatcher doesn't pump his arms." Then he did a little side-to-side head bob. "I avoid the OJ comparisons by acting very *Chariots of Fire.*"

"Anyway," I said. "Thanks for your note."

"*De nada.* How are the teens taking it?"

I told him about Alex and a little about Jule. To be honest, he didn't seem to be paying much attention. I wondered how many psychotropic drugs he was on. In his dreams did he even come close to getting hell right, I wondered? Isabel and Russ never set foot in church. Where were they now? Was the gravel in the cardboard boxes all there was?

"Aaron," I said. "Did your mom go to church?"

"Oh, yes," he said. "A deaconess."

"That sounds like something a female wrestler would coin." I picked up a nickel and spun it on the desktop. "So you think she's in heaven?"

"Undoubtedly. Buck was very clear on that in prison. He wasn't any real theologian but he had salvation covered."

"So where do you put my gang?" I said. "What would Dante do with them?"

Aaron looked at me long and hard and I could see his enormous chest rise and fall. "Andrew," he said, "Dante is for shit in your situation. Seriously."

"Why? Why can't I speculate? I have to imagine them somewhere."

"Imagine them here."

"I can't," I said. "I tried but I couldn't pull it off."

"Really?"

"Yes. It was pretty frustrating. You know what it's like to think yourself sick?"

"Then imagine them in the recent past. You have all that time invested. All those days and nights and family-type moments."

"I can't remember them," I said. "I remember last week tops."

"Bullshit," he said. "When was . . . her last birthday?"

"Isabel's?" I said. "In May. Next month."

"What did you do last year?"

"I don't know. We went out for dinner at the Bistro. The boys gave her some stupid shit she pretended to like."

Aaron stood up quickly. His lips were trembling. "Don't try, then," he said. His voice was in a new register. "Don't even try!" For the first time since I met him he looked like a big queen.

"Bijou," I said, "sit down, man." Some of the kids had heard us and were looking through the window. Aaron stood there with his jaw tight and stared at the surface of my desk. "Aaron," I said. "It's okay, man."

He turned and walked out of the door and nearly collided with Jule and, remarkably, Alex. He froze, staring at them. Their eyes traveled from me to Aaron and back.

"Excuse me," Aaron finally said, and pushed past them. Alex watched him leave even after Jule had come into the office and sat down.

"This chair is four hundred degrees," she said. "Wow."

"He was exercising," I said. Out of the corner of my eye I could see that all activity had now stopped out in the lounge. Alex finally came in and right away I could see something had changed. He wasn't exactly smiling but the stone mask was gone. If anything his face was now lost in wonderment, the way it had often been in the past few years. I was terrified that if I said or did anything I would ruin it, but he spoke first.

"Hey," he said. "Look." He opened a brown paper bag he'd been carrying and pulled out a large plastic ball. It was a Magic 8-Ball. "Ask me a question," he said.

"Was OJ guilty?" I said. But to myself I asked, "Do we have a chance in hell, the three of us?"

Alex turned the ball over and then back, furrowing his brow. His dark hair fell into his eyes and brushed the sharp bridge of his nose. He squinted and blinked and waited for the answer.

"It appears so," he read. He looked up and beamed at me as if he'd just returned from Delphi. Jule put her hand on his upper arm. He shook the ball again. "Ask me another one," he said. "Go ahead."

Dear Lord, I loved them.

3

I think if it wasn't for the accident I would have been a lot more skeptical of Dwayne, Charlie, the Teen Scene, and the whole nine yards. If it hadn't been for the accident maybe Rosie and I would have had a conversation about it sooner than we did.

It was in May, only a few weeks before school got out. Kenny had come and gone again with remarkably few repercussions. Alex was preparing to spend the summer with him and figure out where he wanted to go to school next year. Jule was spending time reading and practicing meditation and being generally secretive and shy. I walked around a lot with my Discman headphones on listening to JJ's compilation disc. It was superb; too good. I wept openly at times, ducking into a corner or ATM or alley.

On a Tuesday morning I sat with Rosie in the bar by the golf machine and she chain-smoked her Trues. I'd stopped by mainly to check in—she expected it and I was only too glad to. She'd given me a car, after all. Not the Cadillac but a Tempo that was easy to drive, soft on the corners but otherwise substantial. Jule and Alex both would be ready for their permits soon, she said, as if I didn't need a car for groceries and general getting around.

"So, who's staying for the summer?" I asked her. Generally she lost some staff in May and she always complained when someone left but always cheerfully hired them back in September.

"Ginny," she said. "Robert. That tool Phil. Becca."

"Wow," I said. "What ever happened to internships?"

"They're too stupid. Phil's restoring some fucking old pickup truck. His parents own like nine dairies and I have to add up his drawer for him."

"He's good, though," I said. In the old days I'd watched him handle the whole bar two deep with no back. He was a natural, and I still admired that about anybody.

"Hey," Rosie said. "I did some asking around about that place you work. Pretty interesting, all in all. Apparently they had money problems and the city cut them off and doesn't have anything to do with them."

"It's a private nonprofit or something like that," I said. "There's some endowment from an old lady but they get some other grant money on top of that."

"I didn't hear old," she said. "I heard a lot younger than old."

"Really?" I said. "He told me an old lady in a nursing home gave a shitload of money and the city uses it for this."

"Not the city. They are totally hands-off that place. You kidding?"

"Wow," I said. "Well, I don't think Charlie or Dwayne are embezzlers. She pretends she doesn't live in the attic and he hasn't bought a shirt in five years."

Rosie stubbed out her cigarette. "I mean who cares, really? In light of everything just make the best of it while it lasts."

I watched the golf machine run through its demo for a moment.

"What did you really think back when Isabel said she was going to marry me?" I asked Rosie. "You couldn't tell me anything I haven't told myself."

"I said he's cute and everything, but how does he treat you?"

I groaned. "That's the question St. Peter's going to ask me," I said. "For me that's the big one."

"Not 'What did you do with your life?' "

"I swear I'm going to treat those two kids like royalty," I said.

"Because you're afraid of hell?"

"Like royalty," I said.

"If I was you," she said, "I'd be figuring out how I was going to deal with solitude. That's going to be the hardest if you ask me."

"I don't know, Alex might stay. He might come back after the summer."

She shrugged. "To stay with you? He doesn't have any friends. He loves his dad. I wouldn't count on it."

"To stay with Jule, maybe. They're pretty close."

Rosie sat back a little, looking theatrically surprised.

"Whoa," she said. "You don't think there's any way in hell they're going to let *her* stay with you, do you?"

"I don't know," I said. "I think there's a medium chance."

"There's *no* chance," she said. "And you should be thinking about what's best for her, not you."

"It's not best for her to move. It's not best for her to go live with dotty Aunt Tana in Cedar Falls. Next year she'll be a senior. Shit, she could go to college today if she wanted to."

Rosie snorted. She had spread her knees on either side of her chair, not unlike a tensed sumo wrestler.

"Listen," she said. "You've never been to family court. You'd last like ten minutes there. What, you're going to petition for adoption?"

"Of course not," I said, my face growing tight. "I'll do the same as Isabel did—custodian, supervisor, whatever. I know there's a term for it."

"Oh, there's a term for it," Rosie said. "You think everyone is stupid, don't you?"

I started to look for the exit. "No, but I think a lot of people don't know what they're talking about."

"Hey," Rosie said. "I'm not your mother, I'm not an agent of the court, I don't know what the hell I am. But I've seen you flat on your ass more times than you've seen me."

"What does that mean?"

"It means you're no more able to take care of a couple of teenagers than Pee Wee Fucking Herman. It means she looks like she's old enough and God knows she and Russ were probably screwing like crazed weasels but if you think that girl is in any way yours you have another think coming."

I stood up. "You stopped making sense back at the St. Peter thing."

"Sit down, sport," she said, and I sat. "Those two are going to need you. You don't see it but I do. They're going to need you, but not the way you think."

"That's all I'm saying . . ." I said.

"Shut up," she said. "Did you have a brother or sister?"

"A brother," I said. "He's in Chicago."

"No kids of your own, right?"

"That's right."

"Do me a favor and take that do-rag off your head. Jesus, you lose your backwards baseball cap?"

"I was playing basketball," I said, which was a lie. I started to get up again. This was grossly unfair, I was sure of it. The bitch could keep her squeaky Ford.

"You own a suit?"

"Yes."

She sat quietly and breathed at me that way that fat people breathe, in through the nose and then out through the mouth with that little apneic catch in the throat.

"Exactly what problems are you ready to deal with?" she said finally.

"How can I answer that?" I said. "How could anyone?"

"What keeps you up at night?" she said. "Who can you say no to?" This time she stood up. "My ex-husband was a cokehead farm boy. He got cleaned up and it was like night and day. He spent time with our kid, went to church, got a promotion. He really hit the ground running, you know?"

"That's good," I said.

"Yeah?" she said. "You never met a bigger baby in your life than he was. He was kidding himself, and you seem to me exactly the same as him."

"You're . . ."

But she wasn't finished. "You remember that part of the Bible where wise old King Solomon gives the baby to the whiny bitch who, like, folded immediately? My husband didn't know what hit him when I took his kid away from him. His picture of everything was clear as a bell, him at the center of this little clean universe, everything revolving around him. Where is he now, you're wondering? Beats the hell out of me. He loses the case and he's gone. He went for half, you see?"

"You totally lost me," I said. But she was already heading back to the office. She stopped for the capper.

"You're heading for a fucking fall if you think you're a match for what you're going to come up against," she said. "I don't care if you don't drink, don't smoke, don't play with yourself. You're like Mr. Magoo, walking out on one of those skyscraper girders. You think you're lonely now," and then closed her office door behind her.

I sat and watched one of the waitresses wrap the silverware for the setups. She sat in the corner wrapping and watching a soap opera on the TV over the bar, her mouth slightly open. She was one of those generic midwestern blond weak-chinned wide-hipped flat-assed no-swallow sorority girls. Next to her another girl who could have been her sister was reading *King Lear* and drinking a Diet Coke. I couldn't help wondering why the two of them were here and Isabel wasn't. How desperately they would be missed if they got picked off, snuffed. How they seemed less than real. Maybe it was the *Lear*. Are you babes of stone!?

That night in bed Jule had one nightmare after another and then just as the sun was coming up she bolted out of bed and threw up in the toilet. When she came back to the room I felt like Rosie was sitting there with us, shaking her head. Jule slid into the bed on the other side and faced away from me.

"Did Isabel know you were pregnant?" I asked. She shook her head without turning over.

"Did Russ know?

She shook her head again.

"How did Rosie know?"

She just shrugged. I lay back and stared at the ceiling for a few minutes. Four or five things occurred to me to say and I let each of them pass. After a few minutes I dressed and left. It was a beautiful morning; I headed for the river, for the footbridge to Hancher Auditorium. Some of the trees closest to the water had budded out and the ragged grass was spotty with their light-green droppings. Sun-starved undergraduates lay on their backs with their eyes closed and their books covered with dew. A girl sat reading a letter and weeping.

The river was fast and high and littered with debris. From the bridge I could just about see the spot on the other side of the river, just beyond the art museum, where Izzie and Russ had hit the semi. I had avoided driving past it, going clear out around on the interstate anytime I needed to go to the mall. I thought about all the death errands I'd run the last few weeks. I'd gone to the impound yard and emptied the warped trunk of the Renault—a gym bag of Izzie's and a pair of Russ's soccer cleats from the previous year, clotted with hard gray mud. I'd bagged some clothes of Isabel's that I knew Jule wouldn't want—her uniforms and some old suits I never remembered her wearing. I'd spent several annoying hours with the probate lawyer, who complained endlessly about the lack of a will clearly stating beneficiaries.

The corpse of either a small dog or a woodchuck floated underneath the bridge, spinning slightly in the eddy created by one of the pylons. When had it stormed so hard? Iowa City was just downstream of the dam. Had they opened it up for some reason?

The crying girl suddenly gathered up her books and ran off. She stumbled up the bank and disappeared into Stanley Hall. Some lumber—broken two-by-twos—floated underneath the bridge.

"Hey," someone said behind me. I turned. It took me a few seconds to filter the person into the present. It was Carl, Isabel's former patient. I'd forgotten he worked at Hancher—some kind of flunky administrator or paper flicker.

"Carl," I said. "How the hell are you?"

"I have a cold," he said. "My back is out. It's May and I've used up my prescription allotment for the year, believe it or not."

"Carl, you look pretty good to me. If I was you I'd be worried about the flood." I peered over the railing just as a broken cooler floated by.

"Flood?" he said. "I didn't hear anything about it."

"They're not going to announce it, I heard, so as not to create a panic. It's a mild flood. There's a very good chance the dam will hold. They're practically certain."

Carl leaned way over the railing this time.

I pointed at a pale object swirling lazily beneath the surface. "Is that a foot?" It sank out of sight almost immediately.

"Good Pete," Carl said. Just then the weeping girl reappeared, still crying, and ran past us on the bridge at a decent clip.

"She's overreacting," I said. "I don't think that's helpful at all."

Carl pulled a piece of paper out of his pocket and hurled it over the side, then crossed quickly to the opposite rail and watched it float away until it was out of sight.

"It's a half mile between bridges," he said. "That was seventy seconds, which makes this current forty or so miles per hour."

"Is that a record?" I said. "How fast can water go before it starts taking out bridges? Maybe we should get off this thing."

"I have to get back to the office," Carl said.

I nodded and gazed over at Hancher seriously. "They have a right to know," I said.

He shook my hand and scurried off. His back looked fine to me.

I stayed on the bridge for another half hour, mentally cataloging the flotsam: more lumber, plastic recyclables, paper and cardboard. A stranger came up next to me and held on to his information for nearly a full minute before he spilled it.

"It's all from that dump truck that rolled into the river," he said. "What a mess."

"Lots of trucks ending up in the river these days," I said.

We both stood there for a while and watched the garbage flow by. In that time no fewer than four of my ex-professors strolled by. Not a single one of them appeared to recognize me.

I imagined that afternoon that I had a therapist. I imagined this therapist to be a woman; late forties, brilliant, wise to the inner complexities of certain men and of course patient, nonjudgmental, and Jewish. She sometimes brought her small dog to the office, where it dozed at my feet.

"I loved her sweet ass," I'd be able to tell her. She was that good. "I loved it as it grew. It made her seem more like a woman to me."

"How exactly do you see yourself, in relation to the baby?" she'd ask.

"How do you mean?"

"I think you know what I mean. There are quite a few choices."

"Father figure," I said.

"Not grandfather figure?"

"I beg your fucking pardon?"

"Stepgrandfather?"

"I know what you're doing," I said.

"You were the stepfather of her partner," she said. "Technically . . ."

"You're getting off on this," I said. "I should charge you."

She pressed a button on her remote and her CD player started in on Simon and Garfunkel's "Hazy Shade of Winter."

She fast-forwarded it to a specific verse and then looked at me significantly:

> *If your hopes should pass away,*
> *simply pretend that you can build them again.*

I countered with the following verse, how it was the springtime of my life, and all that. I loved that part. "Jesus," I said to my imaginary therapist, "why do I need you? Just give me the disc."

In a different session we do that old routine where I fall back and she catches me. Her little dog doesn't like this therapy and hops around, ass in the air, yipping. I fall back and she catches me. I fall back and she catches me. After a while she puts a soft armchair behind me and pours herself coffee out of a thermos.

"That's very cynical," I told her. "I actually think that's the definition of cynical."

She nodded. "You could get one of those MEAN PEOPLE SUCK T-shirts and give it to me on my birthday."

"I'm not whining," I said.

"You're not whining," she agreed. "Why are you afraid of grandfatherhood?"

"Because I'm thirty-two and childless?"

"That's very astute."

"You mean interesting," I said. "It's very interesting."

"It's not that interesting," she replied.

"You agree I'm too young to be a grandfather?"

"No, I agree that you are childless and thirty-two."

"You have to crawl before you can walk. Rome wasn't built in a day."

"Babies are a lot of trouble," she said.

"I took care of my brother's baby for a while when he and his wife were in an ashram."

"That was very nice of you."

In my fantasy my therapist then let me off the hook by quoting Woody Allen, something about the heart listening only to itself.

It fit nicely with the Simon and Garfunkel.

On the way home I ran into Dwayne, almost literally. He was coming out of the bank clutching a manila envelope.

"Dwayne," I said. "Hey."

He squinted at me in the sun. "I thought you were a student I once had," he said.

"It's not impossible," I replied. "I've taken just about every class in the catalog."

"It's getting hot," he said.

"About time," I said. He nodded and I nodded and I pretended I had to go off in the opposite direction. When he was safely out of sight I doubled back through the alley but misjudged and found myself walking about a half block behind him. Why not? If the guy wants to feed me a line about an old lady and an endowment he deserved to be followed.

He made three stops on the way to the Teen Scene: the drop-off bins in front of the library, the Kum & Go across from the

Bistro, and the paint store across from the Foxhead Tavern. I waited until he was out of sight and pushed open the door to the paint store. It was cold inside.

"Did my boss just come in here?" I asked the kid next to the machine that shook the paint cans.

"There was a guy in here," he said. "Was that him?"

"He was supposed to get latex enamel. Did he get latex enamel?" I asked.

The kid shook his head. "He got some mineral spirits," he said. "He's bought mineral spirits a bunch of times."

I pretended to be annoyed. "Can we return that?" I asked. "Did he use the credit card?"

"He had a twenty-dollar bill. But you can still return it."

"Great," I said. "I'll chase him down. When I come back I'll have some questions for you about latex enamel." Outside the paint store it had clouded over and everything started looking very March again.

When I got home Jule was still in bed. I was due at the Teen Scene in a half hour. She was lying on her back with her hands flat and fingers curled. Her belly was very flat and her big toes touched together. Her eyes were closed and her lips were parted a little.

"Hey," I said. "How are you?"

She opened her eyes slowly and tilted her head toward me. "I'm fine," she said. "Your mom called."

"What did she say?" A few days after I'd thrown the phone against the wall Jule had talked to her and told her what happened. I still meant to dial her number but never found the time.

"She talked about when you were a little boy," Jule said. "She went on and on."

"I'm surprised she remembers. Half the time she was stoned."

"I was meditating," she said. "A pretty simple one. It was good."

"You know they might make you leave, right? I don't know but maybe they'll take the baby."

"Why?"

I was stumped. "I don't know . . . you're a minor. You don't have a legal guardian. You haven't finished school."

"I live here. You're my guardian. You're old enough."

"Jule," I said. "We're sleeping in the same bed. I can barely keep my hands off you. That's not a guardian."

"I would marry you if you asked," she said. "What could they do then? I don't even care if I finish school."

I sat down on the bed next to her. Her T-shirt/camisole was pulled up and revealed the soft white of her belly and a small mole that hovered above her belly button. I leaned over her and brushed the hair off her forehead.

"Isabel and I used to do some crazy stuff in bed. I know this sounds stupid but it was grown-up stuff. It makes no sense here in the daylight but all I can say is that marriage isn't . . ." I fumbled for words.

"What?" she said. Her chest, smooth and sharp and perfect under the light cotton, rose and fell.

"It isn't innocent," I said. "It's like signing up to live in a glass house that you carry with you. People come in and out but the two of you carry it around like a shell, and the glass gets all dirty from the inside . . ."

"I can do stuff," she said. "You'd be surprised."

"I know," I said, holding up my hand.

"When did you lose your virginity?" she asked. "How old were you?"

"Nineteen," I said.

"I was fourteen," she said. "And it wasn't Russ."

"I didn't think it was."

"So you don't have to worry about me like that."

"Listen . . ." I said.

"You think you and Isabel were the only ones fucking in this house?"

"Of course not," I said.

"Alex would laugh," she said.

"Fine. Why would Alex laugh?"

She lifted her head up from the pillow a little, her eyes widening. "You're kidding, right? You don't know about that?"

I lay down on the bed next to her. "I may not be up to all this intrigue," I said. "I can't take it."

"He's not in love, and he's careful," she said.

"I don't want to know. I do but I don't."

"He's afraid his dad will figure it out."

"I know how he feels."

She rolled over and put her head on my chest. "I'm not afraid of weird sex or growing up too soon or any of that. I'm pregnant and I want this baby to have a father that's alive. What's so wrong about that? You said you'd take care of me."

"That's different . . ."

"It doesn't have to be. You want me to blow you? I'll blow you right now."

My heart sank but I swear to God my dick jumped. I saw myself putting my hands around the throat of my imaginary therapist and throttling her. Jule stared down at me.

"Slide down," I told her, pushing her gently over onto her back. "Further. Close your eyes." I pulled off my jeans and Jockeys in one move. She started to raise her hands but I pushed them away. "No," I said. "No hands."

I hoisted myself up and put one forearm on the bookcase headboard. "Keep your eyes closed," I said. With her chin up and her eyelashes lying flat on her cheeks, I placed my dick against the side of her face, just under the perfect cheekbone. It was as close as I could let myself get. I shook like a child.

"It's hot," she breathed.

"Don't say anything," I said. I could see her jaw start to clench. She kept her mouth shut tight and I could feel the air forced out of her nostrils. I didn't know what to do so I moved to the other side of her face, as if I were a king and she was my fresh little vassal.

"Are you thinking about your baby now?" I said.

"No," she whispered. Her hands traveled up to my hips. Somewhere far away the phone began to ring. She took my dick gently in her fingers and pushed it against her cheek. "It's like a bird," she said. "I can feel its heartbeat. Can you feel that?" The phone rang and rang.

"God DAMN it," I said. "Jesus Christ God DAMN it." And then I was sobbing. I put my head in my arms on the bookcase headboard and Jule held my dick against her cheek and I sobbed uncontrollably. My body spasmed but she held on, drawing her knees up, covering me up as best she could. And still the phone rang.

"I want to talk to my mother," I said between gasps. "I just want to talk to her. Where the hell has she gone?"

4

I not only ran into my ex-professors all the time, but into various ladies of whom I'd had carnal knowledge. Iowa City was that size town. Most of them had graduated or taken better jobs elsewhere or otherwise disappeared, but a few were still kicking around. Who knows why. The schools? None of them had gotten married or had kids. None of the guys my age had kids; how did the race survive? Nobody born between 1960 and 1972 seemed to want to replicate themselves. Seventy-year-olds in Riga were having quintuplets, fifty-year-olds in the United States were starting families, but the odds of finding a thirty-three-year-old dad with a graduate degree were lower than finding one without a cell phone shoved against his ear.

I, however, had been raising teenagers and now was looking forward to a baby with which I could, apparently, have any relationship I could conjure up. I was a widower, a stepfather, a step-grandfather, and a cleaned-up drunk. All by thirty-two. I'd be lying if part of me didn't think that was a substantial life résumé in the School of Hard Knocks tradition.

But once I quit drinking, in that long winter when I wasn't seeing Isabel, I'd had very little contact with women. In the early days I spent quite a lot of plastic money on phone sex. In just a few weeks I'd rung up nearly three thousand dollars in Visa debt, which appeared on my card as charges from "Custom Graphics." I never paid that bill. This was back in the days when they sent just about everyone who was about to graduate from college a Visa card with a three-thousand-dollar limit. I claimed I never received the card and I never heard any more from the little bank in Delaware. Maybe they went under.

In the month and a half I availed myself of Custom Graphics I dealt exclusively with a girl named Ruby, who was exceptionally talented in phone bed. She had an incredible repertoire of run-ups to orgasm. In a month and a half of three-times-a-week trysts, she repeated herself possibly twice. Some of my favorites:

I can't believe the way this chemise feels against my nipples. It's so cool in the air-conditioning it's like wearing ice cream. They're as hard as gumdrops. Would you like to bite them?

I just got back from the gym so I'm a little sweaty. I normally just wear these tights which have these little holes in them but today they split a little up the middle. It might be easier to get them off if you reach down and . . . that's it. My God, they just fell apart!

I just feel so, stiff tonight, I need to stretch. You know how my kitty stretches? She puts her front paws on the carpet and lifts her little bottom in the air and just stretches. That's the way I like to stretch—my fingers in the carpet, my ass in the air. Are you back there? Rrrrddddddd (she could purr!).

Even though I'd put my dick on Jule's cheek we'd never gone any further. We slept in the same bed and sometimes I pushed myself up against her and she pushed back but neither of us followed through with it. She was pregnant, she was sixteen, did that have anything to do with it? I don't know. No matter what, though, I wasn't getting any, and I was a little crazy.

One night I went to a Parents Without Partners/AA mixer at the VFW hall. Actually I spent about twenty minutes there before I figured something out; women with kids were sexy. Women with kids had a nice way of moving. Women with kids were interesting to listen to. I suppose I had always thought that Isabel was some kind of incredible exception; I was wrong. In ten minutes I had a conversation going with not one but three beautiful women; Charlie's Angels with minivans and underwire bras. I never even caught their names. One was a Realtor with a full upper lip and a nice bead of sweat in the little dent in her throat. In ten seconds she had correctly ascertained my birth sign, my birth order, and my age. She could have worked in a New Age carnival.

"You," I told her with feigned authority, "are thirty-one, a middle child, and a Libra."

"That's amazing," she said.

"I also have perfect pitch," I added.

"Give us an A," one of the others said, a dark-blonde beauty in a black blouse and with a tiny wad of gum that she chewed somehow without it becoming annoying.

"I can't reproduce a note, but I can name any note played. That air conditioner? That's a D, mostly."

"That's not fair," the third one said. She was a copper-skinned Indian with cheekbones so sharp they were almost like Barbie tits under her eyes. "How could we tell if you are right?"

I shrugged. A truck horn sounded from outside. "That's a chord," I said. "Can you hear the A and the F?"

"You're lying," the sweating brunette said.

"Prove it," I said. She was getting aggressive. She was staking the claim.

"Well, for one thing, I'm thirty-nine, a Cancer, and an only child."

"That's three things," I said. All three of them laughed.

One of them asked what I did for a living. You could tell what she really wanted to know: drunk or divorced, or both.

"I counsel teenagers," I said. "And I'm a musician."

"You look like a musician," the sweaty one said. "I'm a dancer."

"Really? What kind?" I said.

"Arthur Murray," one of the others piped up. "You like the cha-cha?"

"Absolutely," I said. "My swing needs a brushup, though." The DJ was playing some Bruce Springsteen and the sweaty woman grabbed my hand and pulled me out in front of the speakers. She was good; I remembered most of the moves from the wedding video. She swung her goods around nicely and smiled through her very white teeth. I enjoyed the hell out of myself. With very little of my brain I figured out the way I would steer her into bed, right there while I was dancing. It seemed a very natural progression of thought. Maybe that was why dancing was so popular.

When that song was over the DJ started in with the Police and I bailed for the refreshment table. The other two Angels tapped in their high heels out to the middle of the floor, where all three of them tossed their hips around and shook their hair and I actually felt my knees tremble. Warm Pepsi foamed over my fingers.

I was still at the refreshment table when I saw Rosie appear in the doorway, wearing a green dress and some kind of strange tortured hairdo. I edged behind two guys with beards and polo shirts.

"Humvee at three o'clock," one of the guys muttered.

But it was too late; she'd caught me in her initial room scan. I stood at the table as she approached.

"Hey," she said. "Fancy meeting you here."

"Please don't rag me out," I said. "I needed to be around grown-ups."

She showed me her palms. "*No problemo*, stud. None of us are perfect, right?"

"Is perfect," I replied, turning my attention back to the ladies on the dance floor. There were about thirty people in the joint; they were the only three dancing. The two bearded guys were watching them silently, gripping their sodas like fire poles.

"Wow, they let hookers in here?" Rosie said behind me. I ignored her.

"I happen to know that Mata Hari there is a teacher," she said. "Look at those tightass jeans she's got on. Slide a credit card in the back pocket and they'd go off like a fricking bomb."

"I'm screwing Jule," I said. I had meant to say, "I'm NOT screwing Jule," but it came out that way. It didn't matter, she hadn't heard me, apparently. The music was pretty loud.

"When that song came out I was in college," Rosie said over the speakers. "The guy I married was studying to be a minister, even though he was a sex and drug addict."

"I was in the eighth grade," I said. "My brother sat on the record and broke it. Remember records? I don't think Jule's ever seen one."

"Did she mention that while you were poking her?"

I turned to Rosie. "What?"

"Did she mention that I called over there?"

"No," I said. "Do you want to dance?" It seemed like the only way to shut us both up. We walked out to the middle where the three moms were dancing and stood and jerked around and swung our arms a little, she in a very eighties style, me in a kind of crappy nineties style, and the DJ slid into a Nirvana song which of course was undanceable to anyone who wasn't preternaturally spastic.

Rosie had destroyed any erotic fantasy I had been entertaining about the moms, either individually or as a group; not by her presence or even her dancing, which was pretty damn good, but by her talent for making me seem—even to myself—like a reptile. I fought the feeling off as best I could by attempting to dance in such a way as to give the impression that I was squiring all four of the females at once. I probably only succeeded in looking faintly gay.

Once that song was over we all cleared off the dance floor. I started to make motions like I was leaving and had to restrain myself from signaling the sweaty mom that she ought to leave too. Rosie wandered off to chat up a woman who had the wind-tunnel appearance of a botched face-lift. The blonde Angel in the black blouse suddenly tugged my sleeve. I leaned forward.

"Don't go," she yelled. "You're the only guy here with real hair."

"I've got to get home and let the baby-sitter go," I said.

"Yeah?" she said. "How old are your kids?"

I pulled on the little hairs under my lip. "That's a complicated question," I said. "I'm a stepdad."

"Oh," she said. I started to move away but the Indian woman in the tight jeans was blocking my way. Rosie flicked her eyes at us from a few yards away. The DJ had chosen that moment to kick out his plug or something because the music was suddenly gone and the chatter echoed off the concrete walls.

"Is your wife older?" the Indian woman asked.

"My wife died," I said. All three of them made purring noises of pity from somewhere in their breasts. I thought of lionesses, wondering if they made small talk with the wildebeest before quartering it and dragging the pieces home. Just moments before they'd seemed like a harem; now a hint of panic had crept into my central nervous system. I had a sudden desire to go find Alex, the way I used to. I needed to find Alex and throw a football around and pretend Isabel was going to show up and make it all calm down.

I lowered my voice so that it wouldn't carry over to where Rosie was standing.

"I'm here from the AA side," I said. "I just thought it would be good to go out. It was actually the kids' idea." In unison all six of their eyes narrowed a bit, it seemed, as they factored in this new information. The sweaty-sexy one put her fingers on my forearm. "My husband died of ALS. If it hadn't been for Jim Beam I wouldn't have made it through."

The other two nodded as if this made complete sense to them. I glanced at Rosie and she'd heard; she rolled her eyes a bit.

"I've got to go," I said. "It was great hanging with you guys." I backed away, turned, and walked straight to the door like I was expecting to take a couple of rounds in the spine. I felt like Frederic Forrest in *Apocalypse Now:* "Never get off the boat . . ."

It was the middle of the next week when I got two bits of important news in a single fifteen-minute period. The first was that the family court wanted to visit the house to check up on Jule. That came in a letter that I hadn't had the heart to open until breakfast. Just like Rosie had said, the forces of virtue were starting to circle, probably at the behest of the vice principal. The second was that Dwayne had disappeared.

It was June 6, two weeks before the end of school, two weeks before Alex would be heading north and my grace period would be over. Apparently it was also the anniversary of D Day. Sixty years earlier my grandfather had landed at Utah Beach without

a scratch and died on a hospital ship three weeks later of the
Russian flu.

I found out about Dwayne from Lourdes. She called me at
eight-thirty in the morning. She was crying. "Come here, please,
very soon."

When I got there Lourdes and Charlie were sitting out on the
back steps. "Dwayne's flown the coop," Charlie said.

"How do you know?" I said. "I mean, is there a note or something?"

Charlie nodded. She handed me a piece of graph paper folded
into quarters.

> *I'm out of here. Really out of here. See you in the funny
> papers. Dwayne.*

I folded it back up and handed it to Charlie.

"Did anyone call him at home?" Lourdes and Charlie looked
at each other.

"Yes," Lourdes said.

"Well, shit," I said. "What does this mean?"

Charlie shrugged. "Business as usual, I guess. Nobody's indis-
pensable." But there was something false in her voice.

"But don't we have to tell somebody?" I said. "I mean, he was
the director, right?"

Charlie nodded. "There's a board."

"So we should tell them? How soon should we tell them?"

"Listen," Charlie said. "We have a couple of problems you
may or may not know about."

I backed up a step and held up my hands. "I'm not receptive
to bad news right now," I said. "If this is bad news, you know,
e-mail me . . ."

"Andrew—"

"I've got a social worker coming to take my children away in a
week. My wife's ashes are sitting in a box at the funeral home
and I still don't know where the checkbook is. Really—"

"Andrew," Charlie said, "Dwayne is my son. Farley is my maiden name."

"Okay," I said. "I get it. Really?"

She and Lourdes both nodded.

"I'm not worried about him so much. He's able to take care of himself. I'm a little worried about how we can keep this place going."

"I need this job," I said. Suddenly Charlie seemed to me more maternal; knowing she was a mother made her immediately less eccentric. She was just a mom.

"I know," she said.

"So we can just keep going, right?" I said. "I mean, it's not like he took the keys with him, right?"

Charlie nodded absently. "I said we had some problems. I've been putting off dealing with them but I think it's time now to think about a reorganization. In the meantime we need a warm body to fill Dwayne's hours and begin a search for a new director."

I could see Lourdes and Charlie draw back a bit to take me in. I'd gotten dressed in a hurry, so I wasn't up to my usual Teen Scene dress standard. I was wearing my baggy-ass shorts with the camouflage and hammer loops. I was wearing Russ's basketball jersey named after some NBA player who'd knifed a hooker after the All-Star game. My hair was slept-in and rank. I had dried milk in my soul patch. I sat down on the steps next to them. "So we hire somebody?" I said absently.

"It's tricky," Charlie said. "We don't want anyone who will ask a lot of questions. We need to keep this boat afloat until I can figure something out. I know I can get us six months but at some point we're going to have to show a new plan. Our charter barely got renewed last year. We do have you now, thank God, with your education. That helps."

"Shit," I said. "I need to graduate, it sounds like."

Charlie and Lourdes both looked a little shocked.

"You don't have a degree?" Charlie said.

"I could have two BAs by December," I said. "Not in social work, of course, but it's a start."

Charlie just looked miserable.

"I guess now we have one more problem," I said. "Dwayne more or less told me it didn't matter."

Charlie shook her head slowly. "We're running quickly out of options."

"Charlie," I said. "You have to tell me about where the money comes from. Not some old lady bullshit. I'm part of this now."

Charlie and Lourdes exchanged a look.

"It's mostly Ford Foundation and Pew and the rest of it is from Lourdes."

Lourdes nodded. "My brother sent it to me from Ecuador. I was to buy bonds with it."

"I changed my mind," I said. "I don't want to know." They both stared at me for a minute. "You mean to tell me this place is essentially a front? For the first time in my life I actually have a job and it's at some kind of fucking boiler room? Do you pay the kids? How much does JJ pull in?"

"Don't be ridiculous," Charlie said. "I have a Ph.D. in social work, I don't know what Dwayne told you but he has a doctorate as well. My husband had several books and hundreds of publications. He was on the national Teen Scene board. He helped found the organization."

"I don't know what to believe. Why do you need her brother's money, then?"

Charlie looked grim. "My husband lost most of the endowment and the operating funds on the riverboats. Lourdes knew about it and told me about the money just before the 2000 audit. They had a lot of questions about the withdrawals and they put us on probation. That's when the city called it quits. Now you know what everyone suspected but couldn't prove."

I sat down next to them and nobody said anything for a few minutes.

"You really have a Ph.D.?" I said.

Charlie nodded.

"What was really wrong with Dwayne?"

"He's made a tremendous amount of progress," Charlie said. Lourdes nodded vigorously. "It was really amazing."

I sighed. "You have the place upstairs to keep an eye on him, don't you?"

"It was the easiest thing. I do have a house on Davenport. It was just easier to be here so that he wasn't alone with the kids."

"What did he tell you about me?"

"He said you were an ABD in psychology. That your MA thesis was quoted in Hillary's book."

"You could have looked that up," I said.

"I knew he was lying. I never left you alone here with the kids, either."

"Don't fire me," I said. "I've got a social worker coming to the house in two weeks. I'll lose everything if I don't have a job."

"Home visit?" Charlie said. "My dissertation was on home environment. I can help you there."

"How about my job?" I asked.

She was quiet for a moment and Lourdes looked embarrassed. "I'm going to put out a search for a new director and then fall on the mercy of the national organization. I don't really have much of a choice. That will mean, even if the place is able to continue, that we'll no doubt be invited to leave. Let's say January or February. After that it doesn't look good."

It never does, I thought. It never does anymore.

The smart thing to do a half hour before a home visit by the family court is probably not screwing the sixteen-year-old you're attempting to gain custody of. Any chimp would know this. Any fool. We came so damn close if Alex hadn't been downstairs I can't say what would have happened.

Jule was changing into a skirt right in front of me the way she always did and lost her balance and we both reached out to keep her from falling over. The skirt tore and she landed in my lap. Could happen to anyone. I wrapped my arms around her waist from behind and buried my face in her hair.

"We've got no chance in hell," I said. "Why are we even letting this person into the house? She'll probably show up with a marshal like when they come to repossess your car."

She got into her dress only about ten minutes before the social worker arrived. Alex was slumped in the swaybacked sofa, corduroy-panted and petulant. He was one week from leaving for Alaska, and I was no nearer finding out who he was sleeping with than when Jule had mentioned it. Whoever it was, she didn't seem to have much of a hold on him; he'd packed for the boat a week earlier and slept with his bag under his bed.

Monica the social worker turned out to be a dead ringer for the girl I'd accused of polluting my urethra thirteen years before. She was young and shrewd and polite and before ten minutes was up I knew the last chunk of my world was hanging by a thread.

She sat in the living room and the three of us sat on the couch facing her. I was in the center of the couch so the whole thing caved in at the center. Alex and Jule sat on either side of me, a bit higher; it was as though we were being interviewed in the Vietnam Memorial.

"I have to tell you first of all that I'm only here as a due diligence," she said. "This isn't part of an investigation or court action or anything that severe."

"Oh, sure," I said with a chirp of agreeability in my voice.

"And please," she said, "let me offer you my condolences on your loss."

"Oh, sure," I said again, stupidly. Then, "Yes, of course."

She had opened her mouth to speak again and held it there for a moment when I interrupted her.

"I should tell you next," she continued, "that we're mostly interested in determining whether the environment is safe. Not about every little detail or checking up on how much television everyone is watching."

"Okay," I said. "Just routine, then."

She hesitated. "There's been some interest in the situation from Julianne's school."

"He's a strange guy," I said. "If you mean who I think you mean. He's taken a weird interest in Jule ever since she started at that school."

She held up her hand. "I don't think we should get into that. But the inquiries did set off a kind of chain reaction, you should know. I won't be the only one meeting with you about this."

"What are our chances?" I asked. "I mean, if you give a good report, will that be enough? We're a family, even though we might not fit the common mold. We just want to carry on as best we can."

She looked grim. "A positive report from me is just a temporary measure. The court is going to want a lot more information down the road. You should get a lawyer, in my opinion."

I started to object but Jule cut me off.

"I'm pregnant," she said. "If I don't stay here I'll drop out of school and have the baby in a welfare hotel."

I closed my eyes rather than look at the social worker. On the other side of me I could feel Alex stiffen.

"Oh," the social worker said. "That's, well, a bit of a problem."

I opened my eyes. The social worker had scrunched up her face, no doubt doing the massive internal calculations social workers do to read the future. Probabilities that the father figure sitting before her was nailing the minor no doubt were key.

"I don't suppose there's any chance that you're joking?" she finally asked.

Jule shook her head.

"My stepson was the father," I added helpfully.

"Am the father," Alex said. "Not was, am."

I opened and closed my mouth. "Alex," I said. "That's not necessary."

Monica the social worker held up her palms. "Look," she said. "Farce doesn't play well in family court. Why don't we stop all this nonsense?"

Alex shrugged. "Give the baby a blood test or an amnio or whatever."

The social worker stood up. "Listen," she said. "What you three need right now is for me to report that this environment is suitable. God knows you've been through hell."

I stood up too. "Listen, do you have to write this up? Can we start over?"

She shook her head. "How old are you?" she asked. "It says here you're thirty-four."

"It's wrong. I'm thirty-two." I smiled at her. "Unless it's better that I be thirty-four." She was actually quite pretty in a douche commercial sort of way. Unbelievably, she returned my smile.

"Listen," she said. "I'm a contract worker. All I'm here to do is make sure Jule is in a safe environment. I shouldn't have said any of the rest. Please just reassure me for today."

Jule stood up next to me. "Andrew always did all the work around here. He took care of all of us. He did all the cooking and cleaning and laundry and shopping."

Monica the social worker looked around the living room and kitchen. "Can you show me around?" she asked. We all nodded.

She put down her bag and I walked her through the house, opening the refrigerator, the closets, the bedroom doors (none of which she entered), the back door to the alley. She stood there for a moment looking out.

"We call the place Dogland," I said.

"Are there a lot of dogs?" she asked.

"The street name," I said, pointing at the corner sign.

"Is that what that means?"

"Well," I said, "the real Prairie du Chien is actually in Wisconsin. I think this street is sort of an homage to that."

"It's a great street," she said. "Way out here is nice."

The four of us went back inside and sat at the kitchen table. I gave Monica the social worker a cup of coffee.

"I'm not doing you any favors," she said. "I'd have to see crack vials in the corners for them to come and take Jule away immediately. But like I said, with the pressure from the school you're going to need a lot of luck to keep this going past Labor Day." She raised her hand when Jule started to speak. "Regardless of any health concerns which may or may not be present. I can write this up as Eden and it wouldn't make any difference." She took a drink of her coffee.

"If she's still here in September will they actually come and remove her?" I asked.

"Probably," Monica said. "I don't actually know how they'd handle that."

"But if they didn't do anything until November, for some reason, and she turned seventeen . . ."

"I'll be eight months pregnant," she said.

Monica shook her head. "That's *not* a plan," she said. "Pregnant or not."

"Why not?" I said. "A year after that she gets her trust. She's in better shape than I was at her age."

"Listen," Monica said. "Let's say you really are pregnant—not that you told me definitively—"

"I did," Jule said.

"She is," Alex said.

"Shhhh," I said. "Let her finish."

"And the father is or was another sixteen-year-old . . ."

"Fifteen," we all said together.

"Fifteen-year-old," she continued. "And you decide to have this baby."

"I am," she said. Jule's eyes were narrow and her lips drawn. She seemed to be holding her breath.

"Then you'd better be settled in your aunt's by Labor Day."

"Why?"

"Because if you are not in an approved custodial situation and you are pregnant you will probably be remanded to the custody of the court until delivery."

"You're kidding," I said. "They'd hold her against her will?"

"They would commit her to a group home," she said. "There aren't any bars on the windows but damn near. She'd be considered a runaway otherwise."

"Fuck that," Alex said suddenly. "We'll get married."

We all looked at him.

"Alex," I said. "You won't even be here, remember?"

Monica was slowly shaking her head back and forth. "If I wasn't sitting here, I'm not sure I'd believe this. Where were you all when I needed a dissertation topic?"

"How old do you have to be in Iowa to get married?" I noticed my fingers were squeezing my coffee cup and I tried to relax them.

Monica sighed. "Without parental consent seventeen." She looked at Alex. "Sorry, my friend."

"This is crazy," Alex said, his voice rising. "We'll all go to Alaska. Come try to find us there."

Monica shook her head again. Her face was starting to get red. "You say Jule's got a trust fund? It would be impounded. Any adult who took her across state lines would be in violation of the Mann Act. You guys are living in a nightmare, I know, but you're not making it any better. I said I was planning to file a report that the household is suitable, but if I think there's a chance for flight I'll go straight to the judge tomorrow."

"Don't do that," I said. "There's one thing we haven't thought of."

Jule and Monica and Alex, all breathing heavily, turned their attention to me.

"What if Aunt Tana moved in here?" I said. "She takes custody right away here and when Jule turned seventeen and got custody of herself, old Aunt Tana could move back to Cedar Falls."

Everyone was quiet for a moment. Monica reached into her bag. "Do you mind if I smoke?" she asked.

"No," we all said together.

She pulled out a pack and went through all the machinations, smacking the pack against her palm like she was getting ready to deal stud. All the while I looked at her body under her suit. It was one of those women's bodies I was always partial to with dark-haired women—on the generous side. Her hands were small and her shoulders full and soft. She was wearing only a decorative ring on her right hand. She knew I was looking at her and kept her eyes down, all attention on her cigarette prep.

When she had taken the third drag she put it down in the saucer I'd gotten her.

"You," she said to me, "have to come see me tomorrow. I'll look into that plan but I have office hours tomorrow and I can't come back."

"You're a professor?" I asked.

"Adjunct," she said. "Don't get me started."

"I'll be there," I said. "Just tell me when."

That night in bed Jule and I finally had sex. It was inevitable, and I convinced myself it was okay, since I was planning on having a lot of sex with Monica the social worker in the near future.

She said she loved me. I said I loved her. We did a few slightly erotic things that might or might not have been in her and Russ's repertoire. It was the middle of the night and we'd found each other by the gold light from the streetlight outside the window.

"Andrew," she'd whispered to me. "In November we can get married. There's so much good that can happen to us."

But I had been musing about Monica the social worker and my comprehension was on a five-second delay. I raised myself up on one elbow and looked the girl over. She was lying on her back on top of the bedspread, her legs slightly bent over at the knees. In that light her skin was like the inside of a seashell, beautifully smooth and streaked with light shadows. Her face was somewhere between a Vermeer maiden and a pop star.

"Jule," I said to her. "Where do you think they are? Your parents and Izzie and Russ?"

She rolled over my way and her perfect hip rose up beside me. I put my hand on top of it, just at the hint of bone.

"I think they're right here," she said. "And they're looking at us with all kinds of pity."

"Pity?" I said. "Why pity?" The word had opened a cold slice in my spine.

"Because now they know why we're put here in these bodies, and how we're just going to waste our lives freaking out about what we do with them."

"Jule," I said. "What's the absolute worst thing about me? You said you wanted to get married."

"You're afraid of beginning and endings," she said. "You start everything in the middle."

I let that sink in.

"Whew," I said. "That doesn't seem so bad." I brushed some hair off her forehead. "Do you want to know the worst thing about you?"

"No," she said. "I already know the worst thing about me." Her sixteen-year-old's conviction was remarkable, I had to admit.

"Which is?"

"I'm afraid to be alone."

"That's understandable," I said.

"You'd think so, right?"

I gently pushed her over and moved on top of her.

"This is a beginning," I said. "And you're not alone."

She smiled there in the streetlight, but it wasn't a smile of agreement. It was a smile of patience, the way a parent smiles at the opinions of a child.

I don't know why that was reassuring, but it was. I slid her camisole halfway up and she did the rest.

5

Aaron's place at the Greenwood Apartments wasn't as bad as I expected. Apparently a lot of the furniture had been left over from the previous tenant—the couch was one of those vinyl and plastic tube creations that skittered around when you tried to sit down. An upholstered armchair with fringed trim had a shiny spot on the seat and back. Compared to Aaron's apartment my place was Ethan Allen.

He came out of the kitchen with two glasses of orange Kool-Aid.

"No Fudgsicles?" I said, and instantly regretted it.

He hesitated and then handed one to me.

"And your little girlfriend is with child," he said. "Kind of a complication, no?"

"I was kidding, Bijou," I said. "I'm an asshole."

"I'm now an expert at reading faces," he said. "You've come here to confront me about something."

"No," I said. "I've come to ask you something crazy, but I'd hardly call it a confrontation."

"Remember, I'm younger than you," Aaron said. "Considerably."

"I . . . you're what? Twenty-four?"

"That's right," he said.

"The thing I'm going to ask you has nothing to do with age," I said. "Well, very little, anyway."

He sat down in the fringed armchair and I heard the springs groan beneath him. He sipped his Kool-Aid and stared at me.

"How's the job going?" I said.

"Gypsum," he said. "The bane of my existence. You know what gypsum is?"

"Not what the cabbie does to the blind guy?"

He smiled at that. "Think heavy," he said. "Unwieldy and breaks if you drop it."

"If it's not a plaster Buddha it must be some sort of building material. Probably toxic."

"Probably," he said.

"I hate your job," I said. "It's awful. I'm sick of hearing about it already."

He cocked his head to one side. "I got a raise," he said. "I'm growing attached to the place."

"Attached to gypsum? I would totally believe you if it wasn't for the fact that gypsum sounds like the *E. coli* of the lumberyard. You can do better."

"Wow," he said. "You'd be amazed to see what your aura looks like now."

I peered up at my eyebrows. "I see blue," I lied.

"You used to run track," he said. His voice had taken on a distant, musing tone. "I'd bet on it."

"I'm sure I told you that at some time in the past."

"A relay? The mile?"

"I was third leg," I said. "As far as I know we still have the school record."

"Did you always get a lead?"

"Yes," I said. "I always got a lead and I always kept it."

"Until now," he said.

I moved a little in my plastic/vinyl chair and it made the obligatory farting noise.

"This is getting a little too subtextual for me," I said. "I was hoping I could talk to you about maybe coming to work at the Teen Scene."

He was quiet. I couldn't tell if he had even heard me.

"Didn't see that one coming?" I said.

He took a deep breath. "Even in a situation comedy the idea of me working in a youth program is too extreme to be taken seriously."

"It would be temporary. Like me. By winter we both would have to have moved on."

"I would imagine my parole officer would have a few questions."

"Tell him you're the janitor. He'll buy that."

Aaron tilted his head back and roared, very suddenly and very loudly. I nearly jumped out of my chair. After a few seconds he put his hand over his mouth.

"I'm sorry," he said. "Just sometimes the things you get away with saying . . ."

I feigned puzzlement. "Isabel said something like that right before she was killed."

"Was she smiling?"

"I don't know," I said. "It was dark."

We sat in our chairs for a while.

"Question," Aaron said, "I've been meaning to ask you."

"Okay," I said.

"Is it hard for you not to drink?"

I don't know if I was more surprised by the question or by my reaction. My throat immediately constricted and the chair groaned under me.

"No," I said. "Not really."

Aaron nodded. "Is that unusual?"

I focused for a second on a car parked outside the window. "Are you concerned I'm going to start drinking again?" I said. "I . . . it's never occurred to me to go have a drink. It's not in my wiring anymore."

He nodded. "That's pretty impressive. Your aura has changed, by the way."

"I can't explain it," I said. "I had a personality that craved alcohol and I don't answer to that personality anymore. There's no room in the life I built for myself."

"It was that easy?"

I nodded. "Yes," I said. "It was that easy. Now can we talk about the job?"

"I think I get it. You can't advertise this job because you'd have to explain the real setup or else find someone really stupid, is that it?"

"That's it," I said. "We need a co-conspirator. By next year the place will be under new direction, totally legit, and off-limits to the likes of us. That's the plan, anyway."

"I don't have the clothes."

"We'll go shopping."

"I get tired easily."

"You can work the early shift."

He drained his glass of Kool-Aid. "You know the last thing I said to my mom," he said, "was 'I'll miss you.' You know what 'I'll miss you' really means?"

"No."

"It means 'Fuck you for breaking this up.' 'Fuck you for tearing down what we built.' Pardon my language."

"I'm not sure I believe that."

"It's true," he said. "Trust me."

"What does 'I love you' mean?" I asked.

He smiled a little, then. "It means 'I'm an asshole. My breath smells. I dare you to do something about it.' Like embracing that guy you don't listen to who tells you to take a drink. 'I love you' means 'I can't be trusted but I insist you try.' "

"That's hardly romantic."

"Romance has nothing to do with it. Asking someone to love you is akin to asking someone to be your new parent. Sex with a life partner is more incestuous than we like to believe."

"Do you think a sixteen-year-old can understand that?"

"Of course," he said happily. "Not everyone is like us."

"True," I said. "But what does this have to do with working with adolescent kids?"

"Kids never say, 'I'll miss you.' They either say, 'Don't go,' or they say, 'See you later.' When they say, 'I love you,' they think it's a compliment."

I stood up out of the plastic and vinyl chair. "Bijou," I said. "Welcome aboard. God help us both if someone actually asks us for advice."

"You're right about that. We have lives to protect, don't we?"

I didn't ask him what he meant by that.

Monica's office was in North Hall, overlooking the river. As soon as she closed the door it was clear that everything we did that afternoon would be foreplay. She had on makeup and a white translucent blouse such as you saw on television lawyers.

"Wow," I said. "You clean up extremely well."

She colored a little but tried to shrug it off. "If I was tenured I could dress like Alice B. Toklas," she said. "Don't get me started."

"I bet you get a lot of apples from your students. Or hits of ecstasy. Whatever they're giving these days."

"What did you give your teachers? Birth control?"

I shook my head. "I was very shy. I didn't date any professors until I was twenty-five."

"I don't think I want to hear about it."

"Okay," I said. "Have you had a chance to think about what I said? If I could get Jule's legal guardian down here for six months or so, until after the baby is born and she turns seventeen, do you think that would work?"

"That depends," she said. "How out of it is she?"

"Aunt Tana? I've never met her but I think she's presentable enough. What kind of scrutiny would we be under?"

She moved her mouth around and moved her head from side to side—those kinds of mannerisms she was probably trained to spot and interpret as role-playing.

"It's actually a brilliant idea," she said. "With the parents' chosen guardian occupying the same house, same environment, same schools and all, it's a good setup."

I nodded. "Great."

"*You'd* have to leave, though."

I opened my mouth to speak but she giggled first. It was a very sexy giggle. I felt like I'd taken a quick shot of something. When I'd walked across town to the Social Work building I'd had little on my mind but the previous night with Jule. But that had been flushed out of my system quickly enough.

I sat up a little higher in my chair. "Listen," I said. "You said you were just hired for the one day, right?"

"That's right."

"So giving advice for the future is okay?"

"That depends," she said. "What kind of advice?"

And it was while I was forming a reply that I looked out her office window and saw that curve of road across the Iowa River, and then I felt it again; my breath started to come a little fast, my throat got tight. And I said the first thing I could think of.

"My wife was killed a month ago," I said. "A little more than a month ago."

Her hand went to her collar. "I know," she said. "I don't know what kind of advice—"

"No, I'm sorry," I said. "I was just thinking out loud."

"That's okay."

"Because I haven't really spoken to anyone about it."

She turned her head to the side a bit and gave me a slight sideways look. "I'm not . . . have you thought about a therapist?"

And then just like that it seemed to pass, as if some huge airliner had briefly crossed between me and the sun. I took a few breaths and tried to reevaluate the scene there in the social worker's office. For a moment I couldn't remember her name.

"Jule is pretty mature," I said. "I don't know what her file says or what you gathered from talking to her."

Monica the social worker looked at me for a long time. What had I said? "When you get your MSW," she said, finally, "you have to do fieldwork, like student teachers do." She picked up a pencil from her desk and put it back down. "There's so many times when you go out and come back wishing there wasn't such a thing as men."

I nodded but let her finish.

"So," she said, "I can't say I have a clear picture of Jule but I'd be electrocuted before I'd tell you what was in that file, if that's your concern."

I took a deep breath. "I didn't come here to con you or anything," I said. "I can tell you all the reasons that were floating around in my brain if you want, but that's not one of them."

"I swear," she said. "I swear . . ."

"Monica," I said, and saying her name like that was a chance, for sure, since I'd never used it before. But it worked. Of course it worked. Women marry murderers in prisons, they fall in love with hermits who order them up over the Internet from places like Latvia and the Philippines. You touch them, you say their names, you show strength in your right hand while hiding your left.

"Monica," I said, "I don't care if you make me feel like Ted Bundy—which you have—I just came to get some help and to talk to you again."

This time it was her turn to apologize. "I'm sorry," she said. She looked at her hands and stroked one of her fingers lightly with a fingertip. It was a challenge or an invitation or both.

"Well," I said. "What I think I'm going to do is get hold of Aunt Tana and make her an offer she can't refuse."

"There are no guarantees . . ."

"I know. But like I was trying to say earlier, I really believe Jule would be the kind of person who could manage her own affairs—with guidance—at seventeen. I wasn't, maybe you weren't, but she is."

"I was a mess at seventeen," Monica said. "A basket case."

"Me too. Is it considered sociopathic to still harbor murderous resentment toward a couple guys in my high school homeroom?"

"Totally."

I laughed and showed her my hands, palms up. I had read about that. The pleasure in her face showed through the guilt. I waited for the feeling of dread to come again. It didn't.

"Listen," I said. "I'm a former drunk, an overeducated, underemployed widower with exactly one friend. I don't get out much. Half the time I leave the house I can't remember where I set out to go."

"If this is a job interview we're not hiring," she said.

"If we went out for coffee in public I'd promise to wear black. Like Scarlett O'Hara."

"She didn't love her husband," Monica said evenly. "And you might find it hard to believe, but I can get dates without checking through the obituaries."

I reached across the desk and held out my hand. "Call me Ted," I said. She looked me in the eye and then took my hand weakly and let it go. Her palm was warm. "Take my advice about the therapist," she said.

"If we do have coffee will you promise to wear that blouse again?"

Her mouth parted and her teeth flashed.

"We're not having coffee," she said. "And you don't drink. I'd need about five glasses of pinot grigio to get through a night with you, I imagine."

"Who said anything about a night?"

She flushed and I stood up. "Hey," I said. "Clearly I have about ten seconds before you call campus security. Seriously, thanks for your help. I can't help being an asshole but I do appreciate it."

"You're not an asshole," she said, opening the top drawer of her desk. She pulled out a business card and wrote a number on the back, then handed it to me. "But I am. Do me a favor and don't call for at least six weeks, okay?"

I took it and gave her an eyes-wide-open smile. "Where was I going again?" I asked.

When I got home I found Alex up in his room surrounded by clothes. He was sitting slump-shouldered on the edge of his bed, his feet resting inside his open suitcase.

"I was thinking of getting you a duffel bag," I said.

"Your mom called," he said. "Jule's at the library."

"Wouldn't that be easier on a boat, a duffel bag?"

"The boat's got these metal chests for clothes," he said. "It's hard to describe."

I sat down in the desk chair across from him. "How long is the flight again?"

He shrugged and wiped some hair out of his eyes. He had let it grow and it looked good long.

"Alex," I said, "you know since you're not identical twins with Russ you wouldn't pass the paternity test as the father, right?"

He shrugged again. "Fuck those people," he said. "You look at them and you can tell they don't know anything at all. Dad says Inuits get married at thirteen."

"I think it will be all right. I'm actually going to try the plan where we bribe Aunt Tana to come down here and live for six months. Don't worry about us."

He looked up at me. "I'm coming back," he said. "I'm not living in fucking Alaska in the winter."

For a moment I couldn't speak. "That's great," I was able to croak. "Is it just because of our lovely weather?"

He smiled a bit and I could see Isabel looking at me through him. "Funny," he said.

"You know, what you said about being the father wouldn't be far from the mark. If everything goes according to plan there'll be a kid here with an open slot. We could be like Old Dad and Young Dad."

He looked at me strangely. "Jule says there's two worlds, you know?"

"She does?"

"Yeah. She says there's two worlds, the one you wanted and the one you made. You never heard her say this? She says it all the time."

"No," I said.

"I don't know what it means exactly," he said. "But you know the first one is impossible, right?"

"I'm not sure I believe that," I said.

"I do now," he said.

"Alex," I said, "why the Platonic dialogue? I'm practically weeping that you're coming back but I get the feeling there's something you want to tell me."

He shook his head. "It's not bad news or anything like that." He moved the suitcase back and forth a bit with his foot.

"You having second thoughts about going to Alaska for the whole summer?" I said.

He hesitated and then nodded.

"Can you do part of the season, just the mackerel or the haddock or the fish sticks part?"

He shrugged again. I thought about the day I met him and Russ in Starbucks and how unrecognizable those two slackers had become. For a while I'd fancied it was my influence but I knew better. Last summer they'd come back with less cash and more purpose in their expressions than the year before. It had been a hard season, lots of work and not a lot to show for it. Russ had gotten a nasty cut and infection and Alex had suffered food poisoning. They cleared only about fifteen hundred apiece.

"I've been laboring under the delusion that there might be someone here that you'd miss," I said. "You know, besides the lovely yours truly."

He nodded, just slightly. "It's not a big deal or anything really worth talking about," he said. "This person doesn't want me to go but all I really think is that I'm leaving Mom behind. Or that something will happen while I'm gone."

I reached over and squeezed his leg above the knee. "Karmically we're set here," I said. "We'll worry more about you guys out on that boat, believe me. I'm setting aside a shitload of money for the phone bill."

"We can e-mail now," he said. "It's cheaper, Dad told me."

"I'm going to graduate in the winter," I said. "Did I tell you?"

He looked surprised. "Really? What kind of diploma are you getting?"

"I haven't decided. I could probably get two, that's how smart I am."

"Cool," he said. "Mom said the reason you never graduated before was because you weren't challenged enough."

"Well," I said, "I guess it's like Jule says, there are two worlds. The one where you've got it all figured out and the one that lets you keep believing that."

He stood up and began to drop clothes into the suitcase.

"Did you take everything out and start over?" I asked.

"I had nothing but shirts," he said. "You know I have like two pants?"

"You need pants?" I said. "Really?"

"I was wearing Russ's before," he said. "I don't want to anymore."

I couldn't help but admire the metaphorical depth of that statement.

"So we'll get you some pants," I said. "You want to got to the mall or handle this on your own or what? Maybe this mystery girl would help." I knew as I said it that I was nearing Hugh Beaumont territory but for some reason I didn't mind.

He dropped a few more shirts into the suitcase, each one from higher and higher up. They landed like they do in fabric softener commercials, nearly in slow motion.

"Jesus," he said with a suddenly tired voice. "You of all people."

"Me of all people what?"

He lay back suddenly on the bed. "This is one fucked-up family," he said to the ceiling. "My dad calls fags 'shitdicks.' So did Russ. 'Did you see that shitdick over there?' 'I wonder how sore that shitdick's asshole is.' "

I didn't say anything for about half a minute. I was suddenly feeling sick to my stomach, like a sustained downward lurch in an elevator. I didn't want to feel that way. There was no reason. Alex was Alex was Alex. But the scenarios tripped through my imagination like comic book frames: Alex with his fingers on a boy's face. Alex's lips on a boy's lips. Alex and a boy walking and fighting and talking on the phone and sitting in a car. I started to say something but he beat me to it.

"Don't get all weirded out," he said. "I'm like ninety percent virgin, okay?"

"What does that mean, ninety percent virgin? You only buttfuck from the ankles down?" I was surprised at the edge in my voice; it was hard and a bit shrill. My hands were trembling and had quickly gotten cold.

"The word is 'shitdick,' " he said. "Try it."

"Hey, fuck you, Alex," I said. "Half the social work apparatus in Iowa City is already staking out this house. Your dad probably hates my guts and I'm going to be out of a job in a few months. I'm sorry if finding out that a minor under my roof is taking it in the ass is upsetting to me."

Alex sat up and looked at me with utter incredulity. "I'm stupid," he said. "I'm fifteen and I don't know shit. I can't do calculus and I can't make a free throw . . ."

"Stop it—"

"But I'm not blind," he said. "You've got this stupid plan for Aunt Tana to come down here and not notice you and Jule banging each other on the kitchen table and you're pissed at me for a few stupid hand jobs? I mean, he's your fucking friend."

"I'm not pissed at you," I said. I took a breath and lowered my voice. "I'm pissed at me. I'm pissed at me. I . . ." And then the final frame of the comic book came into focus.

"Oh, boy," I said. "I am totally not the man for this."

Alex angrily dropped a few more shirts into the suitcase. The last one landed half in and half out. "Nobody said you had to be," he said. "Nobody asked you to."

"He's not in his right mind," I said. "He's a good guy but he's in a bad place in his life." I desperately wanted to say, "He's too old," but I knew I couldn't. He had reminded me just the day before how youthful he was. Compared to me Aaron was a puppy. Nine years difference for them. I'd done the math for me and Jule. When I was forty-five she'd be thirty or close to it. Not Sinatra and Mia Farrow but still substantial.

"Alex . . ." I said.

"Look, I'm leaving for the summer, okay?" he said. "Can we just not get all into it now? He's not the most important thing on my mind, believe it or not."

"Okay," I said. He had hit the right note. He was leaving for the summer and the relief in that was something I could almost clutch to my chest.

"But Alex," I said. "What is the most important thing, if I might ask?" The adrenaline had evaporated from my bloodstream and I was a little light-headed.

He dropped another shirt and looked at me like I was teasing him.

"The baby," he said. "We got a baby brother coming, or did you forget?"

"Brother?" I said. "How do you get brother?"

His face went deep red. "I meant nephew or whatever. For you I don't know. I don't want to know."

"You shouldn't worry about it," I said. "Jule is very healthy, we're lousy with hospitals here, the baby's got good genes."

"And Mom and Russ were just getting shoes," he said. He held up his palms like he was comparing weights. "Getting shoes. Giving birth. Pardon me if I stay a little worried."

"God, Alex," I said. I was choking up and I fought it off. "When I was fucking fifteen all I had to worry about was if my dad missed the beer I stole. You constantly blow me away, man."

"Yeah, well . . ." he said. But I could tell he was pleased. Thank God he could still be pleased to be considered mature.

What was I going to do for the entire summer without him?

That evening Jule and I took a walk out behind the testing complex in the fields they were trying to coax back into native prairie grass. There were some thistles and new, hard green burrs and the smell of the grass and fetid black soil that wafted up was not unlike a new bag of dope. Not the smoking of it, but the gut-level thrill of sticky wet buds in a clean new bag. "But Your Honor," I would say, "I never intended to smoke it, I just wanted to smell it." But I hated walks generally and any pleasant associations wore off quickly.

When we got far enough out behind the old windbreak of poplars they'd left standing we held hands. Jule was wearing some stretchy pedal pushers and a white blouse with the tail out—totally Ann-Margret/*State Fair*—and she walked next to me with her elbow locked and lots of twisting of her hips and fingers. She was happy about something.

There were tufts of short wiry grass here and there and we found one big enough for the two of us to sit on.

"What names do you like?" Jule said about three seconds after we sat. I didn't answer her. There had been a bunch of things I'd wanted to do that afternoon around the house but Alex's outing had thrown me off and now I just felt nervous. I was going to present Aaron to Charlie in the morning and I didn't know what I was going to do when I saw him. I was considering withdrawing my offer but there was nobody else. The Teen Scene had already been closed for two days (for "staff enrichment" we'd said in a note on the door) and we needed to get it back on track if I was going to be employed for the next six months.

Did I care that he was fooling around with my stepson? I did. Did I want to interfere? Did I have any right to? Should I tell his father? Should I get Aaron's parole revoked? What a fucking liar—"homosexual sex is a base urge" my ass. All that and I had papers to notarize and bills to pay. There was no food—I hadn't shopped since Alex was leaving. He was back there alone on his last night and I was sitting on my ass in a rank field of allergens with a pregnant sixteen-year-old girl whom I couldn't think about without feeling queasy.

"I like Cassidy," she said.

"I like Phil," I said. "Or Stan. Leo. Atticus."

"Yuck. How about girls' names?"

"Leonora. Sybil. Any warm-weather month is good."

"June Bergman?" she said. "It's too close to mine."

"How about Isabel, or your mom's name?"

She shook her head. "Uh-uh. She gets her own fresh start. Or he."

"When's the last time you went to the doctor?"

"I'm going again next week. You can come."

"That might be a bad idea. Let me think about it."

We lay back and stared up at the sky, but not before I caught a glimpse of my watch.

After a few minutes Jule reached for my hand again.

"What do we do if Aunt Tana doesn't come here?" she said. "I don't want to go away. If they make me choose between taking off and going to Cedar Falls I know which one I'd choose."

"If Aunt Tana doesn't want to come down here, then we give her a lot of money to let us get married," I said. "I get my degree and find a job somewhere and Alex comes home and we carry on."

She sighed. "Why does it sound so impossible when you put it that way?"

Because, I said to myself, you'd have to be an idiot to think such a thing was possible. "Giving Birth/Buying Shoes," as Alex the Hand Job Prince had so succinctly put it.

We lay there for a while and as the minutes passed the sky turned darker and darker like a Polaroid developing in reverse. The only question became whether or not it would all end in a brilliant flash.

"Did you ever call your mom back?" Jule said. "She's called like a hundred times."

"No," I said, feeling sick inside. "I can't right now."

"Why not?"

I closed my eyes and all I saw were flashes of red. "It's too hard to explain," I said.

part three

1

Aunt Tana didn't need a moving van. She didn't need a lot of suitcases. All she needed was the entire backseat of her tar-streaked Hyundai. She agreed to move in for six months—until the end of the year—in exchange for ten thousand dollars and a new car when Jule turned eighteen and got her insurance payout.

"I could have taken all that money anyways," she said to me on the phone. "I sent those checks and I could just as easily of cashed them and gone to the French Riviera."

What a perfect mercenary she'd turned out to be.

By the end of August, Alex was only e-mailing once a week and calling even less. Jule was showing a bulge in her belly. Charlie and Aaron and I were keeping the Teen Scene afloat mostly by luck. Dwayne hadn't sent his mother a single word of his whereabouts, and my mother had stopped calling altogether. July had been a scorcher. The washing machine had broken down. I'd torn up Monica the social worker's business card then looked her up in the campus directory just to make sure I could.

Everything was going pretty well until the day I tried to register for my final nine credits and the registrar told me every class I needed was full, no waiting list. I didn't think I was making a scene at all but suddenly the registrar was crying. She kept shaking her head and crying and pushing the return key on her keyboard. I left with nothing to add to my two hundred seventy-four credits and no promise of anything in the spring either. It was only the beginning.

I had gotten Jule an engagement ring at Zales and had spent a few hours in the library checking up on Iowa State law just to make sure we could do it. We could. Even without Aunt Tana's approval (which we were certain we could purchase anyway) we'd be able to petition the court and would stand a good chance if I was any judge of case law (and why wouldn't I be?). We'd had several conversations about the various pluses and minuses. Over the summer as her stomach softened her face also filled out down around the jaw, squaring off her cheekbones in such a way as to make her look twenty-five at least. She cut her hair on the short and professional side, wore shirts with collars, walked with her back straight and her toes pointed a little outward.

"Andrew," she said to me one night after we'd done this fantastic thing where she pretended to be a Romanian track star, wearing Alex's sweats with the strategically loose elastic waistband. "We should be playing music soon for the baby. I need to start some different meditations. We should be getting ready."

"Sure," I said. Some lint from the sweats had stuck to my tongue and I was propped up on my elbows trying to trap it between my fingertips.

"I don't want to miss too much school, so I'll have to pump and you'll have to bottle-feed."

"Roger that," I said.

"We'll need a pediatrician. I've got a recommendation from my OB and he'll page him when we're in the delivery room. I mean, if there is a delivery room."

"There might not be a delivery room?"

"I'm going to interview midwives."

"We can't," I said. "Our bed is too uncomfortable. There aren't enough outlets in here. We'll blow fuses right and left."

"Funny," she said.

"I want a hospital with the works," I said. "Lots of machines—ultrasounds, infralights, defibrillators. I want a full-body scan just for me."

"I hate hospitals," she said. "They're no place to bring a life into the world."

"You say that now," I said. "Let's just take things a little at a time." My dick hurt but it was just taking a time-out, like one of those football players you see on the sidelines bent down on one knee. This was the week before Aunt Tana showed up and we knew after that things would have to cool way down.

"Nadehzda," I said. "Amerikanski judge ready for triple jump."

Somewhere during this next time she did something she hadn't done once in the month and a half we'd been fornicating; she put her finger very very close to my asshole. Damn close. Suck-in-the-breath close.

The noise I made was something like "yuh," or more like "shuh."

"Okay?" she whispered in my ear.

"Sure sure sure," I said. But I wasn't sure in the slightest. What the hell was she doing? She was only sixteen. Her fingers traveled back across my ass and I stopped breathing altogether. What kind of meditation centered on pleasuring the rectum? What would her OB say about that? Her goddamn midwife?

"Tell me if it's good," she said.

I reached behind me and grabbed her wrist. "It's very good," I said. "Too good."

"Too good?" she said.

I slid off her and turned to lie on my side. I was just in time;

my terrified dick popped out of her like a newborn puppy out of an Airedale.

"I'm old-fashioned, maybe," I said. "I may not be ready for the *Kama Sutra.*"

"Okay," she said, without the slightest hint of embarrassment. "That's okay."

"I mean," I said, "maybe later."

"Okay," she said. "Only . . ."

"Only what?"

"I think you might want to get some training or at least some breathing—"

"Some training?"

"The *Kama Sutra* is more of a, you know, spiritual guide. You'd have to be able to do some simple breaths . . ."

"I don't believe this."

"I'm sorry," she said, and now she was embarrassed. "I don't always know when you're kidding."

"I feel like an idiot," I said. I rolled on my back and my dick, cold now, flopped against my opposite thigh. "You and Russ were into the *Kama Sutra*? No wonder you're pregnant."

In the half-light from the street I could see her lips go tight. "It has nothing to do with that."

"Well," I said. "It has a little to do with it."

"A lot less than you'd think," she said, now looking out the window.

I let her stare out the window and I wondered if Monica the social worker would want to put her finger in my ass. Probably, but that would be fine, I decided. After all, she had a master's. To be fair to Jule, I'd put my finger in or near her asshole once or twice, not particularly on purpose but not altogether by accident. I had fantasized about more than that but when push came to shove my sexual experimentation was mostly concerned with apparel and role-playing (although once I'd asked Isabel to blow me in the bathroom, not because it was titillating but because she'd been sitting on the lid of the toilet watching me shave and one thought had led to another).

I reached out and brushed some hair from Jule's forehead. "Besides being a big baby, I'm sexually uninitiated, it looks like."

She shook her head a little. In the mustard-orange glow from the streetlight her eyes looked blackened and her teeth gray, like a youthful refugee or handbag model.

"I'm sort of worried," she said. "Sex is just one part, you know, of a life together. What about all the rest?"

"You mean the cool electronic gear?" I said.

"Funny," she said. "You know what I mean."

"We build all that," I said. "It all comes together bit by bit."

"Is that how it happened with you and Isabel?" she said.

As if she didn't know how it had happened with me and Isabel. Whatever Isabel and I had built we'd done it right out there in front of them, for better or worse. If Jule hadn't gleaned any wisdom from the life we'd had, then there wasn't any more I could bring to the table this time. I hadn't been thinking that far ahead; I didn't want to.

And just like that she was crying. I had made two women cry in one day. With the registrar it had clearly been some sort of hormonal imbalance. Here with Jule I could only imagine.

"What's the matter?" I said.

"Oh," she said, "I was just thinking about them. It's crazy."

"What's crazy?" I said.

"It's crazy that I was thinking that if we were going to make this new family and everything, wouldn't it be easier if we had Isabel and Russ to help us? Isn't that sick?"

"Sick, no," I said. "It's not like we had all this time to coast and figure out how we're going to cope and everything. It was like the next fucking morning that I got hit with the fact that Alex was leaving maybe for good and Rosie took like three seconds to tell me they'd be coming after you. We've been put on the defensive from the start. What do they expect?"

She looked at me. "What does who expect?"

"Them. Anybody. Society. Al-Qaeda, I don't know."

"I have a hard time seeing it," she said.

"In a little while," I said, "this part will be forgotten. We'll remember the way it was before. It will be like we skipped this part."

"But I don't want to skip this part," she said. "This part is important."

"I don't really mean skip it," I said. "I just mean that all of the good stuff to come will overshadow this part. It's just the way our minds work. People forget the details of pain, the exact feeling of loss. It's probably an evolutionary advantage."

"I don't forget," she said. "I remember everything."

"Did you ever break a bone?" I said.

She nodded. "I broke my collarbone."

"Can you make yourself remember exactly how it felt? Exactly how the pain was?"

"Yes," she said.

"Well," I said, "I'm not going to say I don't believe you."

"I think you just did. Don't get mad."

"I'm not mad," I said.

"You're all scrunched up," she said. She reached over and touched my shoulder. "You're hard as a rock."

"Look," I said. "You're an amazingly mature person for sixteen but things look a lot different from my side of thirty."

"When I'm thirty-two my child will be sixteen, same age as me. I'll be the parent of a teenager."

"It's not so hard," I said.

She fooled with her fingertips on the bed in front of her.

"I mean," I continued, "I do have some experience there."

"I'm really having a hard time seeing it," she said quietly.

"You said that already. Seeing what?"

"There's a blank when I go to look there."

"Who were you with before Russ?" I said.

"Before Russ?" she said. "Before Russ I was thirteen years old."

"You said that Russ wasn't the first. You should get your story straight."

She sat up. "Me?"

"Yes, you," I said. "Is there another knocked-up sixteen-year-old in the room?"

At that she did a truly remarkable half roll off the bed and was heading out the door, bare-ass, before the dent eased from the mattress. It was great. I wanted to be alone and she took off. Isabel would have—in the old days—cried, and later on kicked me out. I lay there with my little scared dick and listened to make sure she didn't leave the house but didn't otherwise move a muscle.

Aunt Tana's arrival could be compared to the docking of a small boat to an aging cruise liner. She pulled up in her Hyundai just as I was returning from the grocery store.

Considering how many times she tried to maneuver her car up close to the sidewalk and the sound her rims made as they grated on the curb I half expected her to be blind or at least extremely batty. She was neither.

Aunt Tana was a seventy-year-old ex–Dairy Queen and Laundromat owner and was sharper than I was at just about anything worth mentioning. She reminded me of a little white female elderly George Jefferson. In the month since I called her she'd made contact with a lawyer, the State of Iowa Office of Child Services, and the local county office of juvenile affairs. She'd notarized a half-dozen forms, made two recorded statements, and had scheduled two follow-up interviews for September. She even used a Palm Pilot for Christ's sake.

"Andy," she said to me as I was putting the groceries away, "what do you think of all these tattoos?"

"You've got tattoos?"

"No, I do not. I mean on girls. Half the girls I see have some kind of bird or something tattooed above their butts. At least I think it's a bird. It's symmetrical and looks like it's got wings. I hope those things are temporary."

"I don't think so," I said. "It's a fashion."

"Would you put your Johnson in some tramp who's been stuck with dirty needles? I mean, if they have that little respect for their bodies, heaven knows what's crawling around in there."

I remembered a girl I'd palled around with a few years before who had the barbed-wire tattoo on her ankle. I asked if it had hurt and she said yeah, but not as bad as the tongue stud she'd had to have removed. She showed me the little dimple in her tongue and described the resulting infection and all I thought about was the Brian Wilson song "I Just Wasn't Made for These Times."

"Tana," I said, "it's not like it used to be, not even a few years ago. People take precautions, but you sort of assume the other person has the same crap in their system as you do."

"How romantic," she said. "So for a whole generation intimacy is the same thing as sharing a public bathroom. What kind of marriages will they make?"

"Well," I said, "we'll get by."

She frowned. "My niece—Julie's mother—would have been forty this year. How old are you, if I might ask?"

"Thirty-two," I said.

"My husband was nearly twenty years older than I was. He came by the house and sold my father cleaning supplies. I don't have any problem with it."

"Problem with what?"

"You two get married or not, I don't care. I'm not a judge."

She just sat while I finished stocking the shelves and then joined her in the living room. She was sitting in the good chair like she was still a guest but getting used to it, I suppose the way someone would sit in a chair in a boardinghouse or hospice.

"Do you think it's a mistake?" I asked. "We kind of think of it as continuing a family that had already started."

"Does Julie have any tattoos?" she asked.

"No," I said.

"Did your wife?"

"Also no. And neither do I."

"What do you have in common?"

"Me and Jule? We live together. We like it here. We love our life."

"What did you have in common with your wife?" Aunt Tana rocked a bit in the chair, a little forward, a little back.

"We liked to dance," I said. "We liked movies. We loved her kids—the boys."

"And Julie."

"Yes . . . she wasn't technically Isabel's kid."

"Do you think your wife loved Julie?"

"Oh, sure," I said.

"You both did?"

"Yes," I said. "Of course it was a different kind—"

"I would hope so. If not, that would make your late wife a dirty lesbian or something."

She sat in the chair and looked like she was talking about people in movies. She wore sweats and her hair was trimmed close and her glasses were about nine years out of style.

"I can't come out of this looking anything but shitty," I said. "So what's the use?"

"Nobody's going to care, if that's what you're afraid of," Tana said. "Or are we saying the same thing?"

"Jesus," I said. "I don't know what we're saying."

"Well, I'm saying why would you feel the need to get married? You were married once and look how that turned out."

"You're here to help, right? I mean, you came all this way to help us?"

"Of course," she said.

"Then we'll get married if it's all right with you. You can

leave after the wedding or after Jule's birthday, whichever you want."

"And that's your plan?"

"Yes, that's exactly the plan, unchanged, I might add, since we last spoke."

She smiled and she didn't even have to ask. I started ferrying her stuff into the house, into Russ and Jule's old room. There were piles and piles of it, wrapped in the gossamer plastic she'd no doubt saved from her dry cleaner days. It was like carrying angels' clothing, full of static electricity and all fluttery around the edges.

Aaron took about nine seconds to become twice the youth counselor I or even Dwayne had ever been. The kids all talked to him, hung out in the office, bared their Paxil-laced souls. They looked into his dime-sized pupils and poured their hearts and worries into his shaved head. Like a goateed Buddha, he became the new soul of the Teen Scene. All in about a week.

We'd only spoken about Alex once, and that was outside in the shed once when we were changing shifts and I needed to show him where to find the poster frames. He followed me, ducking in through the sliding wooden door. Inside, the broken skateboard ramps were leaning against the side of the shed where they'd been abandoned after my first day.

"Bijou," I said, "how does parole officially end?"

He looked a little surprised. In the few days I'd spent training him I don't think I'd ever asked him a question. The longest conversation we'd had was about the enormous cell phone, and if it could be used to bludgeon an intruder.

"Like everything else," he said. "It goes on for a while, runs out of steam, and then there's a ceremony to see if it's really and truly dead."

"Well," I said, "I'm sure sorry I asked."

"With a hearing," he said, an apologetic tone in his voice. "Just a judge this time, I've been told. He gets all the reports and if they check out then he just ends it."

"It was a terrible risk you took," I said. "This is the first time I haven't felt like scratching your eyes out about it. I was walking here scared to death of Aunt Tana and I thought for the first time that in your case nobody would have to prove anything, probably. Just someone sees you with Alex and mentions it to your parole officer and you're gone."

His expression was amazingly blank. He looked as though I'd been talking about parking fines.

"Why are you worried about Aunt Tana?" he said.

I shrugged. "She's got all the cards, and I gave them to her."

"What makes you say that?"

"She can take Jule away whenever she wants. She can tell the court that I've been banging her. She can hold up the marriage. She can keep all the money, probably, if she wanted to."

"Why would she do that?"

I shrugged again. "Why would I tell the police about you and Alex? Maybe she doesn't get it and thinks the kid should be left alone."

And then Aaron's face split into a wide smile. "I wondered when you'd say something like that."

"Like what?"

"Like that everything could be lost for the right reasons, and everything could be gained for the wrong ones."

"Is that what I said?"

"Would you mind terribly if I quoted Ecclesiastes right about now?"

"Yes. What happened to Dante?"

"You're joking, right?"

"Go ahead," I said.

" 'The end of a thing is better than the beginning. It is better to go to the house of mourning than the house of feasting.' "

I pushed at the skateboard ramp with my toe and it toppled off the wall and hit some paint cans that had been slid underneath, almost knocking them over. I moved them a little closer to the wall, one can of thinner, actually, and one of mineral spirits.

"You know," I said, "the only thing I remember from that book is how nobody can make something straight that God made crooked. Which, of course, is why I never bother to try."

"Well," he said, "I should clear up one thing. When I asked you why you said that she had all the cards, it wasn't because she doesn't have them. I was just wondering why you think you were the one who gave them to her."

"You're right about that," I said. "She's really the one who had them all along."

"And she'd be stupid to give them up without getting something in return."

"She can't do anything about Jule and the baby," I said. "She can do a lot but she can't do anything about that."

Aaron laughed a little through his nose. "That's for sure. Amazing, huh? You got to hand it to her."

"Who?" I said. But Aaron had already grabbed the frames off the wall and was heading back across the driveway.

It was later that same afternoon that we came up, jointly, with the Big Idea to get the Teen Scene through the fall. With the funds Dwayne had pocketed we were running about two thousand dollars short and wouldn't be able to make it to Christmas when we would pull the plug and let the board reorganize. I had offered to cut my salary but Charlie had refused; I was still the director and my salary went into the books. Everything had to look right until the end of the year.

Charlie and Aaron and Lourdes sat around the desk and I stood in the corner.

"How about a casino night?" I said. Charlie shook her head. "Bachelor auction?"

Aaron spoke softly. "My high school band always held a street fair in the parking lot. It was a pretty good deal."

"Car wash?" I said. "Dog wash?"

"Burglary?" said Lourdes softly. We all looked at her. She seemed quickly embarrassed.

"Did you say burglary?" Charlie said.

"I think that's not the right word," Lourdes said. "Where do you sell cakes?"

"Bakery?" Aaron said. "You mean a bake sale?"

She nodded.

"That's a lot of fucking brownies," I said.

"The Haunted House last year was on its way to making nearly thirty-five hundred when we had to shut it down," Charlie said. "We charged seven bucks and everyone loved it while it lasted."

"Five hundred people at seven dollars a shot?" I said. "That seems a bit ambitious."

"We've got the location," she said. "We were pulling in a lot of kids from the bars. We had probably a hundred high school and junior high kids from word of mouth alone. With the security everyone stayed very well behaved."

"But five hundred?" I said.

"We were going to be open from seven to ten for three nights," she said. "We stay open until eleven this time and we can do it."

"Who are the ghosts and shit?" I said.

"The kids," Charlie said. "Last year JJ was the master of ceremonies. He was spectacular."

"I don't know," I said. I had been one of the people standing on the sidewalk the year before, watching the police mill around and wondering what kind of screwup the Teen Scene had pulled off this time. I was tempted to go with Lourdes's idea—the first one.

"The truth is," Aaron said softly, "we can't do anything that requires a large constituency, like a bake sale or silent auction. It takes years to get the contacts together for a good street fair, and weather can ruin it. A Haunted House just takes a handful of people to bust their asses and some working capital."

Charlie nodded. "Last year's cost two hundred in supplies and three hundred for the two rent-a-cops. We put it together in two weeks."

I was still looking at Aaron with incredulity. *"Constituency?"* I said. *"Working capital?* A month ago you were driving a fork-lift and complaining about gypsum."

Aaron, again, leaned back and laughed with his mouth wide open. "Wisdom is better than strength," he said. "Nevertheless the poor man's wisdom is despised, and his words not heard."

"Fine," I said, "whatever." It was clear that they were in agreement. "Shitdick runs the show, then," I said to myself. I felt my hands shaking. So much could go wrong, I thought. Five hundred people wandering through the Teen Scene. Drunks, kids, geeks, flamers, jocks, farmers, frat boys. What would the tableaux be? Headless citizens, axed co-eds? Traffic accidents, botched abortions, bear mauling victims? Surely, I thought, as God is my judge, this would be tempting fate.

When I got home Jule was standing in the kitchen and without saying a word she handed me the cordless phone.

"Hello?" I said.

"Hey, stranger," my mother said. "Long time no sprechen."

"Hey," I said. "What's up?"

"You're really really really pissed at me, that's what's up."

"I'm not," I said. "It's been crazy here."

"Andy," she said. "I shouldn't have said that. I've got the biggest fucking mouth . . ."

"Said what?" I said. "I don't even remember."

She was quiet for a moment. "I wanted to talk to you about your dad," she said.

I looked at the phone and my finger nearly pressed the Talk key to hang it up. My dad was dead, too, and as long as I hung up the phone it couldn't be proven. But I put it back against my ear.

"Okay," I said. Everything was so out of control. How did it ever get this bad?

"Georgette is pregnant," she said. For a moment I couldn't remember who Georgette even was.

"Sacajawea?" I said.

My mom's voice lightened. "Seems more appropriate now than ever, doesn't it?"

"How long?" I said. "When is she due?"

"Hey," my mom said. "Don't get mad. It's a good thing, don't you think?"

"I'm not fucking mad," I said. "I don't care if everyone is bound and determined to screw up their lives. What difference does it make?"

"Listen," she said, "I just thought you ought to know. She would like to have a ceremony in November and would like for you to come up if you can."

"What kind of ceremony? Is she going to hold the baby up in the air and get some kind of Great Spirit blessing?"

"I don't know," she said. "I didn't ask. I think it might actually be half wake, half baby party. That is, if your father doesn't turn up by then."

"Look," I said, "I have my own child coming in November. I can't make any promises."

She didn't respond to this at all.

"This isn't news to you," I said. "Jule said she filled you in."

"Yeah," my mom said. "She filled me in. Just come if you can. I'll tell Georgette it's probably a no."

"Very probably," I said.

She was quiet for another couple of heartbeats and I almost said goodbye then.

"Andy," she said. Her voice was tiny. It didn't suit her at all.

"What?"

"I'm thinking of retiring," she said. "I told Isabel the last time I talked to her. She probably never had a chance to mention it."

Why, I wondered, of all the things that were going on, did that make me want to bawl? "But you love teaching," I said. "Why would you want to retire?"

"I'm tired," she said. "It's a long drive. They cut one of my sections and some bitch is teaching Deepak Fucking Chakra."

"Chopra," I said.

"Whatever. Something's changed."

I nodded and wiped my nose. "Kids today," I said. "They're clueless. Somebody really let them down."

"I'm not a goddamn social worker," she said. Only now it wasn't funny.

"Mom," I said. "Hang in there."

"I don't know," she said. "I just don't know. At least Shakespeare had a good fucking run, in the end."

"Don't talk like that," I said. "Not now, anyway. I'll call you later."

I shouldn't have hung up on her. I knew it and Jule knew it. She looked at me silently and I couldn't meet her eyes.

"It'll be all right," I said. "Trust me."

2

The week before Jule went back to school for her senior year, Tana and I met with the vice principal and she spent the first twenty minutes complimenting him on his appalling choice of artwork. I hadn't even noticed these pictures on the previous visit. He was some sort of odd mix of Camelot and science fiction fan, apparently, and he had a half-dozen prints on his wall that reminded me of early seventies album covers.

"That must be your favorite," Tana said, pointing to a blue-toned seascape with a young girl in waist-high surf wearing a tiara and embracing a dolphin. Several oddly familiar planets were suspended in the atmosphere above them like wrecking balls.

The vice principal ran his fingers through his beard. "That's the expensive series," he said. "I could sell that one on eBay and buy a car."

"Wow," I said. "Is she some sort of queen or something?"

"Yes," he said. "And the little girl is her daughter."

I looked closer, trying to hide my smile.

"The waves are so delicately done," Tana said. "That's something you can't fake."

He looked with us for a few more moments, the blue reflecting in his seamless bifocals.

"Okay," he said finally, looking around on his desk for a folder that was lying right on top. "Status report, I suppose."

Tana and I sat down politely. He opened it and pursed his lips self-consciously. At that moment I would have bet that he was looking at that day's lunch menu. He seemed to be that kind of guy.

"Did the social service people talk to you?" I offered.

He nodded sharply but didn't raise his eyes. Tana raised the tips of her fingers, just barely. I sat back.

The vice principal closed the folder and leaned back in his chair.

"Well," he said. "I don't really have anything to bring up, honestly. She seems to be doing well. Our counselor and the lady from the city both seem to think she's got herself in a pretty solid place, all things considered . . . ."

Still Tana said nothing. I literally bit my lip, and we both sat there. I forced myself to look at the point of his chin, nodding slightly. From outside the office door came the echo of a single pair of heels making its way down the empty hall. In a week that hall would be full. In two days Alex would be back. In just a few minutes we'd be out of there.

"One question," Tana said. We both looked at her. "What are you planning to offer as far as support?"

He looked a bit uneasy. "Support as in . . . ?"

"Prenatal. I imagine she won't be going to gym. Would you provide any sort of alternative to dodgeball?"

He started to answer but she cut him off.

"I'm pretty familiar with ADA rules—" She looked at me. "Americans with Disabilities Act." I nodded. "—but not so familiar with Special Education law. I would imagine some flexibility in testing might be appropriate . . . ."

The vice principal at some point had picked up a pen and was scribbling as she spoke.

"... and perhaps near the end some help with books and lockers. One would hate to see a premature delivery caused by physical stress."

He was nodding but I could see the hinge of his jaw quiver.

"She's in AP classes," I said. "If you could assist in getting her a convenient SAT date."

Then we sat there as the vice principal caught up. "Yes," he said, finally. "I got that, I think. I'll speak with the dean about most of these. I don't see a problem."

But Tana had twisted in her seat and was staring at a painting of some sort of war council in an enormous gothic antechamber. Two of the half-dozen figures in the painting were humanoid. There was also what was clearly a carp wielding a bow and arrow, two praying mantises in religious garb, and a lemur with a spyglass. Outside the high open arches of the castle you could see the tips of islands trailing off into a black ocean.

"The distribution of elements in this scene is just about perfect," she said. "Their quest must be quite dangerous."

The vice principal's tone was reverent when he answered. "It's called 'During the Time of the Last Days.' " Tana and I nodded. I wondered if the carp was the first to buy it, considering how impossible it would be for him to accurately draw back a bow.

"There's clearly a lot of influence here from the *Divine Comedy*," I said. Aunt Tana shot me a look. The vice principal shook his head.

"It's actually quite sad," he said. We looked at it again for a few silent moments.

"Those waves are pure Eakins," I said, but Tana had me by the elbow and she held on to it until we'd said our goodbyes and were out in the sunshine.

"Ouch," I said. "There are actual nerve endings there, you know."

"You, sir," she said, "are one prize specimen."

"Fine. Stick up for the bureaucrat."

"Let me ask you a question," she said. "How would you feel if someone came into your home and critiqued the pictures on your wall like that?"

"We don't have any pictures on the wall."

"Exactly, Mr. Critic," she said. "Exactly." We climbed into her Hyundai and were silent as we back drove toward the house.

"Drop me off at work," I said. "Left here." She expelled me at the curb and left with a squeal. Inside Jule was already there, sitting in the office with Aaron. Through the observation window I could see him speaking and her nodding. Another Aaron fan, no doubt. JJ and his girlfriend were in the back on the couches. He was reading something too advanced for him and he didn't even look up as I passed. Since Aaron had started I was persona non grata to the kids. I had asked JJ if he thought he could put together another disc for me and he'd said, "Sure," but I could tell he didn't want to.

I walked past the open area and into the office. Jule got up when I came in and looked like she was about to give me a hug right there and then but she must have seen the look in my eye. Whether or not JJ or Lourdes or anyone else suspected we were an item or not, I'd made it clear that we'd show nothing at work. I squeezed her fingers and dropped into the open chair.

"Aaron," I said. "I'm worried about our society."

"Our secret society here or society in general?" he said.

"General society. You remember when you had to read *The Scarlet Letter* and 'A Rose for Emily,' and the poor bastard teaching them talked about how society was the antagonist and all that malarkey?"

"I was a music major."

"We read both of those last year," Jule said.

"Anyway," I said. "If you wrote 'A Rose for Emily' today, you'd have to set it in space."

"A Tang for Emily?" Aaron said.

"Why?" Jule asked.

"I don't know," I said. "Maybe because if you were in space you couldn't just say, 'Later,' and hit the road. You would actually be stuck with people."

"Is someone leaving?" Aaron asked, and it looked like he made nervous eye contact with Jule for a second.

"No," I said, "but I was just up at Jule's school and I swear the place was like what I figure those bigass conference centers are like. They sit there all summer basically sharpening pencils and waiting, then after Labor Day a bunch of you come in with your baggage and agendas already set and they just provide the tables and chairs and buffet lunch and a place to plug in your laptop."

"Better than the baby-sitting you get in college," Aaron said. "It does seem like they have it backward, though, doesn't it?"

I looked out through the observation window. "Where is JJ going next year?" I said. "He's a senior, right?"

"I don't know," Jule said. "I go to West High, remember? Those guys all go to City."

"He wants to go to Cornell," Aaron said. "Michigan is his fall-back."

"Aaron," I said, "a couple of months ago you called JJ the quote Motormouth Jew unquote. How do you know all this?"

"He brought his mom in yesterday and we talked a little."

"You're telling me JJ brought his mother in here to, what, be counseled by *you*?"

He looked me calmly in the eye. "It wasn't an appointment or anything. We just rapped for a half hour or so."

"About?"

"Jazz. Richard Wright. Astral projection."

"You're lying about the last one, you bastard."

"The last one, yes."

I looked at Jule. "What were you talking about when I came in?"

"Death," she said without a blink.

"And?" I said. "Are we for or against?"

"Both," they said together. They seemed very pleased with themselves.

"In which case or cases are you two in favor of death?" I said.

"Not exactly in favor," Jule started, and then she looked at a point behind my shoulder. I turned and saw that JJ and his girl-friend were hanging by the door. God knows how long they'd been there.

I turned back to Jule. "You were saying?"

"Just that 'in favor' doesn't really describe it."

"More like respectful," JJ said. He and his girlfriend had taken a tentative step into the office. "In the Upanishads—"

"*Fuck* the Upanishads," I said. "Fuck Ecclesiastes, fuck *The Way of a Pilgrim*, and fistfuck the Bhagavad right in the Fuck-ing Gita. Jesus Christ, which of you is Franny and which of you is Zooey?" They all stared at me. I couldn't get my fingers un-clenched so I stood up.

"Fine," I said. "All right. Hey, I've got to get to work here, folks. Why don't we break up this little kaffeeklatsch?"

"We're waiting for Charlie," Jule said.

"Yeah," JJ's red-haired girlfriend said. "We're supposed to talk about the Haunted House."

"We are?" I said. "Since when? It's not even Labor Day for three days."

"It's on the bulletin board," JJ said.

My eyes were starting to lose focus, so I sat back down and closed them.

Aaron spoke from the desk. "We got a bulletin board from Staples," he said. "Everyone thought it was a good idea so we can keep track of who's doing what. It's back there on the wall."

I kept my eyes closed and just shook my head. "Fine," I said. "I'd like to handle organ donation and police reports."

Aaron shot back with one of those great big laughs and I

opened my eyes and after a few seconds I smiled in spite of myself.

"You know," I said, "let's do a little Death Poll, since we're on the subject. Grandparents and hamsters don't count. Me, dead wife, dead stepson, and father missing, presumed dead." I looked at JJ's red-haired girlfriend. "You?"

She hesitated and looked at JJ, and he gave her what might have been an encouraging look.

"Dead best friend," she said. "Dead favorite cousin."

JJ followed up. "Dead father."

When Jule started to open her mouth I suddenly wanted to stop the whole thing but I couldn't.

"Dead parents, dead boyfriend, dead stepmother." For a second I was sure she was going to say something else, but she didn't.

"Dead father, dead mother," Aaron said.

"Dead husband, dead parents, dead sister." It was Charlie, across the open door from JJ. "Is this some sort of initiation?" she asked. "Is there a secret handshake?"

Everyone was quiet for a second and several people were looking at me.

"Hey, Charlie," I said. "Don't mind us. It's just kinda dead in here tonight."

Aaron roared again, Charlie smiled, and the first meeting of the 2003 Teen Scene Haunted House Committee had officially begun.

That night in bed Jule was asleep or pretending to be when I got upstairs. The last few nights I'd taken to spontaneously running my fingers and palms across her belly. It was a cliché all right but a powerful one. A pregnant belly could never be confused with plain old flab, at least on a normal-sized person. It was as if she were one of those drug couriers you read about, except instead of swallowing little balloons stuffed with heroin she'd swallowed a couple of kilos. Her tits were firmer, swollen at the base, and her rump had muscled up in anticipation, probably, of the stress her thighs were going to take on soon. In short, her body had caught up to the rest of her.

I slid up behind her and ran my hand up over her belly from underneath. She took my hand and held it in front of her, curling slightly around it. Ah, awake after all.

"Alex comes back tomorrow," I whispered.

"That's like the fifth time today you've said that," Jule said. "Next you're going to ask me if I want to come along when you pick him up."

"What's your answer? I always forget."

"No," she said. "I'm going to check out this childbirth class at the Emma Goldman."

"Really?" I said. "They do that there?"

"Listen to you," she said. "The suspicion is just dripping from your voice. If I wanted an abortion I wouldn't have waited until my fifth month."

"That wasn't what I was thinking." What I was thinking—what I always thought when I heard the name Emma Goldman Clinic—was lesbians, secretive gynecological discussions, and middle-aged professional women in slacks with their hair pulled back severely. And maybe a little mind control. And only after that abortions.

I'd never gotten anyone pregnant, I was sure of it. Perhaps I was sterile; I certainly couldn't be accused of being careful. I'd had the luck or good fortune to have slept mostly with women who didn't particularly care for me; with the exception of Isabel and now Jule, the most positive thing that could be said about the vast majority of my previous sex was that it was consensual.

"Alex is going to flip when he sees you," I said. "When he left you were just this little girl." Jule squeezed my hand.

"I don't think there's any question Alex should be best man, do you? The only other candidate is Aaron and family comes first."

She didn't answer and it took only a few seconds for me to figure out why. Under the tequila tent Russ had played that part perfectly, or nearly so. I remembered the way Jule had looked at him standing there reciting his toast to the little motley crew. That had been nearly a year ago, and there was no way of knowing how many times Jule had wondered if she and Russ would be standing there someday the way Isabel and I were. It must have seemed at the time like they had forever to figure it out.

"We don't have to have any of that," I said. "We can go to the county courthouse, just the two of us, let some of the clerks or whatever witness it."

"November first," she said. "My birthday is the twenty-ninth, so let's do it on the first. I don't care who's there. I really don't."

"I just thought of something. We'll be busy doing that stupid Haunted House on the twenty-ninth."

"We'll call that my party," she said. "That's fine with me. It seems silly to worry about it this year with everything else happening."

I knew her well enough by now to note the false ring in her voice. But I wasn't surprised. No woman really wanted her birthday forgotten. I'd just have to figure out how to surprise her.

"Hey," I said. "What do you think of Aunt Tana these days? Is she the same or worse or what?" She'd been in the house less than a week but I was ready to call it a success. Three months would be a breeze; come November she'd be counting her money and we'd be counting down the last few weeks until the baby came.

"I don't know," Jule said. "You mean is she better compared to before?"

"I was just thinking that she's pretty easy to get along with all in all. She stays out of the way, has all of the custody stuff down pat."

"She's a business owner," Jule said. "She's used to dealing with junk like that. You'd have to be."

"Hey," I said, "maybe we should get some advice on what to do with your money next year."

There was a momentary hardness to her, like a ripple. I was pressed against her back and I could feel it, no question.

"It's invested," Jule said.

"I realize that," I said. "But we'll have to get acquainted with those investments pretty quick when it comes into your name. Maybe you'll want to keep the same investments, maybe not. All I'm saying is we'll have to study up."

"It's my money," she said.

"Hey," I said, making sure my voice sounded properly injured. "I never said one syllable about it not being your money. It's yours and always will be. I was just offering my services if you needed help."

"I may not do anything with it," she said. "I may need it for college. I may give it to my baby. I don't want to think about it."

I separated myself a little from her and rolled onto my back. "Technically," I said, "the money is supposed to be used the same way your parents' income would have been used, to pay your bills until you're old enough to get a job and a career and all that. It's not an inheritance."

Her voice was steely. "I didn't say it was. I just don't want to use it. I'd rather get a job right now."

"You may have to," I said. "I'll be out of work at the end of the year. Even if the Teen Scene survives the audit there won't be any place for me there."

"So get a different job," she said. "You'll have graduated by then, you'll have a head start on everyone else."

"Sorry," I said. "It doesn't look like that will happen, either. I couldn't get into any of the classes I needed to."

She rolled over onto her elbows and shot me a look of pure disbelief. "What does that mean? They won't let you graduate? Is that legal?"

"Well," I said, "it's not a question of letting me. There are some requirements that I never bothered—"

"Like what?"

"Second-semester Russian. Middle English poetry. One other one."

"You can't get a degree without second-semester Russian?"

"Not if your only foreign language was first-semester Russian."

She looked at me skeptically.

"Pravda," I said.

"There's no way around this?"

"Not to my knowledge."

"Did you talk to the dean?"

"I beg your pardon?"

"You have deans there, right? Don't you see the dean if you have this kind of issue?"

"Look," I said. "It's not like high school. The dean runs the college. He doesn't check for forged notes from Mom."

"Who does? I mean, who takes care of it when the only courses you can possibly take to graduate after ten years are full? Don't they want you to get a degree as much as you do?"

"I suppose I could appeal or something, or see if I could substitute a Russian lit class or something."

"See?" she said. "There are options. I bet you could take something else besides midwestern poetry, too."

"Probably," I said. "Look, I'll talk to the English department tomorrow. But don't get your hopes up. These bastards can be pretty rigid."

"If they won't give you the classes then graduate on the Internet or something. That's just ridiculous."

"I made the registrar cry," I said. "At least I think I did. I don't think I had better start asking for favors there."

"What did you say?"

"I don't remember." I had probably insulted her. I honestly couldn't remember. I made a note to go back and apologize, or at least send her an e-mail. I'd forgotten that she once expedited something for me when I was having trouble getting my Pell grant.

Then a completely unwelcome thought popped into my head. If I graduated then I'd lose my student loan deferment. I'd already used up my grace period.

I wanted to put a pillow over my head. "So, anyway," I said. "Not to change the subject, but Alex is coming—" I had almost stopped myself this time.

But she was staring out the window, lost in some kind of calculation or meditation or something. I decided that I was talked out and laid my hand on top of her hand for a quick squeeze, then turned over and faced the door. I waited for her to object or say anything at all, but she didn't. I didn't hear her move at all before I fell asleep.

Rosie had a cold and she was in a foul temper to begin with. The golf machine was on the blink and unplugged and the place was about to open for lunch with a missing waitress.

I'd been to the English chair's office and, it turns out, the dean's office that morning and had gotten my affairs in order with only the slightest effort. I was whisked into an independent study with a professor emeritus for my English requirement and I was safely tucked into an already overcrowded Soviet history seminar for my foreign-language credit. My other hole, an arts workshop, had been fulfilled with a little sleight of hand by the chair. She gave me credit for a jazz improvisation class I'd taken six years earlier, even though it was technically theory. It hadn't been offered for so long the classifications had changed, and she was none the wiser. The whole thing had taken an hour and a half, including my sheepish visit with the registrar, who acted as if she'd never seen me before. I got another loan deferment, and even, thanks to a brochure tacked up on the waiting room bulletin board, scored an Iowa Adult Returning Student (IARS) grant—nonrepayable—for fifteen hundred bucks. It was a good morning.

"Rosie," I said, "you were right about the Teen Scene. It's not crooked but they've got some money problems."

"No shit," she said. "I heard they were behind on their taxes, on top of everything else."

"They're a nonprofit," I said. "What taxes?"

"Property taxes, dumbshit. They get a break but it's not free. Plus if they get audited and they lose their tax exemption they're very screwed."

"They're going to reorganize after the first of the year, turn it over to the board, and let them bring in whomever they want. It's a big mess."

"It's a bit ridiculous," Rosie said. "Since they expanded the rec center there's really no need for the joint."

"Well," I said, "one of the founders is dead and the other wants to retire. Plus the director split."

"Who's the director? You mean that pudgy fella with the comb-over?"

"Dwayne," I said. "He took off a few weeks ago."

"I saw him yesterday," Rosie said. "If we're talking about the same guy."

"You saw him yesterday? Where?"

Rosie relayed how she'd seen Dwayne or his doppelganger using an ATM in Coralville. She'd taken an interest in him because he was on foot, using one of those drive-up ATMs. But she couldn't be one hundred percent sure.

"Too bad he never worked for UPS," I said. "You'd have his ass committed to memory."

She shook her head dismissively. "Nope. I don't go for shifty bastards like that. Dumb is okay, evasive is something else altogether."

I knew why she'd said that; it was her way of telling me that I could come in there once or maybe twice more, but that she'd decided on the makeup of my character, and it wasn't for the better.

But she wasn't finished. "Plus I heard he was hospitalized for a while after his old man died. Tried to off himself or something."

"I don't think so," I said. "I think they would have told me this." Of course they wouldn't have. Who was I kidding?

"Listen," I said, "I really came in here to get some advice. I have to figure out what to do with Isabel's ashes. Alex is coming home tonight and I think it's time to get this one done."

"She never said anything ever?" Rosie asked. "It never came up?"

"That's the trouble," I said. "She owned plots—she and Kenny have two down around the corner from us."

"So buy him out, maybe. You could put both of them there."

"That's what I was thinking. I didn't know how it worked. I mean, I can't buy him out for his spot if that's where Russ would go. It's his son, not mine. And Isabel already owns her half."

"You haven't said anything to him at all?"

"Not really. He may have other ideas. Although he was the one who told me about the plots, come to think about it."

"Look, I'll be honest," Rosie said, pinching the skin above the bone in her nose. "I don't think either of you rates a side-by-side with Isabel. Neither one. If there are two spots it should be her and Russ. The rest of you will probably go on and get hooked up with other people with bad taste in men. Sit him down and tell him that's what you want to do. It's easy, it's paid for, nobody gets their feelings hurt."

"You make it sound so easy," I said.

"It is easy," she said. "You just want to make it complicated to suit yourself."

"Hardly."

"Just do the right thing," she said. "The two of them belong together. Let the rest of you figure it out some other time."

This time when she left me sitting there the place was full. Iowa City had opened up in the last few weeks and gorged itself on humanity. Kids, parents, scholars, professors, shoe store owners, cops. The town was full again, everyone had money. As soon as I stood up, the hostess, a girl I didn't recognize, motioned for a threesome to come sit down. Life had started over again, as it always did.

Alex came down the ramp swinging his backpack next to his feet the way an aviator would swing an unopened parachute. He was tanned and his hair was long and pulled back in a ponytail. In the car he looked like he could barely contain something— his mouth worked and no words came out. Sometimes when I looked over he had a small smile curling his upper lip.

It had been a good summer, Alex brought back over four thousand dollars. As in the past years, he also brought back a bit of a swagger and a scoffing no-bullshit attitude which I'm sure was the prevailing zeitgeist in Prudhoe Bay.

"Hey," I said as we took the exit off the interstate a few blocks from Dogland. "You're going to need some clothes for school. You want to go to the mall tonight or tomorrow?"

He shrugged and slid down a bit more in his seat. "Sure, whatever."

"I got a birthday present for you. I was hoping you'd have called."

He didn't answer.

"Hey," I said. "You're taking driver's ed this fall, right? Let me know and we can go and get your permit anytime you want."

This perked him up a little. "Can I drive to school?"

"Not until you're a senior," I said.

"That's bullshit," he said. "I'll just park on the street."

"Fine with me," I said. "As far as I'm concerned if you get your license you can drive anywhere you want. You'll probably have to kick in some money for insurance, though."

He shrugged again. "No problem," he said. "I can cover that."

"Things might get tough in the winter," I said. "I'll probably be out of a job. We have some insurance and you have money from your dad and Jule gets some too, so if I can just score a new job we should be okay."

"I heard you were graduating."

"You did? Who told you?" I hadn't spoken to Alex since early July.

"I got an e-mail," he said. "I think it's pretty cool. You'll be set."

"Right," I said, "a bachelor's degree is practically a seat on the board these days. I actually may go to graduate school."

"Why?" He had turned in the seat to face me, and rocked a bit as we pulled into the driveway.

"Why graduate school?" I asked. "Do you know what graduate school even is?"

"Yeah," he said. His face was hard. "It's for people who either don't have a life or know pretty much exactly what they want to do. Which are you?"

I looked at him as I shut off the motor. "How old are you again? You sound like your mother."

His face colored a little but he kept his mouth tight. "My dad started all over. He worked in a cannery to get enough to buy the boat. He lived in his truck. He almost died because he had to have his appendix out and couldn't afford to go to the hospital until the last minute."

"I know this story," I said. "You guys always left out the part where he ran away when he and your mom got divorced."

"Yeah, but he came back," Alex said. "Mom said he paid every bit of money he owed and more."

"He's a hero," I said. "I'm a dumbass. Is that the whole point to this story?"

"Whatever," he said. "I forgot how you were, dude."

"How I am? Exactly how am I? Can you answer fast, because I wanted to get a head start laundering your dumbass underwear and making your dumbass dinner, if that's all right with you."

"Hey," he said, "it's your life, dude."

I opened my door and climbed out. The grass was long and without even going into the house I went into the garage and dragged out the dumbass mower. Inside I heard Jule squeal with delight when she saw Alex. She never squealed; she wasn't that kind of kid, that kind of woman, that kind of whatever. At least, I hadn't thought she was.

I pulled the mower out and raped my rotator cuff starting it. It was the Sunday before Labor Day, and I wished to God it was Christmas. By then it would all be over; the wedding, the legal hassles, the baby, the end of the Teen Scene. The motor belched and chugged a few times, the rotor underneath taking a few lame hacks at the crabgrass, and then it died with a great shudder. It wouldn't restart for anything.

3

The month of September was the blur it always was; school starting, sororities chanting and singing on the sidewalks, football games, the first cold snap and the gassy smell of the furnace starting up for the first time. There was music and a candlelight thing on the eleventh that sucked, the way those things probably always do in college towns, where the general populace doesn't believe deep down that death really exists.

Once a week at the Teen Scene we had a Haunted House meeting, complete with storyboards by JJ and a running budget tally by Charlie. Aaron had gotten the permit somehow, dropping off documents that he'd forged with Dwayne's name. We'd started putting some junk in the attic, collecting props we'd need, ordering fake blood, and rounding up mannequin fragments where we could find them.

We'd been arguing about the theme one night for forty-five minutes (Charlie wanted a real Haunted House with vampires, Aaron had his heart set on a Phantom of the Opera thing, etc.) when I just stood up and said, "Teen slasher film." Everyone in

the room was struck dumb for about four seconds before erupt-
ing in a cheer. It was unanimous; the theme would be gore, and
lots of it. We made posters with the words Teen Scene on them
and the "Scene" crossed out and replaced by "Slaughterhouse."
Tuesday, Wednesday, and Halloween Thursday; eight bucks a
head. "May be too intense for pre-teens," I added. "Don't come
on a full stomach" was in small print at the bottom. My old boss
let me do up the signs myself for the cost of the Gatorboard and
vinyl. At least as far as the signs went, it was looking to be the
most successful event ever put on at the Teen Scene, which
wasn't saying much.

JJ and his girlfriend and some of the regulars recruited heavily for staff and volunteers, and nights at the Teen Scene were
hopping from mid-September on. Aaron and Charlie and I were
all pretty much sharing the evening shift—there was that much
to do. JJ and the kids were sneaking vodka in their Slurpees but
we let them get away with it. I had begun to be very impressed
with them and had even mentioned to JJ's girlfriend that there
might be some baby-sitting money to be had in the spring. She
thought I was kidding, apparently, because she laughed behind
her hand. She was, more than I had figured before, a bit of a
flake. But she worked her flawless seventeen-year-old ass off on
whatever project needed to be done. She no doubt had a perfectly tuned prescription, and I envied her.

Jule was rounding out; we'd had our last sex a little more
than a week after the OB said we should stop—actually about
two weeks. Her face had squared off impressively; her hair had
darkened, her voice was huskier, and she developed a new,
secrecy-flavored manner of smiling around the edges of her
mouth.

We'd begun to accumulate baby things as well; in fact, we
were nearly set just by accepting castoffs from a couple that had

worked with Izzie at the convalescent center. Once when we were unloading their little truck I slipped and said "we" when referring to Jule's baby. It was happening more and more and lately I had stopped caring almost altogether.

I read a few books in Prairie Lights about childbirth and midwifery. I scanned them, anyway. I have to admit I was dumbfounded at the sheer gore potential of the average birth. Forget the pain of contractions, which I could at least begin to classify in recognizable terms as somewhere between severe abdominal cramps and being gut-shot; I read passage after passage about episiotomies, spinal taps, forceps births, breech, transverse breech, and inverted double transverse breech deliveries. Caesarean sections I simply passed over. We'd passed on the amnio and passed some other test for spina bifida with flying colors so I figured once the creature was delivered the worst would be over—then I read the part about changing the dressing on the cord and, if a boy, the foreskin. The book went on to mention the high probability of vomit and defecation during delivery; the small likelihood of a miscalculation of anesthetic leaving Jule with an overcooked cauliflower for a brain. How the child's head might come out shaped like a Vienna sausage. The chances of a blue baby. The chances of a purple or ashen baby. The battery of tests the team of specialists would inflict on the little worm before Jule or I would get to touch him or her. The remote possibility that surgeons would have to split Jule's pelvis with the Jaws of Life. The possibility of hermaphrodism, autism, mongolism, etc. The one thing not a single book mentioned was a caul. I was determined to find out if children were still born with cauls, and not a single book mentioned them.

Once, I skipped out of my Russian seminar on *The Petty Demon* to sit in on a sonogram. I hated it; every second was torture. The Caribbean woman manning the thing was a chatterer and Jule fidgeted and looked away from the monitor a lot as the radiologist or sonologist went through her checklist, telling us how "groovy" the shrimp's spine was, how sure she was what sex he/she was but wouldn't tell us if we didn't want to know. I hated her because halfway through she zoomed in and printed this odd little shot showing all ten toes.

"This is very rare," she said, "all ten toes in focus at the one time. You don't usually see this very nice like this." She leaned over and ripped the printout from the little box. She leaned way the fuck over me and put it on the table next to Jule.

"I can take that," I said, picking it up.

"Oh, sure, oh, sure," the sonologist said. "That's okay." She never printed another one that afternoon, and Jule didn't say a word the entire time.

At home I put the ten toes picture up on the refrigerator and held it up with the Pizza Hut magnet. The next day it was gone and nobody would admit to taking it.

As September moved into October the days shortened and Jule slept more and more. Alex left early and came home late; most nights everyone was sacked out when I got home from the Teen Scene; in the morning they were all gone soon after I got up. Tana had more or less taken over my domestic duties of shopping and laundry and general cleanup. As a result the bathrooms were noticeably cleaner, the towels were softer, the underwear whiter, the water glasses less spotted. Everyone had a packed lunch waiting for them, complete with little Goldfish snack bags and Oreos. In the back of my mind I suppose I realized that I had been something less than a domestic wonder in the past year or so. I tried to feel guilty about that but couldn't dredge up too much concern. I'd kept the Board of Health from the door; that must have counted for something.

A week before Halloween we had a dry run of the Haunted

House—staff manning their stations, kids standing in for customers, actors playing their parts without makeup, lights down, that sort of thing. I'd turned out to be the art director of the entire project, positioning everything, figuring out the flow, the names of the various rooms, the interactivity. The way I had it set up, customers would enter through the back door and get their tickets in the little kitchen area before entering the hall through a heavy curtain. From there they could go into the basement (theme: *The Silence of the Lambs*) or proceed to the front room diorama and then up the stairs. We had three rooms upstairs, or a total of six scenarios, with the basement counting really as two since the old boiler room was separated by a wonderfully decrepit old brick doorway. In between rooms we'd have roving volunteers in hockey masks, ice hooks, that sort of thing. We'd also serve pop and chips.

We had JJ and about nine others slated to suit up to man the rooms. The costumes were minimal: some surgeon's scrubs, various lumberjack shirts, that sort of thing. We'd already gotten some of the props at that point, except for some actual organs one kid said he could score from the Coralville Meat Locker. We'd spoken to the gun store next door about overflow parking and had even gotten the okay to tap into their outdoor socket if we started blowing fuses.

After I finished my walk-through, all fifteen or so of us sat around the front main room for a debriefing. At that point it was clear to me we would be short of props and I was worried.

"Anything you can get your hands on," I said to the Meat Locker kid (which was how I remembered him). "Just nothing, you know, disease-ridden."

"I know I can get pig hearts and heads," he said. "Probably not guts."

Some of the girls moaned in disgust. The kid looked embarrassed.

"Hey, you laugh," I said to them, "but let me tell you something. Nobody's going to fall for that old "Close your eyes and put your hands in spaghetti" crapola. We'll need real viscera or we'll have half of these bastards asking for a refund."

"I've got some fake eyeballs," one of the kids said. "My dad got them on eBay. They were recalled or something."

"We'll spread those around liberally," I said. "Maybe drop one or two in the occasional Sprite."

"I can score a whole kid mannequin from Younkers," a girl said. "We'd have to be careful with it. But it looks pretty real and it comes apart."

"Bring it," I said. "Anything else?"

One of the other kids' dad was a surgeon and he'd already said he could loan us some old tools like bone saws and stuff but he repeated the offer again, I suppose to get a little recognition. I ignored him.

"Remember, girls," I said. "Costumes are on the skimpy side. You'll be inside so don't worry about being cold. This is a teen slasher movie, so the sluttier the better. Get some Wonderbras from your moms and if you aren't already tattooed from asshole to elbow get some temporary ones. Magnetic piercings are not a bad idea, either."

Most of the girls snorted at me and rolled their eyes.

"All right," I said. "Remember that next week we'll have a few more things going for us, so I expect a lot less yawning and a bit more method acting, if you know what I mean."

JJ raised his hand. "You mean you want me to reach down and find the homicidal medical student deep inside me?"

"I mean," I said, "that we'll have the smoke machine and the dark and the music and blood. If you all stand there like you're too cool for words it will be a long fucking night."

Charlie grimaced. "I don't think all this foul language is necessary," she said.

"Fine," I said. "Just everyone remember that we're shooting

for a PG-13 and above crowd, so we can scare the crap out of these people. They've paid more than they'd pay for a movie, remember. Some of them will be drunk. Some of them will be high. Some of you guys will be drunk and high." Several of the kids looked at each other and tittered.

"One more thing," I said. "Most of you know Jule. Tuesday is her birthday and I'd like to have some cake here just before the thing starts up. No presents, but just a little surprise and happy birthday and all that."

A few of the kids looked at each other and I heard one or two "Who?"s.

"That's sweet," Charlie said. Another kid, apparently answering someone else, said, "His stepdaughter or something, I don't know."

"But . . ." It was Charlie. "I'm not sure a party . . ."

"Not a party," I said.

"Still," she said. "Maybe . . ."

"Listen up," I said, cutting her off. "I know it's fun to joke and everything but I'm not kidding now. Let's be relatively sober for the real night, okay? I know of what I speak."

The kids all smirked but Charlie shook her head with her eyes closed. So fire me, I thought. Do me a favor.

A couple of days later Jule and I found ourselves home alone. She lay on her back all big-bellied up against the headboard and I sat on the edge of the bed with my feet on the floor.

"Tana's leaving on my birthday," she said.

"Holy shit," I said. "Why?"

"She said that's when it's all over. She said she knew when she wasn't needed anymore."

"Well," I said, "technically that's true. Monica said once you turned seventeen it was pretty much all academic."

Monica the social worker had come by twice in the previous

months; both times to walk outside and talk to Tana alone in the backyard. God knows what the two of them talked about. When I asked Tana she said it was about filing deadlines.

"I didn't say I wanted her to stay, I was just saying."

"Okay," I said. "I thought she would stay at least until the wedding or maybe even for the baby."

"We need a license," Jule said. "I don't want to go to City Hall for a wedding license on my seventeenth birthday and eight months pregnant."

"Fuck 'em," I said. "Who cares what they think?"

"Me," she said. "I've lived here my whole life. It's not what I thought it would be like."

"What what would be like?"

"The moment," she said. "I didn't think the moment would be that way."

"The moment of what?"

She shrugged. "The moment that marks the start of the next big thing, the next journey."

"There will be lots of those," I said. "So many of those you'll lose track."

"How many have you had?" she asked.

How many? "Well," I said. "A few already this year, that's for sure."

"When? Tell me exactly when one of those moments was." She was staring at me open-eyed, her hand on her belly where it pushed open the fabric of her blouse between two buttons.

"The funeral," I said. "The first night we made it. The first time I felt the baby move with my hand."

"You're lying," she said. "How could you lie about that kind of thing?"

"You're hormonal," I said. "Take it easy."

"You never hit on me until your dad disappeared," she said. "You should be thinking about that moment."

"That might be one," I said.

"At the wedding you were totally going through the motions. You mailed that one in."

"Listen," I said. "Let's just get through the next month or so before we get the scalpels out, what do you say?"

She looked away from me out the window. Her breath was shallow; it was probably hard for her to take a decent breath in that position.

"We can put Alex's dad in Tana's room. That may be another reason she's leaving."

"Shit," I said. "I totally forgot he was coming."

"It's on the calendar," she said. "It's all Alex talks about."

"Not to me," I said. "I never see him anymore."

"He's the same," she said.

Kenny was due for a weeklong visit. It was the first time, Alex said, that he could get away after putting the boat up for the winter. Just like everything else, this was happening on the twenty-eighth too. I'd offered to pick him up and nobody had turned me down so it looked like it was a date. It would be a very fun-packed day.

"Well," I said. "Kenny and I have some business to take care of anyway. We'll probably have that cemetery thing then while he's here, if you're up for it."

"I don't think so," she said. "It's just too hard to picture."

"Maybe that's a moment," I said. "We put Izzie and Russ to rest."

She shook her head. "You really think backward," she said. "You know that?"

Before I even got out of bed that morning I was fucked. For one thing I was the last person up, and that never happened. When I was a drunk I'd slept routinely until ten, but since then I woke with the sun. Very rarely had anybody beaten me out of bed.

This morning by the time I'd made it downstairs not only had

Jule gotten up, she'd left. Tana sat at the breakfast table with Alex. Her suitcases sat by the door.

"Hey," I said. "You don't mess around."

She gave me that steady and patient look. "Early worm gets all the birds," she said.

"Okay," I said. "I meant the bags, though. Where's Jule?"

"I knew what you meant. She's got a doctor's appointment."

I cocked my head in polite disbelief. "She was at the doctor's on Monday." Alex looked at her with concern.

"It's all right," I said. "No biggie. As long as Alex gets her to the Teen Scene before the whole thing gets too crowded."

"I'm sure he can manage that," Tana said.

"Yeah," Alex said, looking at his bowl of Cheerios. "I'm cool with all of that."

I sat down and poured myself a glass of Tropicana. "Tana," I said. "We could, you know, always use help when the baby comes. You're always welcome back."

"That's very nice of you to say," Tana said, "but as the lady once said, 'I don't know nothin' 'bout birthin' babies.' "

"Butterfly McQueen," I said. "And you're still welcome."

"I'll keep that under advisement."

"Alex," I said. He practically jumped.

"What?"

"I'm going to head to the airport at four to pick up your dad. You want to come?"

He shook his head. "I'll just come home from school and see you all here."

"I can swing by and pick you up from in front of the school," I said. "Not a problem."

"That's okay," he said. "I got some things to do here."

Sure you do, I thought. Something at the Greenwood Apartments, perhaps? Just let me tell your old man, I thought. I'd love to be the one. But Alex had to figure out his own path. I understood what it was like—at least I thought I did.

———

I managed to get the cake dropped off at the Teen Scene and then make it to the airport only a few minutes after Kenny's flight arrived. I left the car at the curb and caught him just as he was about to head toward the rental cars.

"Kenny," I called. He swung around and for a second I was sure that he was disappointed to see me there. Did he want to rent a car that much? He walked over with this carry-on hanging from his shoulder and a now beardless face. He looked all of twenty without the facial hair, a bit like a bartender or fitness coach. He came up and grabbed my hand without a smile.

"Long flight?" I said, but he didn't respond. He was looking out the window at the car.

"Should I just get a rental?" he said. "Might be easier."

"No way," I said. I actually didn't care one way or another but it seemed appropriate to overdo the hospitality. He was on my turf. His kid had chosen to live with me, not him. I owed him something.

He followed me through the double doors to the curb and I opened the back door and tossed his bag onto the seat.

"Hop in," I said.

He did. "This yours?" he asked as we pulled out onto the highway.

"Permanent loaner, I guess," I said. "Rosie's still paying the insurance. I guess at some point I'll need to take that on, since the kids will be wanting to drive it."

"That would be pricey," Kenny said. "You may want to think that one over."

We'd made it all the way into town and were in sight of the VA hospital when I realized that I had taken a wrong turn and that if I didn't do something we'd be forced to drive past the spot where Isabel had died. There was only one way to get off so I took a quick right up an access road that led behind the basketball arena.

"Whoa, *shit*," Kenny called out, grabbing the dashboard. I'd turned so quickly I hadn't noticed the guy walking along the shoulder and we missed him by only four or five feet. I brought the Tempo to a stop there on that access road and shoved the shifter up.

The guy was wearing a fake beard and a pirate suit—a bandanna on his head, red sash around his waist, and a Lone Ranger–type mask. He was a chunky guy and walked with his feet pointing a bit out. He'd hesitated a bit when I careened in front of him but now was progressing past the rear bumper without a glance in our direction.

"What's going on?" Kenny said. "You look like you saw a ghost."

"I changed my mind," I said. "I want to go the back way."

Kenny nodded slowly at me. "It's okay with me either way. I don't especially want to pass by there either."

I sat there for a few seconds and watched the chunky guy continue along the shoulder. It was the way his baggy pirate pants hung off his ass that made the connection for me. I quickly rolled down the window.

"Dwayne," I yelled. "Hey, *Dwayne*."

He stopped and turned around, his hand on the hilt of his hollow plastic scimitar. His mouth dropped open and he stood half on the curb and peered through his mask at me.

I waved my hand at him in a beckoning motion. "Come here, man," I yelled.

"Who's that?" Kenny said next to me.

I ignored him. Dwayne stood for a few seconds and then turned and continued on. I watched until the high concrete retaining wall hid him from view.

"Who was that?" Kenny repeated.

"My old boss," I said. "He kind of disappeared on us."

"Guy looks like a lunatic," Kenny said. "So he's in hiding or whatever?"

"I guess so," I said. "I guess maybe he's come out now."

"Does he know it's not Halloween for a couple of days yet?"

Apparently not, I thought. I put the Tempo in gear and trudged up the hill and circled the VA parking lot a few times before I found the back way out. I kept my eye out for Dwayne all the way up Burlington but I didn't see him again.

Poor bastard, I thought. He ran away from home at age forty and this was as far as he got. But still I wanted very much to talk to him.

4

I knew they were gone the moment Kenny and I pulled onto Prairie du Chien. It wasn't just that the Hyundai was missing from the curb; it was something else, maybe the way Kenny sat in the passenger seat with his hands formally on his knees after we'd come to a stop. Maybe the way Alex sat on the back steps smoking a cigarette.

I got out of the car and just leaned against the front fender. Alex didn't look up and Kenny finally opened his door and came around his side of the car and sat down next to Alex on the stoop. I suppose I could have pushed through them to get into the house but I was sure there was no point.

"Okay," I said, running through the entire cast of characters in my head. "I'm guessing everyone in town is in on this?"

"In on what?" Alex said. Only then did I notice his duffel bag on the step behind him. His brand glistening new duffel bag that I had bought for him in the spring.

"I get it," I said. "Kenny, can you just tell me the whatever—the bottom line? Do I still live here? Does anyone still live here?"

He took a few moments to answer, pulling a little on the edges of his chin where his beard used to be.

"Andy," he said. "First, this is no conspiracy of the kids. Part of it was my idea. It was only decided like this in the last two weeks."

"You expect me to believe that?"

"I don't expect anything," he said. "The truth is that Alex is no relation to you, Jule is no relation to you, and the baby is no relation to you. I think somewhere along the line you forgot all that, man."

"What are you talking about? We were getting married to-morrow," I said. "Or the next day. Today is her birthday, if you didn't know."

"I did know. I knew all of that. Did you get the license yet?"

"Where did she go?"

"Yeah, I didn't think so."

"Alex," I said, "where did they go? Back to Cedar Falls?"

He shook his head. "They're going someplace in Texas," he said. "Some couple is paying for the whole thing."

"Some *couple*? Hey, Ken, this is your grandchild, my friend. Some fucking yuppies in Texas are going to buy your flesh and blood."

He nodded. "I'm aware of all of this, buddy. I talked to them."

"You talked to them? What did they give you?"

"What did they *give* me? Nothing."

"Oh, *please*," I said. "You get rid of the poor asshole who's been taking care of everyone and in exchange for this . . . this *baby pimping*, you get, like, Grandpa rights for perpetuity. Tell me I'm wrong."

He started to answer but I waved him off.

"Ah, forget it, man."

I looked around me and, lacking any better plan, opened the Tempo door and sat on the driver's seat. I started going through the entire dramatis personae in my head. Rosie probably had a hand in it; as did Monica the social worker, the lying bitch. Charlie was in on it since she had been so weird about the party; ditto Aaron, my best and only friend.

"Alex," I said. "Why didn't anyone just talk to me?"

"We were going to," he said. "But you've been acting crazy again. I had to talk to my dad. We made Jule go see that social worker."

"I'm just stressed, Alex," I said. "It's just me. I'm always like this. You of all people . . ."

He was crying. "That was *before*, you fucker. It was okay back then because Mom would come back and you'd be, like, normal again."

"I'm the same," I said. "It would have been the same. It was all working out."

"God," he said. "What's the matter with you? You're fucking *hopeless*. Nobody saw it but me and I covered for you. You know what that was like?"

"You're lying," I said. "Why are you lying? It was good, you wanted to come back here."

Alex just craned his neck forward and wiped his sleeve across his face. "I was wrong, it's not right here. I can't explain it. I'm not going through that again."

"Through what again? It'll be fine. I promise."

"Listen," Alex said, "you don't know what you're talking about. You never did. You think everything can last forever. It can't. Yeah, you can always get another job, or make some more money, or, you know, buy a wooden leg if you need one, right? You lose, like, a *life* you had, and it's *gone*. You're supposed to start over, like we all did after."

"After? After what?"

"After you came along," he said. "After *you*." His voice was slick with hate. "And I'm not going to do it again, not here."

"You," I repeated. My voice was coming from somewhere

deep in my lungs. "You fucking little . . ." But I stopped myself. I don't know why. He wanted me to say it, I could tell. He wanted me to out him. He was daring me. But I didn't.

"Hey," Kenny said, standing up. "Just take it easy."

"You take it easy, Captain Fucking Queeg," I said. I reached into the backseat and wrestled his suitcase out and threw it onto the lawn. It was awkward and I looked like a clown doing it, but it made me feel better.

"I'm out of here," I said. "If you two are leaving take the fucking airport van." I slammed the door and fired up the Tempo. I nearly dropped the transmission shoving the shifter from R to D while I was still backing into the street. I ended up going back up into the lawn just missing Kenny's suitcase in my arc back to the pavement.

My first stop was North Hall but Monica's door was locked. I dialed her number from a phone in the Social Work hallway; her machine picked up on the second ring and I hung up.

Back in the Tempo I was only slightly more tender to the transmission than a terrorist. I was a block away from the Teen Scene when I noticed someone coming out of Dirty John's grocery and I locked up the brakes. It wasn't the person, it was the little paper sack he was carrying. I looped into the little parking lot and entered through the back door. Three and a third minutes later I was back in the Tempo with a paper cup of ice magically transforming itself into a portable Dewar's rocks. The ice was smelly tap water ice, but it was still the best drink I'd ever had. I drove with one hand on the wheel and the other in my lap.

I drove straight to the Teen Scene and tried to get into the back without anyone noticing me, but there was too much activity. Light was fading quickly and everyone was scurrying around. Some of the high school volunteers were hanging chili lights in the lounge over the ticket table. One girl I barely recognized was counting ones into the tin money box. No grown-ups were in sight.

JJ was the first to notice me. He had on his hospital scrubs. Of course he looked confused to see me there; *et tu*, JJ?

"Hey," I said. "Aaron here?"

He shook his head.

"Cake and everything ready?"

He turned and pointed to the corner of the entryway. The white box still sat where I'd left it. Of course it did. Everyone was in on it. All of them.

"Okay," I said. "I still have to go home." I took a drink from my cup. "I had an errand, so I'll dash back over there and pick up Jule. I know there's a shitload to do but see if you can just get the cake out of the box and onto a table. No need for a big deal but I want her to see the cake."

"Okay," he said.

"Back in a few, buddy," I said. He just nodded, looking down at the cup in my hands.

I got back in the car. Let them all wonder, I thought. Nobody gets the satisfaction. Not one of them. But then I climbed out and left the car there in the gun store parking lot. I didn't have far to go.

Rosie's bar was nearly empty. Six o'clock was a bit early even in Iowa City. I got my old seat at the corner, moved the setups tray a bit to the left, and waited for the bartender to come back from the walk-in.

When she did I almost burst out crying. She was unbelievably beautiful. She came back from the walk-in carrying two plastic buckets of twists and limes and proceeded to dump them in the bins behind the bar just in front of me.

"Sorry I moved that," I said, pointing to the setup tray. "Am I in the way?"

She gave me a little hair toss when she straightened up. "Nope," she said. "Just don't let the waitresses bump you. They're klutzy."

She was probably thirty, with a broad Scandinavian forehead and honey-colored hair that touched her shoulders. It looked like it had been worn short and she was growing it out. Her eyebrows were nicely arched and her lashes long and dense.

"I'm Andrew," I said. "I used to live here."

"Oh, yeah?" she said. "Were you going to school?"

"I mean here," I said. "My ass, this stool."

She laughed while she ran glasses through the sink. "What would you like?"

"Dewar's," I said. "Just a little water."

"Start a tab?"

"Sure, why not?"

She turned and bent down to get the scotch and I noted the quality of her sleeveless sweater and her perfectly low-slung jeans. Above the little dimples on either side of her coccyx there was, indeed, a small butterfly tattoo.

"You didn't tell me your name," I said when she slid the napkin under the tumbler.

"Carla," she said. "And I've seen you here before. You're a friend of Rosie's."

"I suppose I am," I said. "Although it's more complicated than it sounds."

"Did you used to work here or something?"

"No," I said. "But I may as well have. Can I bum one of those cigarettes?"

She handed me the pack and I shook one out. By the time I looked up she had stroked the lighter.

"Carla," I said. "How long have you worked here?"

"Two weeks," she said.

"Damn," I said. "I could have pretended to be a regular and you wouldn't have known."

"You would have asked about the old bartender."

"Doesn't that bug the shit out of you?" I asked. " 'Where's Jack?' 'What happened to Marcia?' "

She shrugged and lit herself a cigarette. The only other person at the bar was going down on his burger basket. It was pretty much just me and Carla and row after row of bottles.

"Where did you work before?"

"Ames," she said.

"Ames," I repeated. "Is it true that they sometimes herd cows through the streets there?"

She blew smoke out of pursed lips. "Practically," she said.

I stood up. "What should I play on the jukebox?" I said. "Or just tell me what not to play."

"Play anything on twenty-nine," she said.

Disc 29 was a band I recognized from the CD JJ had made for me. I played four songs with unremarkable titles.

"Carla," I said a few minutes later. She was filling up mixers from large white jugs.

"Andrew," she said.

"I haven't had a drink in over two years."

"On purpose?"

I smiled into the ice of my Dewar's. "Good question," I said. "Yes, on purpose, but probably not for the right one."

"How does it taste?"

"Like it was yesterday," I said.

"Why'd you quit?"

"Well," I said, "that's probably not as interesting as why I started again." I looked down at my watch. I'd been there an hour. I didn't feel drunk but my fingertips were cold. I probably shouldn't have skipped dinner.

"Which was?" I waited while she filled a table order. I didn't even bother to look at the waitress next to me. I could hear her snapping her gum two feet from my ear.

"Half of my family was killed and the other half betrayed me."

Carla didn't say anything but I wasn't too drunk to notice a look of cold indifference flit across her face. It was quick and then gone.

"That's terrible," she said. "I'm sorry to hear that."

"So anyway," I said. "*C'est la vie*. People do what they have to."

She looked at me oddly, then. "You want another?" she said.

"Yeah, okay," I said. She probably didn't believe any of it, even that I'd ever quit drinking. She'd heard it all before.

"Look," I said, "I'm harmless, so just out of curiosity is that wedding ring real or just for work?"

"For work," she said. "And yours?"

"It's real," I said. "But it's just a talisman now. Like a monkey's paw."

"Who's the monkey?" someone said behind me. I looked to the side just as Rosie maneuvered herself onto the stool next to me.

"Hi," I said. "I'm walking, not driving."

"Okay," she said. "Shit. Hold it." She got back up off the stool and nodded her head at a couple who had come up behind me. "Here," she said. "Thing feels like a bicycle seat to me."

I watched the couple move onto it; the woman sitting on the stool and the man wedging himself into the space on the other side of her. They were from out of town, probably. My age but presentable.

"Top of the morning," I said to them. "Don't order a Bass, I found a hook in mine once." They just looked sweetly confused. I noticed then that the bar had filled up around me. Bodies pressed against my back. The voices were like a pounding waterfall.

Rosie circled around and took a position across the oak bar from me, causing a kind of roadblock there by the waitress window.

"Hey, tiger," she said to me. "*¿Qué pasa?*"

"If you don't know, you're the only one."

"Then I'm the only one," she said.

"Well, you'll approve, anyway. Alex is going back to Alaska

with his dad and Jule's gone to Texas to have her baby for some couple. I guess it's just me out on the ranch now."

She didn't say anything and just picked olives out of the setup tray. Carla made herself busy at the other end of the bar, where another bartender had at some point begun his shift. Waitresses called their orders over Rosie's ass and Carla mixed and used the soda gun and beer taps over there.

"You're scaring away the customers there," I said.

"Screw 'em," Rosie said. "It's not like it was when you were here. Mostly Greeks and freaks now. I blame you for that."

"Everyone grows up sometime," I said.

"Well," Rosie said. "Did you talk to Captain Worthless about the burial plots?"

"Yes," I said, swirling my Dewar's. "It's all taken care of. I just have to pick a date and tell them if I want a tent for a service. I think no."

"I'd like to be there," she said. "If it's all right with you."

I looked up at her. I was suddenly dumbfounded that something like that was up to me. I knew my head was unsteady so I took a long drink to give it some support on the glass.

"Sure," I said. "You can come. Fuck those others, though."

"They'll be able to visit later," she said. "This is yours to do. You took care of them, you earned the right to do this however you want."

"Just you and me, then," I said.

"Whenever you want, hon," Rosie said. It was the very first time I had ever heard this tone in her voice. It was probably how she talked to her kid. It was very nice. Her face loomed close.

"My Lord," she said. "You're deep in the tunnel, aren't you?" She put her hand on top of mine. It was cold and wet but also soft; it felt very good. "I don't know how people like you end up being people like you, but it's goddamn sad." She looked like she was going to cry. Rosie crying. Unbelievable.

"Rosie," I said. "I'm not a bad person." The couple sitting

next to me had stopped talking and were looking embarrassedly at their drinks. At the far end of the bar Carla looked, if anything, a little disgusted. I wanted to crawl into Rosie's great big fucking lap. But right at that second the highball glass dropped from my other hand and the ice shot off to the side. The woman next to me gave a little squeal.

"I'm sorry," I said. I pulled a piece of ice off their nacho plate and got hot cheese on my fingertips. "Damn," I said. The jukebox changed over at that second to a top 40 song, and just like that it was more than I could take.

"*Fuck* this," I said.

The couple next to me looked shocked. They were probably in town for a football game or a reunion or some such shit.

"Look at you," I said to the guy. "The way you dress, man. You a professional bowler, by any chance?"

"Andrew," Rosie said sharply. "Hit the road. And I mean now."

"In my condition?" I said. "In my condition and you want me behind the wheel? Shame. I wrap myself around a tree and I'd own this place."

Rosie lowered her voice. "Come on back to the office."

I pulled a handful of bills from my pocket and dropped them on the bar.

"I don't think so," I said. I pushed my way through the undergraduates and their fisted schooners and bottles of Bud to the sidewalk outside. Clinton Street was cold and empty; a couple walked past me and I bumped the guy on purpose. His aggrieved reaction was completely satisfactory.

I wasn't going back to the Teen Scene, and I wasn't going to drive anywhere. I was drunk and broke, all by nine o'clock. I was just walking east and somehow managed to walk past the Teen Scene without even trying. From outside the line stretched down the driveway out and onto the sidewalk. The Haunted House was a hit. *My* Haunted House was a hit. I'd broken the curse; the place would have, for the first time, a successful event; folks would have fun, money would be made, children would squeal and laugh. I pictured Aaron inside, presiding over this scene, roaring his great big laugh, exchanging proud glances with Charlie.

I watched people stagger out of the front door and onto the porch. Some of them actually crossed back around to the driveway to get back in line. I walked around to the back door and cut in front. Inside JJ's girlfriend was taking cash and giving tickets. One of the other kids—a girl in an unbelievably revealing Sally Bowles from *Cabaret* costume—leaned over the table and chatted with her. Nobody else was in that room except the line of customers.

"Hey," I said, faking joviality. "A little emergency at home. Where is everybody?"

They looked at each other and then back at me.

"All over the place," JJ's girlfriend said.

"How about Aaron?" I asked.

"He's either in the crematorium or the slaughterhouse. He's dressed like Casanova Frankenstein. I'd check the dungeon, too. He doesn't look happy."

"Good," I said.

Behind her the doorway to the main hall was covered with a black drapery. When Sally let someone in you could see the darkness behind, and just a hint of the red-tinted clouds from the downstairs fog machine.

"Where are the cops?" I asked. "I thought there was supposed to be one out back."

"One's at the Kum & Go getting something to eat," JJ's girlfriend said. "The other one is out front making sure nobody comes in that way."

"How about Charlie?" I asked. "Where is she?"

Both girls shrugged and Sally let another group of three through the doorway. This time I heard squeals and screams over the music.

"What's her costume?"

They told me to look for someone who thinks they look like somebody called Phyllis Diller but actually looks like a very old and crazy version of the housekeeper from *Diff'rent Strokes*. I pushed through the curtains.

The office wasn't part of the proceedings and it was locked and empty. Through the glass door I could see on through the observation window to the main lounge—redecorated as the Human/Animal Transplant Operating Theater. The Younkers mannequin torso was there along with the authentic pig head the kid had apparently successfully scored from the Coralville Meat Locker. I walked down the hall and up the stairs just as one of the paying customers shrieked—she'd been grabbed by the cleverly concealed kid under the blood-and-sheet-covered operating table. JJ the crazed surgeon practically chased a girl up the stairs behind me, brandishing a handful of link sausage. I was tempted to trip him.

"Aaron," I called as I reached the top. The overhead fluorescents had been replaced by a black light tube and it was dark as pitch except for the odd bit of obscenely bright lavender clothing walking around. I pushed my way past a silhouetted gaggle of girls trying to decide if they wanted to go into the room marked Amputee Rape Pit. It was the supply closet, the door locked, but they didn't know that. "That's sick," one of them was saying. "I don't care, that's sick."

"Well," I said to her, "you might try your luck down the hall at the Chainsaw Weight Loss Clinic."

She glared at me in the black light dimness. Her teeth were black.

"Aaron," I yelled. "Where the fuck are you, man?"

I pulled open the door to the attic and stuck my head up there. Empty and dark, the way an attic should be.

Down at the north end of the hall, the Homeless Organs Yard Sale was empty except for the proprietor, a bored kid with a coping saw. A boom box next to him played Anthrax or some shit like that at distortion levels. The kid sat next to a table set up like a buffet with more pig organs and some of the spare limbs from the Younkers mannequin.

"Hey," I yelled to him. "You seen Aaron or Charlie?" I picked up a severed forearm with an effort at nonchalance.

He shook his head. "Maybe he's with the old-time sailor guy?" he yelled back. "I thought it was you with a fake beard."

"Not me. I got hung up and just got here."

"Weird." He twisted the stereo volume down for a couple of seconds. "Something might be fucked up around here. I didn't recognize that dude."

"It'll be all right," I said, and stepped back into the hall. He had just turned the music back up when a dull concussive *thud* moved the floor beneath my feet. Someone screamed over the music and I pressed up against the wall as a stream of white collars and eyeballs streaked past me to the stairs and down.

The Chainsaw Clinic kid came flying out of his room last of all. "What was that?" he yelled.

"What was what?"

"Fucking explosion."

"You sure?" He nodded and pushed past me to the stairway.

"Man, it's nothing," I said, but he kept going and I waved him down the stairs. I moved down the hall to the middle room— usually the encounter room for one-on-one counseling, but for today decorated with bowls of rice pudding, strips of rotting bacon, a Dirt Devil, and—until moments before—a very dirty one-eyed and bearded male nurse. This was, of course, the Budget Liposuction and Plastic Surgery Clinic (Stomach Stapling $10). One of the rice pudding bowls had been knocked to the floor. I left it there.

At the other end of the hall was the last room, the crematorium—Aaron's pet project. This room was the old master bedroom, complete with working fireplace. I kicked my way through the draperies, with the Younkers forearm still in my hand. The acrid smell of smoke registered on my brain indistinctly—the way a siren does when you're walking around with a Walkman on. I covered my mouth with my sleeve.

The crematorium was decorated with shadowy silhouettes, pieces of charcoal, and some very nice papier-mâché skull fragments and femurs painted to look charred. A TV showed video loops of stumbling, flaming stunt men in full burns spliced together with the burning of Atlanta from *Gone With the Wind*. The room attendants were supposed to offer some overcooked spare ribs to the guests and—at a prearranged signal—pop the button on the gas logs—whoosh, scream, etc. All of this happened in stroboscopic darkness.

But now there were only two junior high kids standing in the corner next to the abandoned ribs making out. I yelled over the music (Midnight Oil's "Beds Are Burning"); in the strobe light they opened up like a set of French doors in a very old hand-cranked film.

"Gotta get out," I yelled, just as the music cut off and the room was instantly as black as the inside of a cave. I'd started to yell at the boy again to get out and got a lungful of gravel. I doubled over and in the few seconds it took me to get my breath back some part of my mind did some fast arithmetic, a rush of logic and synapse. The Teen Scene was on fire. The Teen Scene was on fire, it was pitch dark, and I'd lost track of what part of the room I was in. I dropped to my knees and backed up toward the nearest wall. The boy and girl were screaming from the other side of the darkness and somebody close by was coughing madly. Just as I made contact with the wall I realized it was me coughing. I ran my free hand a few yards along the baseboard until I found the blanket over the front window and pulled hard. Yellow light streamed into the room just as a head rolled across the floor—the last remaining portion of the Younkers boy. The top few inches of the window were covered by a foaming drop-ceiling of smoke—it swirled there in the streetlight like amber and gray ice cream.

I dropped closer to the floor and crawled to the door and out into the hall; the couple was ahead of me, skittering like cockroaches to the steps. When they hit the first one the boy just rolled down the stairs like one of those hoops you'd see in bad remakes of *Tom Sawyer*. The girl stumbled after him, her hand on the rail, her knees bumping the treads. I followed her mostly on my ass.

On the first floor there was less smoke but a lot of leftover fog, which made it harder to see, even with the battery-powered emergency lights down there. From the direction of the front door came some loud voices—the rent-a-cops, probably, and they were screaming *This Way This Way This Way*. The crematorium couple and I were headed down the hall in that direction when I heard something from inside the office. The door was now ajar and I thrust my head through the opening, but the room was empty. Then I heard it distinctly.

"911? 911? 911?" It was coming from underneath the desk.

"Aaron?" I said. I crossed into the room, flashlight beams scissoring over my head through the observation window. But under the desk it wasn't Aaron, it was Dwayne, huddled in a ball with the enormous cell phone crammed against his ear. He was dressed in the remnants of his pirate suit; his mask hung around his throat and tufts of beard stuck to his cheeks.

He saw me and put the phone down on the carpet. "I didn't mean to," he said.

"Dwayne," I said. "What the fuck did you do?"

"I just thought I'd set fire to the shed. Just the shed. But I forgot about the turpentine. Those old ramps blew right through the top and caught the roof and the whole east side on fire."

"But why?" I said.

He just picked up the phone and punched 911 again.

"Dwayne," I said. "The fire department is already coming. We gotta go. We can sneak out the back if you're afraid to get caught."

"No," he said. "I'm not afraid to get caught. I came in here, didn't I? I didn't have to do that."

I could feel my throat starting to close up. I squatted lower.

"You can't stay here," I croaked. "Take the fucking phone and let's go."

"No," he said. "My dad died here. It's a good place for it."

"What?"

"He killed himself here. Right where I'm sitting."

"Dwayne, you won't die here," I said. "Life doesn't work out that way." Some smoke just then hit me in the eyes so I dropped even lower to where my head was about even with the edge of the desk.

From somewhere above I heard a crash, then another, and another.

"The fire department is here," Dwayne said, looking at the ceiling. "They're sawing holes in the roof to let the smoke out. My neighbor's house caught fire and that's the first thing they did."

Footsteps sounded in the hall and instinctively I stooped down and squeezed in with Dwayne behind the desk. The footsteps hesitated at the door, then passed.

"They'll be back," I said. "I'm heading out that door in ten seconds. I'll tell them exactly where you are."

"Don't go," he said.

"I've got to, I've got to find Aaron."

"Why?"

"I don't know," I said. Suddenly he grabbed for my pant leg and in doing so caught part of my calf. His fingers were like pliers.

"Tell me what happened with your dad," he said. "I was sorry I left without asking you."

"My dad?" I said. "What are you talking about? Let go of me, motherfucker."

His fingers tightened. "Tell me," he said. "You lost those others. Did he die, too?"

"Nothing happened," I said. "He disappeared. He's just gone."

His face was close. "You know, I was going to burn the whole place down one day and blame the fire on you," he said. "That's why I hired you. Then your whole family died and I didn't have the heart."

"Let go of me," I said. My voice was weak, a four-year-old's. "I'm going."

"Why?" he said. "What are you going to do? What possible plan do you have?" Dwayne's nose had started to run and his eyes sparkled dully, as if coated with a residue. Maybe he was crazy; maybe he was still suicidal. But then again, maybe he was like me, so lost a tiny space in the middle of a burning house could begin to seem like a haven.

I slumped against the floor. "I don't know," I said. Under that desk, with the butterscotch smoke descending on us, it was just possible to believe that death was not the worst thing after all.

"I guess I'm going to start over," I said. "From scratch. What else is there?" After a moment his fingers let up and I pulled my leg away.

"You make it sound so easy," he said.

"I don't think it will be, man," I said. "I think that compared to what's coming, bringing them all back here would be easy."

"But they can't come back."

Of course, I thought. That goes without saying. They weren't coming back, but even if they could—even if it were possible for Isabel to return to me—like Jule and Alex and my father, I'd be willing to bet she wouldn't do it. And who could blame her, really? I hadn't even been able to tell her out loud that I loved her. Christ, who could blame any of them?

Just then there was a crash from the front of the house and a brilliant light flared through the observation window. I dropped to the carpet, thinking it was another explosion. When nothing else happened I got to my knees and peered over the rim of the observation window. The entire front door had been ripped from the frame and the black silhouettes of two figures stood in its place. Scissoring behind them was the brightest light I had ever seen. I picked up my hand, and slowly, like it was someone else's, I waved.

"We're back here," I yelled. "We're right here."

Next to me Dwayne had crawled up to the window and he, too, started waving. The smoke swirled in our hair and around our hands but still we waved.

"Here we are," we yelled, "here we are, here we are, here we are."

"*Stay where you are.*" It sounded like the great booming voice of God himself. And then the two dark figures came crashing down the hall and into the room, two enormous men with face masks and helmets and stiff coats of canvas armor. They hauled me and Dwayne out of there like we were Muppets.

Outside the air was cold and the sky incredibly black and orange. Staring crowds filled the street and sidewalk. When the firemen released us and we stepped off the porch someone came running at me, caught me up in huge arms.

"Oh my God," he said. It was Aaron. "Oh my God, oh my God."

He held me there on the sidewalk, crying, rocking me back and forth. I looked over his shoulder and saw that Charlie was holding Dwayne the same way, rocking and chanting.

"Aaron," I said, trying to pull myself away, even if just slightly. "Why are you crying?" My voice was weak and I couldn't help but end the sentence with a spate of coughing. Aaron held me up and kept sobbing and shaking his head.

"Well, he's gone, isn't he?" he said finally. "He's just gone. Just like that." I'd never heard anyone sound so bereft.

"Oh, man," I said. "Aaron, I'm so sorry."

"What are we going to do?" he said.

Some part of the Teen Scene crashed to earth just then, and a few people screamed and the firemen started pushing us all back toward the street. I half dragged Aaron with me, our arms around each other like prom dates. He sat down on the opposite sidewalk, my only friend, all two hundred pounds of him, and sobbed into his hands.

"It'll be all right now, buddy," I said, my hand on his shoulder. "Trust me, I know what I'm talking about."

And it was finally true.

5

Rosie and I buried Izzie's and Russ's ashes two weeks later. The cemetery had put up a little tent and spread a bit of Astro-turf over the holes they'd dug for the boxes of ash. I had also in-vited Carl the client. The three of us stood there with Eddie the mortician under the tent and then Rosie read an Auden poem that she'd seen a character read in a movie funeral. Isabel had loved the movie but I had refused to see it on some sort of half-ass principle I couldn't remember. Rosie's throat wobbled under her chin as she read it.

When she was done she took this embarrassed half step back-ward and, maybe to compensate, I stepped a little bit forward. In front of me the two boxes on the Astroturf looked as though they would each just about fit a softball inside them.

"My mother," I said, "made me memorize Shakespeare to get my allowance. Which is really helpful in times like this."

My voice was a bit thin but I hadn't stumbled. I had taken two quick shots of Absolut when I heard Rosie's car pull up to the house, and while I knew there would be some real reckoning about that in the days ahead, I was glad at that moment not to be shaking.

"Were I crowned the most imperial monarch,
thereof most worthy,
were I the fairest youth that ever made eye swerve,
had force and knowledge more than any man's,
I would not prize them without her love."

Since I had memorized the lines a part of my mind was left free to gaze around me at the naked trees and rain-streaked headstones as I spoke. It was a pretty nice place, that cemetery. Nothing fancy, lots of trees.

I had no idea where I'd be buried; it seemed conceivable now that I'd get no further in life than Dogland after all. If that were the case it would be nice to be buried right there, maybe not next to Izzie but close enough to be in the running. That was something, after all.

Jule had left a note; Monica and Tana had set her up in an alternative high school in the Tucson desert, where she'd live with other young women who had given up their babies for adoption. She didn't give many details but I didn't need them. Between Monica and Tana it was clear every dot was connected for her. They had planned it for weeks. Jule had agreed only if they promised not to press the charges they'd been quietly working up against me—contributing to the delinquency etc., statutory rape, the predictable ones.

"I'm not afraid anymore," she wrote toward the end. "All of these people died and I'm still here. I'm not ashamed of that and I'm very hopeful now."

And then I realized I'd stopped reciting; had blanked out on the remainder of the *Winter's Tale* speech and couldn't for the life of me remember the *Antony and Cleopatra* lines I'd planned to follow them with. I was standing there, my voice primed to continue, all of them watching me from behind. And so I just quoted the only thing I could pull to the surface. When I finished it and turned around I could tell it had been the right thing, even if just for me.

"So when this loose behavior I throw off,
And pay the debt I never promised
By how much better than my word I am,
By so much shall I falsify men's hopes;
And, like bright metal on a sullen ground,
My reformation, glittering over my fault,
Shall show more goodly and attract more eyes
Than that which hath no foil to set it off."

After a few minutes of milling around the little tent I walked Rosie back to the Tempo parked on the cemetery path. We'd agreed earlier in the week that I'd give it back. I didn't need or particularly want it; she was uncomfortable with the arrangement since I'd fallen off the wagon. I didn't blame her.

"Okay, Shakespeare," she said, putting on her gloves. "You'll come by sometime?"

"Not for a while," I said. "I'm going up to Oregon for a week and then I have to get ready for finals."

"Be careful up there," she said. "Don't get mixed up with those survivalists."

"Too late," I said. She climbed into the Tempo, fired it up, and chugged away.

And then this very odd thing happened.

Carl and I were standing there on the sidewalk watching Rosie leave and we were about to split up, him back toward town, me the other way, alone now, out to Prairie du Chien. It was a very quiet moment.

"Well, thanks, buddy," I said, reaching out and shaking his

hand, which was surprisingly firm. All of a sudden I had trouble speaking. "I appreciate it," I managed to add.

We gripped hands and he held on for an extra moment or two, his eyes wide and friendly. "You know," he said, "I never told you, but I've always been a big admirer of yours."

That statement seemed to suck the very last bit of wind out of me.

"Is that right?" I croaked. I was more aware than ever of how much I really needed a drink. I just had to make it through the day, wasn't that how it went? It was going to be hard, it was going to be very hard.

He continued with a shy smile. "I was actually a big fan. I even voted for you."

I shook my head. It was as if he were speaking Flemish. "You voted for me?"

"For President. That was you, right? At the caucuses? I wrote you in on the ballot in November."

I must have nodded blankly at him a few too many times because he gave me a final concerned look and shook my hand again and then walked away up the street. I just stood there.

For President. A seemingly rational person had voted for me for President of the United States. I said it to myself four or five times as I resumed walking toward home.

Andrew Bergman, widower, underachiever, and alcoholic, for President. Andrew Bergman, Prince of Dogland, gratefully accepts the nomination of his party for President of the United States of America.

Thank you very much, I said, to no one in particular. Thank you, God bless you, and God bless America.